AND THEN SHE VANISHED

AND THEN SHE VANISHED

NICK JONES

BLACK STONE PUBLISHING

Copyright © 2021 by Nick Jones
Published in 2021 by Blackstone Publishing
Cover design by Bookfly Design
Book design by Blackstone Publishing

Printed in the United States of America

First edition: 2021
ISBN 978-1-66503-655-9
Fiction / Science Fiction / Time Travel

1 3 5 7 9 10 8 6 4 2

CIP data for this book is available
from the Library of Congress

Blackstone Publishing
31 Mistletoe Rd.
Ashland, OR 97520

www.BlackstonePublishing.com

PART 1

PROLOGUE

Summer 1997—King's Funfair

The smell of roasting chestnuts and sweet candy, the piercing screams of kids being thrown around at impossible speed. The fair has come to Cheltenham, and it's a big one. It's all Amy's talked about for the last few weeks, and now it's here. My little sister is about to burst with excitement. Seven years old and enchanted by this colorful, sugary, crazy-loud place. We walk among the huge rides, their colored bulbs bright against the evening sky, a warm indigo of summer. Amy smiles up at me, her hand in mine. She looks impossibly cute in a dress she picked out weeks ago, pastel blue, like the ribbons in her hair. Will she remember this night?

We pass a shooting range with a mountainous rainbow of stuffed animals. The vendor is a stout man dressed in a three-piece suit and top hat. He has piercing eyes and a devilish beard, a grown-up Artful Dodger. "Why don't you give it a go, sir?" he inquires, grinning, his accent laced with a subtle cockney twang. "Win the little lady a prize?"

"My brother is really good at guns," Amy informs him.

"Is that so?" he replies, playfully. "And what's your brother's name?"

"Joseph Bridgeman," she says with businesslike candor. "And he'll probably hit them all." She points to the row of targets at the back of the stand.

The Dodger breaks into a kind laugh, attracting interested glances from passersby. Amy has already charmed him. I've seen it a hundred times. A few of my mates have sisters and wish they would spontaneously combust. I like spending time with Amy though. Everyone does.

The Dodger leans forward as though intending to share a secret with her. "It's normally two pounds for three shots, but your brother can have an extra one for free, all right?"

Amy folds her arms. "My daddy says that nothing in life is free."

He nods seriously. "Well, I'm sure your daddy is a very smart man, but sometimes, the best things in life are free."

"The Beatles," I say automatically.

"You can't beat 'em." He nods. A brief reverence for the Fab Four passes between us. "So, you up for it then, Joseph?"

Amy squeezes my hand. "Please?" Her expectant face shines up at me. *How can I say no?*

With my pockets emptied, the Dodger cracks open a gun, loads it with pellets, and hands it to me. "There you go. Hit three targets, and she can have whatever she wants."

I pinch one eye, and stare down the barrel. The sight is fixed at a strange angle. *That will need to be compensated for*, I think, *like a sniper in high winds*. Amy's sights, on the other hand, are locked onto a huge pink bear, her arms folded neatly as she waits for me.

Boys and girls. Fourteen and seven. Chalk and cheese.

"Roll up, roll up, ladies and gentlemen!" the stallholder cries. "The world-famous Burning Joseph Bridges is about to take the stand." It seems I am, and the stakes are high.

I gaze at the small crowd gathered around us, and my heart skips a beat. Sian Burrows, a vision of beauty in stone-washed jeans and a ruffled white blouse, is staring at me.

She lifts a heavily bangled arm, waves, and flicks her huge mane of curly hair over her shoulder. Her makeup is so professional she looks like a woman—Julia Roberts, Madonna, and Sharon Stone all rolled into one. Sian is flanked by her usual cronies, Vicky Sharp and Wendy Nelson, but her eyes are on me. A fluttering sensation swims through my belly. Only Sian does this to me. I've fancied her since the first year of secondary school, nearly three years now. Some people aren't even married that long. I was skinny then, but in the last year I've shot up and filled out. My acne has cleared up too, and finally Sian has noticed me. I haven't kissed her yet. I haven't kissed anyone. But if tonight goes well, I might get my chance. She smiles, confident and playful. I think I smile back, but I can't feel my face anymore.

Amy claps her hands and squeals, "Come on, Joe, win me the big bear!"

Right. I wipe my brow and attempt to steady my heart rate. Rifle against my shoulder, I track one of the circular targets as it shakes its way in front of the sea of toys. I remember what my dad taught me about shooting an air rifle. Relax, and wait for the target to come to you. Aiming a few centimeters ahead, I wait, raise the barrel of the gun to compensate for the arc of descent, and fire. A loud *ding* rings out as the target drops. Amy jumps in the air and grabs my arm. "Yes!" she cries. "You did it, you got one!"

One down, two to go. I rush my next shot, missing the target by an inch at least. I check to see if Sian's still watching me. She offers me a stern but supportive nod, a gesture I acknowledge with a flush of pride. Her friends glare at me. Luckily, Cinderella isn't listening to the ugly sisters. Now I'm more confident and wink at her as I raise my gun. I fire decisively and another target drops with a wonderful sound like a spoon hitting a pan. It sends a ripple of applause through the small audience. All I need is one more shot to win the bear and, hopefully, my first proper kiss.

"You can do it," Sian mouths at me, then bites her lip and flicks her hair again. I raise my gun one final time, breathe deep, wait for the final target to reach the sweet spot, and pull the trigger.

DING!

"Yes!" I punch the air, delighted in my moment of glory.

"There you go, mate," says the Artful Dodger, exchanging the gun for a big pink bear. The crowd applauds. I turn to give the bear to Amy, but she's no longer at my side. A ripple of concern moves through my gut.

My throat tightens. "Where's my sister?" I ask the Artful Dodger.

He looks around. "That's weird. She was right here."

The music from a nearby ride warps and swells along with the grinding power of machinery. A wave of panic washes over me. The fairground seems to close in around me. Heart pounding in my ears, all I can see is a blur of faces, none of them Amy's.

Sian comes over. "She was next to you, I mean just a few seconds ago. She can't have gone far." Her voice is kind, and I can't stand it. I swallow, mouth suddenly dry. Amy said she wanted to go to the merry-go-round next, so I run toward it, dropping the bear. Horses painted gold and red gallop through a thousand light bulbs, mouths stretched into tortured grimaces. Children laugh and scream. *Please, please let her be here*, I beg the universe. *Please let her be safe.*

The carousel spins full circle.

No Amy.

Something's happened to her.

"No," I growl, trying to ignore the terrible thoughts invading my head. I expect she's just wandered off, that's all. Something must have caught her eye. But she was so excited about the bear, and I was on my last shot. Why would she leave?

Someone took her.

I push through the crowd of people. Each strange face weakens me. The sound of the fair is discordant now, screeching sirens, the shrill cries of terrified children, the deceptively innocent tinkling bells of a steam organ. The soundtrack from a nightmare.

Seconds become minutes. Others call her name. I spot a flash of color in the grass next to a dirty generator that bangs away like the blood in my temples. Staggering, I fall to my knees and pick up one of Amy's blue hair ribbons from the mud. I hold it, shivering, but when I try to call her name, nothing comes.

1

Tuesday, December 10, 2019

"Joseph," my accountant Martin says, "are you listening to me?"

"Yes," I say, but I'm not really, which is unfair. He's only trying to help. It's four thirty p.m. Martin has dropped in for a "chat." Never good news. We're in my den, a place I think of as my refuge. I'm slouched in my favorite leather armchair, listening to the rain hammer Cheltenham into submission.

"Have you been drinking?" Martin asks, sniffing the air dramatically.

"No." I have, but not that much. "You were saying the website needs some work."

"No." Martin peers at me over his glasses like a school headmaster. "I said your website is *down*. I checked it this morning."

"Oh," I wince, "that's not good."

"Don't you care anymore?" he inquires carefully. "About the business, I mean."

I shrug. My business is a failing antiques website. My heart hasn't been in it lately, which is a shame because I was good at it, before the dreams came back. I chew my bottom lip. "I was thinking, maybe I should try a different career."

Martin nods patiently, even though he's heard all this before. He's far from just my accountant, he's my guardian, my conscience, and one of the only people who tells me the truth. He used to work for my dad.

As commercial director, Martin ran the property development business, and when Dad left us, Martin took me under his wing. He's never given up on me, and considering that he was the one who got me interested in antiques in the first place, my apathy must be especially difficult for him.

"Why do you do this?" I ask. "Keep trying to help me?"

"Because you have a gift," he says without hesitation, "and when your head is in the game, you're the best there is."

The "gift" he's referring to is my ability to connect with objects. They talk to me. I see things. The official name is psychometry, not that I broadcast the fact. It's spooky and weird but also pretty useful. In the business of antiques, provenance is everything, and if you know which items will be desirable, will be worth good money in the future, then you are unstoppable. I could make a profit in my sleep, but therein lies the problem.

Sleep, and my total lack of it. I'm lucky if I get two hours a night, and it's been that way for months now.

"You seem tired," he says.

I rub my eyes. "It's Amy's birthday this week."

He nods and says quietly, "I know."

I never say it *would have been* her birthday, because we never found her, therefore she isn't dead. My chest tightens, and I exhale loudly. Martin offers me an empathetic smile, an expression I've seen on his face many times over the years. "The dreams have come back, haven't they?" I nod. He walks to the window and stands beside me. "Listen. I'm sorry about the timing, I know things are difficult . . . but we do need to talk about the house."

"The house?" I say, as if we haven't already talked about it a hundred times.

Martin tenses up, jaw flexing. He's in good shape for a man in his midfifties, plays a lot of squash. I imagine that if you took him apart, he would look like one of those sinewy models you see in sports injury clinics. "Your parents' savings are almost gone," he says. "When the money runs out, they could take the house, use it to pay for your mother's care."

I shake my head, watching beads of rain trace their way down the window and disappear. *Money.* When you have it, you don't think about it, and when you don't, it's all you think about. Unless you're me: Captain Denial of the good ship *Penniless*.

"Do you understand what I'm telling you?" Martin asks.

"Yes," I say. "But I don't know what you're worrying about. It will be okay."

"Not it won't, not this time." His voice is cool and direct. "Not if you carry on like this."

I stand, stare at him, and with fake enthusiasm say, "Martin, you're a gent, and I know what you're trying to do, but I now relieve you of your duty."

He arches an eyebrow. "My duty?"

"Yes. Whatever it is you feel you need to do, you can stop now."

"I made a promise to your father," he says seriously.

I hold up a finger. "That's not a conversation we're going to have today." He relents, and we stand in a stalemate. I appreciate that I'm acting like a petulant teenager, but I'm lost. I don't know who I am anymore, and I can't think straight. Grief and insomnia will do that to you.

Eventually Martin says, "I'm not giving up on you, Joseph." He hands me a business card.

"What's this?" I ask, taking it.

"Someone I want you to go and see."

"Oh, come on!" I burst out. "Not this again."

"Her name is Alexia Finch," he replies, unperturbed. "She's really good."

Over the years, Martin has pushed and shoved me in front of various "experts." I know he means well, but what's the point? They can't bring Amy back. I stare at the card, and then back at him. "The last thing I need right now is some shrink poking around in my head, digging up the past."

"She's not a shrink." Martin's voice is calm and controlled. "She's a really experienced hypnotherapist."

"Hypnotherapist!" I snort. "Martin . . ."

"She's good."

"She won't understand."

"You might be surprised." He studies me, expression cool, and then softens a little. "She has her own story, told me she got into therapy because it helped *her* so much."

"Well," I smile sarcastically, "I'm glad someone had a happy ending and everything worked out."

I'm being annoying and immature, but it's true what they say: when we hurt, we take it out on those closest to us. Martin doesn't bite. He has three girls, all in their teens, which means he's a master at ignoring displays of self-importance. He places a hand on my shoulder. "I care about you," he says. "So, I've booked you an appointment."

"Really?"

"Yes. Will you go? Please?"

I fold my arms. "Fine."

"Good, that's settled then." Martin grabs his briefcase. "Oh, and I hope you don't mind, I bought you some essentials."

Essentials? I study him, nervously.

"They're in the kitchen," he says. "Consider it an official bribe. Go and see her."

The bribe is a shiny blender that resembles a space rocket from the sixties and a box full of fruit and vegetables. I put the machine straight to work and blitz apples, blueberries, and bananas into purple mush. It tastes amazing. Until recently, online shopping was my savior. Food delivered weekly is ideal for a hermit like me. All I had to do was nod to the delivery person and sign on the line. But then a really annoying thing happened. My credit card stopped working, and then I kind of ran out of food. Now, thanks to Martin, I have another three days' worth of juicing ingredients. I'm not dead yet.

I turn the business card over in my hands and feel bad about how I treated him. He's been loyal, and I value that, but it doesn't mean I'm going to see the therapist.

The afternoon bleeds into the evening; when you suffer from insomnia, it's all the same. I pick a bottle of red wine from my diminishing stocks and head to the den, leaving the rest of the house in darkness. There seems little point in filling it with light when I spend most of my evenings in one room. My den is my safe place, my escape, and it has everything I need. It isn't a big room, but that's good, makes it easy to keep warm. In one corner is a beaten-up old club chair. It's missing some of the brass studs that adorn its edges. Next to that is a tall standard lamp with the largest, craziest shade I could find. The walls are lined with shelves and cupboards, crammed with books and things I've collected over the years. One section is full of vinyl, and next to my chair is a cabinet that houses my pride and joy: a Rega record deck and valve amplifier.

I'm aware this room sounds like the final resting place of a retired old has-been, but I like it. It's quiet in here, and when I play music, it's like a wave of warm water running through me. I pour some wine into a large glass and scan my record collection. It doesn't take long for a little voice in my head to suggest *Rubber Soul*.

The Beatles seem to have a song for every occasion. My copy of this particular album is a reissue. The originals are nice—I have those too—but the remasters are another thing altogether, clean and rich and warm all at the same time. I pull the 180-gram slab of history from its sleeve, place it on the turntable, lower the stylus carefully onto the vinyl, and sink back into my chair.

The needle finds the groove, and the Fab Four ease my mind. McCartney's vocals on "Drive My Car" soar perfectly above the deep guitars. I pick up a framed photograph from one of the cluttered shelves: Amy, a few weeks before she went missing, hair trailing behind her as she plays on a swing in the garden, a swing that's rusted away now. Twenty-three years, and the pain feels hot and fresh as ever. Music fills the room and the wine goes to work. The folk melodies of "Norwegian Wood" give way to the powerful Motown groove of "You Won't See Me," and the lyrics take me away. Finally, I collapse into my chair. As I drift off to sleep, the Beatles sing of loss, of years gone by and a missing girl they can no longer see.

I know the feeling, boys.

2

I wake, heart pounding in my chest. Blinking away tears, I tune in to the reassuring sound of a stylus bumping and popping around the inner edge of a piece of vinyl. I've been through bouts of this recurring nightmare before, but usually after a few weeks it fades away. Over the last year or so, though, it's become unbearable, a constant replay of the night Amy disappeared. The pain as raw now as the day I lost her.

In the dream I relive every tiny detail, every stupid mistake I made, how I took my attention off her for just a second to impress Sian Burrows and win the bear. All of it is seared into my memory, branded, permanent. I walk to the record player, lift the tone arm, and stand for a while, transfixed by the spinning turntable.

Sometimes I dream Amy never went missing, that we walked home together, and all was fine. On some occasions, my subconscious reaches for hope and I convince myself I see her waving at me from the merry-go-round. I call out her name, but my voice isn't there. I'm empty, hollow. That's when I realize it's a dream, but I'm strapped in for the ride. The carousel accelerates, the wooden horses gallop way too fast, and the music builds to a sickening, discordant crescendo.

When I wake, all that's left is the truth.

She's gone.

They say time heals, but what they actually mean is that you start to forget. It's a natural process, a way for our minds to cope with loss. To their credit, the police did what they could, made appeals, combed the area, put up posters. In the end though, Amy's disappearance became another statistic, another missing kid, another unsolved case. That's probably the hardest thing, the not knowing.

I take a shower, scrubbing my skin in an effort to wash away this hollow feeling. I can't carry on like this. Three hours of sleep a night just isn't sustainable, but what can I do? I replay my conversation with Martin and wonder how long this house will protect me. I can't hide anymore. The past is finally catching up with me.

In the kitchen, I make another smoothie. There's something very therapeutic about mass-murdering fruit. Martin may have known this. The business card he gave me is next to the blender. Alexia Finch, Hypnotherapist. On the back is a list of disorders: anxiety, stress, insomnia, and so on. *Am I really going to do this?* I stare at the card for way too long, rotating it in my fingers. I realize I'm procrastinating, which is another symptom on the back of the card.

I shove it into the back pocket of my jeans and head out.

It's MIDMORNING, AND ALTHOUGH IT'S COLD, the streets of Cheltenham are busy. I hunch down and drift along, deliberately avoiding eye contact with anyone. I enjoy walking, but it hurts to see other people getting on with their lives when you are stuck in yours. For an insomniac, the best time to take a stroll is about four a.m. Most people are asleep, and animals—the ones you don't normally see, like foxes and badgers—own the night. I'm depressed. I do know that . . . and over the last few years I've become reclusive too, but there is still one person I enjoy seeing, someone worth venturing out for. I arrive at Vinny's Vinyl, a regular haunt of mine.

The shop's namesake is a chatty, bald-headed music lover with a passion for all things analog. He's one of my only friends now. The rest have sort of drifted away, not that I've tried to stop them. Vinny's shop has been here forever, and I suppose you could argue that he's a captive audience, but he is always willing to chat and accepts me for who I am. And, perhaps more importantly, he doesn't ask me difficult questions. I walk down the steps and enter. Call me weird, but I find the odor of aging protective paper and menthol cigarettes reassuring. It's not a big place, but Vinny still manages to hold a stock of thousands of records in neat rows. Classic album covers by artists like Pink Floyd, the Stones, and Bob Dylan take up every available wall space. Vinny loves old things, and therefore I like Vinny.

I find him at the back of the shop. As always, he's wearing ancient gray jeans turned up to reveal Doc Martens, and a vintage T-shirt, which today is Guns N' Roses. He's surrounded by pristine cardboard boxes and is ripping the tape from them.

"Cash!" He wipes sweat from his brow and smooth head. "Good to see you."

He calls me Cash because I don't do credit cards. "What are you up to?" I ask.

"Just took in a load of new stock." He grins, pulling an album from one of the boxes. "I thought you might like this one. It's a Beatles tribute album by the Flaming Lips—you know, the *Sergeant Pepper* one?"

"I don't really want it, Vinny," I explain carefully, not wanting to appear ungrateful. "I love the Flaming Lips, but honestly, the thought of anyone covering the Beatles fills me with dread."

"Fair enough." He laughs heartily. "That reminds me, the album you ordered came in yesterday." He heads off toward the storeroom. Vinny is a big guy. He reminds me of a grizzly bear, but is surprisingly light on his feet. He told me once that he goes to Cuban dance lessons. That is something I would love to see. From the storeroom he calls out, "I'm thinking about sticking a coffee machine out there and arranging a little café area. What do you think?"

"Sounds good," I call back, wondering where he thinks he's going to put a table and chairs.

Vinny emerges in a cloud of blue smoke with a record under his arm. He smokes hand-rolled cigarettes with menthol papers and completely ignores the smoking ban, especially when the shop is quiet, which is most of the time.

"It'll be one of those posh vending machines with the brown plastic cups," he says, his eyes glistening with excitement. "I absolutely love it when you have a hot chocolate and the end is all sticky and powdery at the same time." He smacks his lips, groaning with imagined pleasure. Vinny and quality don't always mix.

He hands the album to me. It's the stereo reissue of *Help!*, and I'm looking forward to giving it a spin. I thank him, and he reminds me it's all paid for.

He narrows his gaze. "I've gotta say, Cash, you look like you could do with a coffee right now. Are you feeling all right?"

"I'm not sleeping well."

"The nightmares," he says. "Right? They're troubling you again?"

I nod. Vinny is one of the only people I've told about Amy. "After the last time you came in, Cash, I googled 'minimum sleep requirements for a human.' It's not good . . . you are way under the norm."

Sighing, I decide to tell him what's been going on. "I keep replaying it, Vinny, keep seeing Amy next to me, and then I look down and she's gone. Sometimes it feels like my life is on a loop, like someone just keeps putting the needle back to the beginning of the record. It's been over twenty years and it still feels like yesterday."

"Can't be easy with your mum too. You've got a lot on your plate." I can hear the genuine empathy in his voice. "This bloke I know was a soldier, did two tours of Iraq, and he had a similar thing to you, kept replaying all the bad stuff, got himself into a right pickle." He pauses, and when he speaks again his voice is softer. "I keep telling you, mate, you have DPST. You need to get some help." Vinny means PTSD, and he also means well.

"Martin's booked me an appointment with a therapist," I tell him.

"That's good, Cash. When?"

"Today at two p.m." I shake my head. "I was annoyed."

"Why?"

"He booked it without asking."

Vinny considers this. "He's probably just trying to help. Are you going to go?"

I wander over to a rack of vinyl and flick through it without really looking. "I don't think so. The dreams will stop eventually, it will blow over."

"Good," he grins. "It's only one o'clock. You can help me put this lot away." Vinny continues unpacking boxes while I browse the racks. We don't speak for a while. I consider what he said, and he's right in a way. It's good of Martin to try and help, but he's pushed me into this kind of thing before, and it didn't end well. Eventually, Vinny says, "It's all right to ask for help, you know?"

My chest tightens and I breathe out slowly. "Yeah, I know."

"So what are you afraid of?"

"Sharks," I tell him.

"What?"

"Sharks. People say things like, 'It's okay, the ones around here are plankton eaters,' but I've seen vegetarians eat a bacon sandwich in a moment of weakness."

He laughs, shaking his head. "You know what I mean. Why are you afraid of therapy?"

I look at the floor for a few seconds, and I'm surprised when the truth starts pouring out. "Honestly, I feel like all this pain, this history, has become part of me," I tell him. "It feels as though it's drifted down, really deep, and settled like sediment."

"And you're worried this will stir it all up again?" I bob my head. Vinny walks over and places a hand on my shoulder. "Listen to your Uncle Vincent now. I'm not sure it could get much worse, mate. What kind of therapy is it?" I hand him Alexia Finch's business card. "Hypnosis!" he cries enthusiastically. "I had that once. Brilliant."

"Really?"

"Yeah!" He absently flicks the ash from his hand-rolled cigarette onto the floor, a sticky red carpet that reminds me of a pub. "I had two really awesome sessions and *totally* quit smoking. Just like that. It was amazing!"

I stare pointedly at his hand.

"What, this?" he says, waving his cigarette. "Oh, yeah . . . well, obviously I started again."

"And your point is?"

"It was really, really hard."

"Giving it up?"

"No! Starting again."

"Vinny," I say, "I don't know if this is helping."

"Right." He nods, sagely. "What I'm trying to say is, go and see the hypnotherapist, and if it helps, then that's good." His expression shifts, and he considers me with a serious expression. "But if you decide that for some reason you *don't* want to sleep again, that you want to go back to the life of an insomniac, having nightmares and stuff, then you can." He pauses and shoves his hands in his pockets, eyebrows raised as though he's about to reveal a clever secret. "Hypnosis wears off, you know."

3

The hypnotherapist's office is situated in a quiet crescent overlooking Imperial Gardens. I'm glad Martin paid for this. It looks expensive: a large, imposing front door, pristine white brickwork, paneled windows, and period features. A shiny brass plaque informs me that Alexia Finch shares the building with a lawyer and an accountant. She's in good company, people who charge eye-watering amounts of money, per hour, every hour. My shirt clings to my back, and my heart is pounding. Meeting people. I'm out of practice and the thought of interacting with anyone sends me into a tailspin. Vinny doesn't count because he's Vinny.

After some pacing and a few deep breaths, I head inside and follow signs up to the first floor. I'm greeted at the top of a staircase by a woman, dressed smartly in black trousers and a cream blouse. She looks relaxed, easygoing, her hair tied in a loose ponytail. She smiles with the easy confidence of someone who knows she can put you under with a snap of her fingers. Guess I'm in the right place then.

"Mr. Bridgeman?"

"Er, Joe is fine."

"Great. Hi, Joe. I'm Alexia." She holds out her hand and we shake. "Come on in."

Her office is a large room with high ceilings, decorative cornices, and an opulent crystal chandelier. It smells faintly of vanilla and warm bread. I think her business card should include aromatherapy; I feel better already. The walls are adorned with the usual "I'm really qualified" certificates, along with oil paintings depicting calm scenes of shorelines, sunsets, and gardens. The color of the room is soothing. I suspect it has some pretentious name like "Coffee Breath" or "Buffalo Turd at Sunset." I guess if they just called it "Brown," they wouldn't be able to charge as much. There is a lot of space, it's easy to breathe, and for that, I'm grateful.

Alexia grabs a notebook, and we sit opposite each other at a small coffee table. She pops a pair of black glasses on her nose and picks up a pen. "Many people are quite nervous about hypnotherapy, especially their first session."

"Oh, I'm not nervous," I say, nervously.

"Good." She smiles. "You have no need to be. Everything that happens here will be because *you* allow it."

"You aren't going to put me under?"

"There isn't really such a thing as putting someone *under*. Hypnotherapy is actually self-hypnosis."

"So, I do it?"

"In a way, yes," she replies.

Classic therapist. She gets paid, I do all the work.

"If you don't want to be hypnotized then it won't happen," she says. "It's your choice, and there's no pressure from me. We can just see how it goes." Alexia smiles again, and for the first time in months, my shoulders drop a little. She's unlike other therapists, who all seem to follow a formula and check the clock a little too often. Alexia comes across as kind and appears to be in no hurry. I'm relieved.

"Do you use a pocket watch?" I ask. "You know, to swing in front of my face?"

Her blue eyes shimmer for a second, and she seems to stifle a laugh. "I don't use a watch," she says, "but using an object as a point of focus can be a good idea, a way of distracting your conscious mind so we can get down into the subconscious. That's where the real action happens, below the surface. I imagine it's like we're doing a spot of maintenance, helping the subconscious reprogram itself."

"Like brainwashing," I say.

She nods. "Hypnotherapy is like washing your brain, cleaning away some of the learned behaviors that might be causing problems."

This sets me thinking about some of my learned behaviors, how a rut that felt temporary has become entrenched over the years, deep and established.

"So, tell me, Joe, what do you hope to get out of your time with me?"

I consider the question. I might as well tell her the basics. "I need to sleep."

"You suffer from insomnia?"

"Yes," I admit, surprised by how easy she makes this. She scribbles more notes, pushing her glasses up her nose every few seconds. It's an almost childlike gesture that's strangely hypnotic, which is probably deliberate. I pinch my wrist, double-checking that I'm not in a trance already.

"How long have you suffered from sleep loss?"

"Three months this time," I reply, "but on and off since I was a teenager."

"Right." She chews her lip as she writes.

A clock ticks a steady rhythm. Distant traffic hums outside. A gentle buzzing sensation flutters through my stomach, and for some strange reason I'm reminded of shoe fittings as a child. I used to love the cold metal contraption they measured you with, feeling plastic straps pulled under and around your foot. Maybe it's to do with being cared for, being the center of attention without the pressure of a crowd.

"Joe?" Alexia says.

"Yes?" I reply, blinking.

"You seem to have drifted off a little."

"Did you hypnotize me?"

"No," she says thoughtfully. "I won't do that without your permission."

I nod, examining my hands.

"Do you have any idea what might be causing the insomnia?"

This is the part I've been dreading. That ticking clock sounds a bit louder now. How much do I tell her? Part of me wants to talk, but I'm worried that if I open the floodgates, I might not stop. All the guilt, the loss, might start pouring out of me: absent father, mother in a care home, house on the line. Blah, blah, blah. It's such a tragic list, and although I know it's a therapist's job to listen to people's dross, I really don't want to burden her. I'm bored of my own melancholy.

Alexia waits patiently.

I draw in a deep breath. "I have an online antiques business, and I'm struggling to concentrate, to make a decent go of it. If I can just get some sleep, things might get better."

"Of course, everything is harder without proper rest." She removes her glasses. "I think for your first session, we will work on some breathing exercises, techniques you can use at home." She gestures toward a long leather recliner in the corner of the room. "Shall we?"

I lie down on the chair. Alexia twists the blinds, darkening the room. The room is calm, and she has a way about her that is reassuring, peaceful even, but I have years of tension wound up in me like a rusted spring. There is no way she's putting me under.

She pulls up a chair and asks me to close my eyes. I oblige, and she begins. "Have you ever driven somewhere, arrived, and realized that you don't remember how you got there?" I nod, keeping my eyes closed. "That's time distortion," she explains. "You've slipped into a mild daydream, moved from beta into alpha." Her voice is low and wonderfully calming. "The brain operates at different frequencies, or states, as we call them." She pauses. When she speaks again, her voice is quieter. She deliberately overarticulates the end of some of the words, which in turn makes me focus on what she's saying. "All we're going to do is move from beta to alpha, drift into a relaxed place, and quiet your conscious mind for a little while. Does that sound good to you, Joe? Do you *want* to try and become more relaxed?"

"Mm-hmm," I confirm.

"Good. I want you to count slowly down from thirty," she says. "Start with your eyes closed, and then alternate. Open for a count and then close them again for a count. When you open them, focus on the small dot on the ceiling."

I look up and notice a little black sticker high above us. How did she get that up there?

"There's no rush," she says. "Just take your time. Whenever you're ready."

Drawing in a breath and feeling a bit silly, I start my countdown. "Thirty." Eyes shut. "Twenty-nine." Eyes open.

"That's good," she says. "Try and clear your mind, Joe."

Ah, the classic *clear your mind*. As soon anyone tells me to do that, it fills with a load of noisy rubbish.

"Twenty-eight." Eyes closed. "Twenty-seven." Eyes open.

By the time I reach ten, I can't remember if I'm doing it right, but I don't really want to open my eyes anymore.

"Good," Alexia says, her voice close to me now, just above a whisper. "You feel very relaxed . . . perhaps more relaxed than you've ever felt before."

She's not kidding. I didn't realize how tense I was until my shoulders and stomach unwound a little. And this chair is so comfortable, if I had any money I would get one myself, maybe sleep in it. I feel as though I'm sinking into it now.

"I want you to fill your mind with a memory," she almost purrs. "Think of a place where you felt good, where you felt happy."

I'm surprised when a memory bubbles up easily. "I have one."

"Good. Where are you?"

"I'm walking on a beach," I reply, the past filling my mind like paint pouring into water. The sun warms my face, and the salty air is fresh. It was a good day, a walk with my parents. Bare feet on sand, birds soaring over crashing surf. I'm young, maybe eight or nine. "I'm with my family," I say.

"Okay," Alexia replies, "tell me how you feel."

"Safe," I murmur, softly. "I feel safe."

"That's a good feeling," Alexia assures me. "You *are* safe and in complete control. I want you to hold on to that. You are feeling more and more relaxed now."

Her voice drifts in and out, like the surf. Mum is pushing Amy in a buggy. I'm holding my dad's hand. On the count of three he lifts me into the air with one arm, both of us laughing. My feet flail, then land, and I'm running, warm sand between my toes. I look up. My father is a shimmering silhouette, young and strong.

The memory flickers like sun over a lake, and we shift locations. Same day, but now I'm staring out to sea, the waves crashing over my shins. The water is surprisingly warm, and my feet sink into the wet sand. Within seconds I'm knee-deep, but I don't panic. It's strangely comforting being swallowed like this, like sliding into a warm bath. For the first time in years, everything is exactly as it should be.

That's when I realize that I must have let go, forgotten where I am and everything that happened to me. Sucking in a breath, I sit up in the chair, blinking, confused. For a few precious seconds, Alexia's office was gone, along with my life here, and it was wonderful. I was back in the past, before it all went wrong.

Alexia is quiet for a while, waiting as I adjust. Eventually, she says, "You were nicely relaxed, Joe, but sometimes our conscious mind fights back. It doesn't want to let go. It's completely natural, like falling off that imaginary step as you drift off to sleep."

I breathe deeply, attempting to process what just happened. I don't drift off to sleep these days, but I remember that feeling. I've missed it. I've missed a lot of things.

Alexia hands me a glass of water. I thank her and take a sip. "I was properly under, I think."

She nods. "You did really well. You can use the counting technique at home. It will help you to relax, and when you send your subconscious the right signals, you'll be amazed what you can achieve." She goes back to her notes. "Also, I want you to think about your evening routine and how it builds toward bedtime."

I decide not to tell her that my typical evening consists of moping about, drinking wine, listening to vinyl, and staying awake most of the night. Alexia takes some more notes and explains that I should contact her to arrange another session. I assure her I will, but I'm not convinced I mean it.

She walks me down to the front door, and we shake hands again. It might be my imagination, but my senses feel heightened. Colors appear a little more vibrant, everything looks sharper. Amazing what a few minutes of peace can do.

"Drink chamomile tea and try reading before sleep," Alexia says. "Maybe take a bath to help you unwind. Oh, and no alcohol, of course."

"Of course," I nod. "Sounds like fun."

4

By the time I get home, the sky is a winter bruise of dark gray and yellow. I throw my keys on the kitchen table and automatically walk over to the wine rack. Habit is like an old slipper. Not drinking tonight will be hard. I know that makes me sound like an alcoholic. I don't think I am, but that is exactly what an alcoholic would say, I guess. Genuinely, though, I use alcohol to numb my brain and only ever drink after six p.m.

A functioning alcoholic, then. With OCD.

On the way home, I purchased a box of chamomile tea. It smells like a musty shed but I'm willing to give it a go. I pop the kettle on and think over my session with Alexia. I'm not sure if I will see her again, but she did put me under, and for a while I lost all sense of myself. That was a relief. I've never done drugs, but I imagine that's one of the benefits, losing yourself and forgetting reality for a while. I consider giving my new Beatles album a spin, but that's my old routine. Instead, I drop it off in the den and with herbal tea in hand, I head upstairs.

My house is a four-bedroom, terraced property. Classic Cheltenham, redbrick, regency in style, and well built. My family moved here when I was about five, a couple of years before Amy was born. Dad described it as a proper house, a place for our family to grow into. Now it's just me, rattling around like a ghost. I know being here is keeping me in limbo, but how can I sell it? It's part of me now. As I often do, I pause outside

Amy's bedroom. It's unlocked, but I never go in. Grief is barrier enough.

Through the door, like a warm breeze, I feel it again, the undeniable, magnetic draw of Amy's belongings—toys, clothes, jewelry, photographs. It sounds crazy, but I mean it literally. Objects talk to me. I sense things when I touch them, and sometimes see things as well. Psychometry is exactly the kind of thing I would have laughed at, until it happened to me. The first time was not long after Amy went missing. I was holding one of her roller skates—she really loved them—and I was alone. It was quiet, calm, and I felt close to her again. I closed my eyes and was carried away, but this wasn't a memory or a dream. This was more like watching a film in my mind. Amy was using the roller skate as a train, pulling her toys along in the garden. Then it dawned on me that I was seeing this crystal clear scene from Amy's point of view.

Initially, I was afraid, but curiosity got the better of me. A couple of days later, I tried again and saw the same scene, a replay of the past transmitted through an object. After that, I tried tuning into other things that belonged to her, and they, too, triggered these short films, bright and clear as day. I called them "viewings," because "visions" made me sound like a nutjob. Not that I would tell anyone. This was my little secret. Seeing the past like this, connecting with my sister, brought comfort as well as pain. It was a blessing and a curse to be this close to her.

I figured something else out, too. These replays were always emotional moments for Amy. The joy of bouncing on a trampoline. The pain of saying goodbye to our cat, Claude. The excitement of the day before Christmas. The warm, easy comfort of a family night in front of the fire. Of course, I was always searching for clues to her disappearance, but I had no control over these viewings, no ability to alter what I was seeing. All I could do was watch, and it became addictive. It was like getting to know Amy a little better, spending time with her. But grieving is a process, and I realized eventually that if Mum was right and Amy was dead, then my viewings were holding me back. They weren't achieving anything except anchoring me to the past. So I stopped. I put everything away and tried to forget.

Often, I feel an increase in activity around the time of Amy's birthday. This year it feels particularly strong. I wonder if it's because of the outside pressures building around me—the house, money, my mum. Who knows? I rest my forehead for a moment against Amy's door, and let the moment take its course.

Then I stand up straight again, remembering what Alexia advised me. Read, take a bath, and prepare for sleep. That's exactly what I intend to do.

I pull a book from a shelf, some sci-fi tale. I don't really care what it is. I just hope the words act like magic pills to help me sleep. I read for what feels like ages, check the time, and see that it's only been seven minutes.

How does anyone do this?

For me, a bath should be close to boiling, hot enough to warm your bones, really get them glowing. Steam fills my bathroom. Candles flicker on the windowsill. I undress, slip into the water, and exhale slowly. Nearly perfect. All that's missing is a glass of wine.

My pajamas are cotton, pale gray with light-purple stripes, the attire of a true gentleman. It's eleven o'clock, and although the man in the mirror looks exhausted—no change there—I don't feel tired at all. I'm wide awake, which is annoying. I brush my teeth and gargle. To ensure I gargle long enough, I usually hum random movie themes. Tonight I choose *Indiana Jones*.

Lying in bed, picking out patterns in the cobwebs hanging from the ceiling, I wonder if I should draw a focus dot up there. Who am I kidding? This isn't going to work.

Next to my bed is a retro digital alarm clock. The green digits remind me cheerfully that it's 11:25 p.m. I click off the light and gaze into the darkness. Honestly, I feel more awake than I have all day. Nothing is going to change. I'm a stuck record. It's stupid to think that one hypnotherapy session will do anything. I groan, lie on my side, and watch the clock. The minutes flash by . . . 11:28 p.m.

Alexia's words come back to me. *Send your subconscious the right signals, and you'll be amazed what you can achieve.*

Drawing in a breath, I stare at the two little dots between the numbers. They wink at me, like a cursor on a computer, waiting for input. Matching their steady rhythm, I open and close my eyes. I control my breathing, and when the clock hits 11:29 p.m., I begin counting down from sixty in my head, in time with those little dots. Halfway through my countdown, I feel that sense of losing myself, like in Alexia's office. I don't panic though. I try and let it come, lean into it, stay relaxed. A wonderful sense of weightlessness arrives, and I can't even tell if I'm blinking anymore. As I count down the last few numbers, I feel calmer than I have in years.

Five, four, three, two, one.

The light clicks on.

"Jesus Christ!" I cry, sitting up, my heart skipping around like popcorn in a pan. I'm wide awake now. "Oh, this is useless," I groan, glaring at the light. Why did it turn itself back on?

Then I look at the clock. That's weird. It reads 11:20 p.m. Maybe a power surge?

I freeze and hold my breath, straining to listen. Someone is in the bathroom! A man, humming. A ball of fear rolls over me. What the hell is going on?

I almost call out, but then my fight-or-flight instincts kick in. I leap out of bed and crouch behind the huge laundry basket in the corner of the room.

Whoever the bloke in my bathroom is, he takes a slug of mouthwash and I hear him gargling. And then he starts humming the theme to *Indiana Jones*.

My mouth dries up. Can that be *me* in there? Have I just died? Am I a ghost?

From my current position I have a decent view of the bathroom door and my bed. I hold my breath, afraid of what I might see, but I can't tear my eyes away.

And that's when a version of me walks out of the bathroom.

He's wearing my pajamas. And my *face*.

My sanity does a little wobble.

The man gets into bed—*my* bed—and continues to reenact the last few minutes of my life. He lies on his back for a while, staring at the ceiling.

Together we breathe.

I'm close to hyperventilating. What the hell is going to happen now?

I replay, in my mind, my countdown from sixty, the light suddenly turning on.

At 11:25 p.m. he turns out the light. It takes a few seconds for my vision to adjust, but I can see his dark outline, illuminated in the green glow of the clock. He groans, shifts position, and turns onto his side, facing the clock just like I did.

If what I'm seeing is real, then the man in my bed will start counting down soon. What will happen to me if he reaches zero? I swallow, wondering if I need to try and stop him, but that little rabbit hole is just as scary.

I'm clearly experiencing some form of hallucination, so I decide the best thing to do is absolutely nothing.

Remain calm, Joe.

At 11:29 p.m., my doppelgänger begins his sixty-second countdown. The man, who sounds like me, whispers numbers in the darkness. As he counts away the last few seconds, I hold my breath, eyes fixed on him, unblinking.

Five, four, three, two, one.

The man in my bed disappears. No sound, no special effects, he just goes.

The bed covers settle slowly onto the newly empty space.

The clock reads 11:30 p.m.

The darkness is momentarily drenched in a deep indigo blue that fades quickly, and the clock now reads 11:40 p.m. My mouth hangs open. I close it and for some reason, pat myself down to reassure myself that I'm still here. This is, without doubt, the craziest and most realistic dream I've ever had. At some point, I presume, I'm going to wake up. Unless I just did? Maybe I fell asleep, sleepwalked, hid behind my laundry basket, then snapped awake. Stranger things have happened. Somewhere.

Feeling very wobbly, I drift from my hiding place and sit on the edge of the bed. I switch the light back on, hand shaking like a washing machine on final spin, and feel the mattress. Still warm. I don't move for a while, waiting for my ragged breathing to return to normal. The house is silent, but I need to be sure I am truly alone. Methodically, I work my way through it, checking cupboards, bathrooms, even the loft. It's tough, but I even check Amy's room, which I haven't ventured into for years. Nothing. Whatever the hell just happened, I am alone again.

For absolute certainty, I check the whole house again, and by the time I'm done, it's nearly one o'clock. There is absolutely no way I'm going to sleep now.

In the kitchen, I growl, "New routine, my arse!" and grab a bottle of wine, but then I put it back. After all this weirdness I deserve something a little stronger, more medicinal. Back to the scene of the crime, I surround myself with the duvet and a protective reef of pillows. Pumped with adrenaline, my entire body on red alert, my hands shake as I pour myself a decent slug of brandy.

Slowly, the warming amber liquid goes to work, burning the edges of the twilight zone away and calming my overactive mind. Three glasses down and I'm convinced that this whole thing was just a crazy dream or a hallucination brought on by hypnosis. I drink until I can no longer focus on the room, until it ticks over like a projector on the blink. My head aches, like I've been poisoned. Perhaps I'm coming down with something? Or it could be the brandy combined with a massive adrenaline spike . . . I might even be in shock.

I'm going to call Alexia in the morning and tell her that she's mucked with my brain for the first and last time. For now I concentrate on denying the entire evening and focus instead on two things I know for sure.

Brandy is awesome.

Chamomile tea is evil.

5

Thursday, December 12, 2019

I'm dragged out of a deep slumber by the shrill beeping of a recycling truck. My head feels like a melon in a vice, close to popping. The pain makes sense when I realize the brandy bottle is half empty. According to my digital clock, it's seven a.m., although I'm not sure I will ever trust it again.

Wincing like a vampire about to sacrifice himself, I open the blinds. Dull and gray. Men in fluorescent jackets empty recycling boxes into the back of the truck.

That reminds me—I haven't put mine out. Why can't I remember the simple things? Oh yeah, chronic insomnia.

That said, my weird out-of-body experience wasn't the only unexpected thing to happen last night. I'm not sure when I fell asleep. I can't remember much after about two a.m., but I slept. It's been so long since I've had more than a couple of hours that it's weird to feel restored, even with a hangover. Five hours sleep is a treat, nothing short of a miracle.

My mind wanders back to last night's shenanigans, which already seem distant and absurd. The more I think about it, the sillier it seems.

After a quick shower, I head downstairs, grab a coffee, and end up in the den. It's a mess, and I vow to tidy it up at some point. My old Mac is shoved in the corner, hardly used. I blow dust off the keyboard, boot it up, and google "Can hypnosis cause hallucinations?"

Ten minutes later I'm convinced. The other me in my bedroom was a hallucination, triggered by a self-induced hypnotic state. If I'm wrong, then I've either had a stroke, or Alexia Finch has caused permanent brain damage. Case closed.

My gaze settles on my Beatles calendar, and I immediately feel dreadful because in all the madness, I forgot.

Today is Amy's birthday.

I can see her now, blowing out candles, unwrapping presents, making sure she thanks everyone. She is considerate like that, a stickler for good manners. My sister lights up a room, and the world has been a darker place without her. All these years, and not a day goes by when I don't wonder what happened. Pain mixes with anger as I imagine what I would do to the person who took her. But that kind of thinking doesn't serve me well, and as always, I push it from my mind.

It's time to sober up, to get my game face on, because today I have to play the good son. I visit her often, but always on Amy's birthday. I need to go and see Mum.

FROM THE OUTSIDE BEECH TREES NURSING HOME looks pleasant enough, a low-level modern building set back from the main road. Through ground floor windows, I see Christmas decorations, a wall-mounted television, and numerous residents seated in tall chairs, the kind these places always seem to have. I grimace, suck in a long cold breath, and push open the front doors.

It's quiet, just the sound of the television and studio laughter seeping from the main hall. I recognize the receptionist, who is seated behind a curved desk, making notes.

"Hi Clare, how are you?"

She smiles. "Can't complain. Your mum's in her room."

"How is she today?"

"She wasn't too good this morning, but she seems a bit brighter this afternoon."

I thank Clare, but words can't convey my gratitude for what the staff here do, under difficult circumstances, every single day. There are precious few people in this world who could cope. Beech Trees has nonetheless managed to attract its fair share of them.

The corridor smells of bleach and polish and squeaks underfoot. Part of me wants to turn around because it's painful to come here. I don't, of course. Duty dictates I see this through. There are times in life when you suck it up, get on with it, and do what's *right*.

My mother is a warm, kind, and sensible person. She ran our family, steered us when we went off course, and coped with her fair share of tragedy. It was my decision to put her in here; not an easy one, but necessary, and that means I come and see her. Even when she gets cross, when she doesn't know me, when she says things that hurt, I keep talking to her and I never complain. It's the right thing to do.

It's only midafternoon but with the arrival of rain, the day is nearly done. I enter her room. Mum hasn't turned the lights on yet, and it's gloomy. She's seated next to her bed and she's dressed, which is a good sign. I call her name, and she turns, her eyes glowing like embers in the half-light. She fiddles with a cable down the side of her chair, and then a sidelight illuminates her. She smiles and my spirits lift. Growing up, those smiles were gold. Now they are the rarest of diamonds, and when I see one, I want to cry with joy.

She looks happy, her skin aglow. She's wearing a hat, the paper kind you get at parties. I guess they've had an early Christmas celebration. The hat is positioned at a jaunty angle, and her hair pokes out from beneath, thin wisps of white that nearly reach her shoulders. I remember as a kid how much she, and Amy particularly, looked forward to Christmas, to all our relatives and family friends coming into town. The Bridgeman house was the center of my universe. I can still see my grandparents arriving, coats and big hats, the cold air rushing in with them and their suitcases and presents. My Uncle David was wealthy and always came with big beautifully wrapped boxes and his latest girlfriend in tow, striding in on a heady cloud of perfume. Suddenly our house would fill with excitement and people and love.

"Hi, Mum," I say, hoping for recognition.

"Joe," she smiles. "It's so nice to see you. I didn't think I would get any visitors today."

It's a massive relief. It can sometimes take her half an hour to get my name, and even then, it's as if she still doesn't know me. But today is one of her good days, and that is another diamond.

"How are you?" I ask.

She shrugs. "The food here is terrible, but I can't really remember what I had for breakfast, so it's not all bad."

My mother always did have a rapier wit and—before we lost Amy—a fantastic sense of humor. But, like most of the best comedians, that wit can turn inward, devouring its host. For a long time, she lost her ability to laugh at life, but in the last few years, as her illness bedded in, it has returned. There's nothing good about vascular dementia—stick it on a pile with cancer and motor neurone disease and we can have ourselves a good old bonfire—but it's ironic that the qualities that might have consumed her now appear to be saving her. On bad days, she is all but absent, but on the good ones, she jokes about her forgetfulness and her disease, and it's just impossible not to smile.

She continues. "The fact that I can't remember what day it is or what I watched on TV last night makes this place bearable." She shakes her head. "That said, I'm probably watching the same program over and over, laughing at the same old jokes."

It goes on like this for a while, and I enjoy this version of Mum. It almost reminds me of how it was. But she runs out of steam quickly these days, and after a while we sit in silence, the rain hissing against the windows and joining the distant sound of buzzers and mumbling conversations.

Mum closes her eyes. Her skin is pale and veined with thin blue lines, and she's lost weight, which makes her look frail. Her eye sockets are dark and hollow, and her cheeks are thin, but she's still beautiful. Nothing, no disease, no curse could ever take that from her. When she opens her eyes again, she flashes a weak smile and, although the brief connection is welcome, I see darkness.

"You seem sad, Mum," I say gently.

"Amy's not back." Her fresh confusion is obvious. "She hasn't come home and I'm getting concerned. You know how your dad worries." Her gaze wanders, as though she's woken from a dream. Mum is still talkative and present, but she's suddenly out of sync by over two decades. I remain convinced to this day that losing Amy was the trigger for Mum's illness. This is based on nothing scientific, just a gut feeling and a belief that a long fuse was lit that day, one that smoldered just below the surface and exploded a few years ago.

Mum's expression darkens, concentrating as she tries to navigate her way through the broken maze in her mind, her thoughts slippery like eels, evading her grasp. I've been talking to the surface of a lake, skating over the thin ice of Mum's memory, and now, without warning, she drops silently into the depths.

"Joe seems withdrawn," she says. "He's not like his old self. He's worried about something." I nod and swallow and fight the urge to cry. "Thomas, I'm not convinced that moving him to a new school was the right thing to do," she says. "I know that money is tight but we . . ." She trails off and then eyes me with suspicion.

"Thomas, what's wrong?" she asks, her voice scared and cold.

"Mum," I say, softly, "it's *me*. Joe."

She pulls back, curls her top lip. "Well, I know that!"

I nod again and reach for her hand. I'm relieved when she allows my touch. Her skin is cool and dry as paper. I can't stand to see her looking so confused, and that stupid hat makes things worse. "Mum," I say gently, "would you mind if I borrowed your hat for a bit?"

She takes it off and passes it to me, gripping my hand urgently. "Will you wish Amy a happy birthday for me?"

My throat tightens, but I paste on a smile. "Of course."

"Joe," she whispers, "listen to me." Suspicion falls over her like a cloud. "Something has happened, something terrible."

"Mum it's okay, it's—"

"No, it isn't!" she snaps. "It's not okay! You listen to me. Something has happened, I know it." She looks over her shoulder suspiciously, lips trembling. "Amy is missing, and I'm worried about your father."

The years are converging inside her fragile, damaged mind. As best I can, I calm her and assure her that I will find Dad and bring him to visit. It's a lie, but if it makes her feel better, what harm can it do? In this moment, I will say anything to settle her. If she reacts positively, I will tell her more of the same. Eventually, thankfully, she sleeps, and I slip away.

It's freezing outside. I pull my collar, button my duffle coat, and walk quickly, but I can't fight the loneliness creeping into me like hypothermia. Mum was all I had left and now she's hardly here at all. Seeing her has triggered a fresh wave of money worries. Her care doesn't come cheap. What will the nursing home do if I can't pay? And if the bank takes the house, I won't even have the option of moving her back in.

Nearby a man sits on cardboard, begging. His eyes are young, but his skin is red leather. Even his dog appears to be fed up. The man holds a sign, but I don't need to read it. He needs money, probably just enough to get him drunk so he can forget his worries. If it brings him some happiness, who am I to judge? Maybe he and I will be drinking buddies soon. I dig into my pocket, pull out the last of my change, and toss it into his collection box.

"Thanks, mate," he says in a hoarse voice. "Happy Christmas, yeah?"

6

The light rain turns to sleet that falls in icy daggers and sharpens my senses. Today is always a tough day, but this year it feels especially hard. Mum and I used to get together, talk about Amy, and imagine celebrating her birthday with all of us together. It was painful but it was also galvanizing. My mum and I supported each other, but over the last few years, the safe harbor of my mum's company has eroded, leaving me vulnerable and alone. I wander the streets of Cheltenham for a while, chewing on my thoughts, and by the time I get home, it's five o'clock.

Home. My sanctuary. But for how long?

The house is dark and quiet, yet the air feels agitated, unsettled, like someone has been busy. I don't believe in ghosts or spirits—never have—but I do believe that buildings absorb history and events, that emotions can soak into their walls. How else do you explain the undeniable sense of right or wrong you can feel when entering a building for the first time? My house is saturated with memories: good, bad, mundane, extraordinary. Over the years, it's often been a comfort, but at other times, like today, it makes me uneasy, the energy malevolent. I draw in a deep, steadying breath and work my way through the ground floor, turning on lights and reclaiming the rooms as my own. It's a weird little ritual, but now that my home is bathed in brilliant LED light, I feel a little better.

I end up in the kitchen, drying my hair on a towel. I spot last night's half-empty bottle of brandy and consider downing a quick shot, wondering if it might be the answer.

"But what is the question?" I murmur.

Although it's tempting, I decide that brandy is a bad idea, at least on an empty stomach. Instead, I grab what's left of the fruit Martin brought over and dump it into a blender. It's a healthy cocktail of strawberries, raspberries, and blueberries that *might* have been good for me if I had remembered to screw the lid on properly before firing it up. In a shocking explosion, I redecorate my kitchen in a matter of seconds.

Crying out, I switch off the blender and assess the damage. None of the fruit puree has landed on me, but two walls and part of the ceiling are spattered with a scarily accurate representation of blood and guts. The room resembles the scene of a gruesome crime.

I'm faced with a choice: grab some step ladders and spend the evening wiping the kitchen down, or just ignore it until tomorrow. Guess which one wins.

I head across the hall to the den. Next to my record player is the new Beatles album, still in its Vinny's Vinyl bag. Like a ten-year-old at Christmas, I tear off the protective sleeve, drop the 180-gram slab of heaven onto the turntable, and lower the needle. The music breaks the silence, and I'm cocooned in the warm, loving embrace of the best band that ever lived. The Beatles could almost be in the room with me, the sound from the vinyl is so close and raw. In a swirling harmony, they ask for help and explain that they need somebody.

Don't we all.

I dim the lights, sink into my favorite chair, and gaze at a collection of framed photographs on the wall beside me. My university days, a brief period in my life when I found happiness, an escape, when I made peace with denial. I did my fair share of drinking and partying, but music was my great love. I played keyboard in a band and we often packed local venues. One photograph never fails to make me smile. It focuses on our front man, Mark D'Stellar. His hair is long and he's properly rocking out, guitar hung characteristically low. Mark was a great singer, decent rhythm guitarist, and awesome friend. An excited crowd gazes up at him in awe. He grins back, effortlessly cool. At the side of the stage is a young man in a long coat, slouching moodily behind his keyboard. Me. Happy in a supporting role.

They were good days. Simple.

Most of the people in my gallery of memories went on to bigger and better things. Mark studied advanced physics and has some megabrain mathematics degree as well. My smile fades. I haven't seen him in years. I miss him and I wish things had been different between us, but some things can't be undone.

I massage my temples and try to forget that it's Amy's birthday and that Mum, once the backbone of my family, now lives alone in that place. The Fab Four sing of hiding your love away. I got through another birthday, I assure myself, until next year.

My thoughts drift. The music plays on, and I think ahead to "Ticket to Ride," the last track on side one. Once that's done, I will get up and turn the album over. It's the wonderful repetition of vinyl.

But I don't hear "Ticket to Ride," because I fall asleep.

When I wake up, sunlight is pouring in through the blinds. Wow, that must be the deepest—and strangest—night of sleep I've ever had. I don't remember a single thing! I stand up, stretch, and yawn. I don't feel refreshed at all, but then again, my sleep debt is in the red these days. I shouldn't expect miracles after just one restful night.

In the distance I hear the beeping of a recycling truck. I guess that's what woke me up. I check out the record player. It's empty, the lid is down. No spinning vinyl, no crackling stylus. Leaning next to it is the *Help!* album in its Vinny's Vinyl bag. Frowning, I inspect it and confirm it's still wrapped in its protective sleeve.

What?

My thoughts pick up speed.

If I slept all night, then this should be Friday. But the recycling is always collected on Thursday, just like it was *yesterday*. I can hear the truck's whirring hydraulics, crushing things into a pulp.

I also hear someone in the house, moving around upstairs. Me? It's me up there . . . My throat clicks as I swallow, my heart rate hitting double time. I check the big retro clock on the wall.

Thursday, December 12, 2019—7:05 a.m.

Amy's birthday.

Again.

It's Thursday morning. It appears—and I use that word advisedly—that I have accidentally hypnotized myself and . . . slipped back in time. Except this time, I've traveled back twelve hours! If that's true, then upstairs, there is a copy of me, waking up with a killer hangover.

The alternative is that this is another hallucination. In that case, I'm going mad.

A thought occurs to me as my mind races through how this might have happened. There is one way to be sure. With my heart pounding, I creep across the hallway and sneak into the kitchen, like an intruder in my own home. The lights are off, but I can clearly see the blender, pristine and ready for action on the worktop. The walls are clean, no murdered fruit. Also, no brandy bottle . . . because that must be upstairs with the other me.

My reality slides. I grip the cold, granite countertop, breathing heavily.

I had convinced myself that the "double Joe event" was a dream or a hallucination. After all, how could it be real? How could there be two of me in the same place at the same time? How could I possibly have watched myself disappear?

I couldn't. It's impossible.

Yet here we are. This is real. Soon the version of me currently brushing his teeth will walk downstairs in search of coffee. What would happen if he walked into the kitchen right now? Every time-travel story warns of the dangers of meeting yourself. If we meet, it could implode the world or destroy the space-time continuum. Wait . . . I try to work things through logically, rubbing my forehead. If I did meet myself, I would remember, wouldn't I? The thought makes me sway. I feel nauseous. After a few deep breaths, I pace up and down, pulling at my hair.

Think, Joe, think!

But there's no time. He's coming. I hear the familiar creak of the floorboards. I clear the hall in three light steps, desperately trying to keep the noise of my footfalls as low as possible, and dart into my den. The other me thuds down the stairs, groaning and sighing. I lean my head around the door and catch a glimpse of him, brandy bottle in hand, heading into the kitchen, bang on time. Obviously.

This is off-the-charts weird.

Right, all I need to do is hide in here until he goes out. I think through what I did next, *yesterday*, and nearly smack myself on my forehead. What an idiot! After securing a coffee I came in here! I googled whether hypnosis could cause hallucinations. Desperately, I scan my den for a hiding place. It isn't a big room, but in the corner is an old hat stand, piled with coats and scarves. I wrap a scarf around my face and hide behind the stand. It's pathetic, but it's all I can think of in my panic.

The other me stalks into the room. I watch in nervous silence as he does what I did. He blows the dust off the Mac, boots it up, and taps away. He mumbles, reassuring himself that the whole thing was just some weird dream, triggered by the hypnosis session with Alexia Finch.

Part of me wants to dive out and scream, "Oh yes! It triggered something all right!" Of course, I don't. I stay completely still and focus on not being seen or heard. Thankfully he doesn't spend long on the Mac, shuts it down, and leaves the room without incident. I remain where I am, concealed, not wanting to risk anything. After another ten minutes or so, I hear the front door closing behind him, and after waiting a few more minutes, I wander out into the hallway. I'm dazed and feel jet-lagged, which I suppose is right. I've crossed multiple time zones. Night is now day.

For a while I just stand there, breathing, processing. It's quiet in the house, just the distant rumble of traffic and nearby birdsong. So strange to think all of this has already happened. The people in those cars have made the journey before, they are turning down the same roads, swearing at the same bad drivers, probably laughing at the same jokes on the radio.

This is scary. It's crazy. And yet I find myself smiling because it's also amazing. I've slipped back in time, about twelve hours back. It's Thursday morning again. I know I didn't exactly intend to travel, it was an accident, but I don't really care, and that leads to a couple of obvious questions, both tentatively exciting.

Can I get control? And if so, how far can I travel?

The doorbell rings. My pulse quickens as I press myself against the wall and risk a peek through the kitchen window. I half expect it to be a version of me out there. Who knows how this works? How many Joes could layer up before breaking the universe? I'm relieved to see it isn't me. It's a middle-aged man in a suit, holding some pamphlets. He looks keen, a local politician maybe. He rings the doorbell again and then thankfully gives up on my vote. He wanders off and I exhale loudly. Why am I so nervous? It's my house!

But if I had answered the door, then Thursday morning would be changed forever. Only slightly, but that feels dangerous. I'm no expert on time travel, but who is? I understand one thing, though. I need to avoid changing anything that might affect the outcome of Other Joe's day. There may be rules at play here, and until I understand them, I'm going to be super careful.

I nervously pace and scratch my head for a bit, then decide it's probably a good idea to keep busy. After all, the other version of me doesn't get home until five p.m. It could be a long day if my mind continues burning this brightly. There are a ton of boring jobs that need doing around the house. I find some mind-numbing pleasure in the mundane tasks of tidying, cleaning, and organizing. For a little while I even manage to forget that I am reliving Thursday again, but it doesn't last. Ideas and thoughts crash around, demanding attention, and I'm not hugely surprised when a killer headache wraps its claws around my skull. I head to my bedroom, splash some water on my face, and take two pain killers. I'm tired. My body feels like it's about midnight, and I don't exactly have a positive sleep reserve to call upon. I sit on the bed and attempt to quiet my mind. It's like playing tennis. One side tells me not to change anything, the other volleys with the idea that . . .

If I could somehow get control of this, I might be able to save Amy.

"Slow down, Joe," I tell myself, not daring to dream. Hope is a powerful and dangerous thing. I need to go one step at a time. Luckily, I can't think of much at all now because my headache is getting worse. I curl up in bed, alongside my trusty digital clock.

Two thirty p.m. I've been in the past for seven and a half hours now. Soon, at five p.m. if I remember rightly, the other me will get home, at which point I will need to hide and ensure he completes his loop. *Do not fall asleep.*

Two forty-five p.m. Sleep? With this headache? Fat chance. And now . . . Brain freeze, like when you eat ice cream way too fast. Sounds funny. It isn't. This is getting worse and like the sleet outside, it isn't stopping. A thought occurs to me as I pace the room, clutching my poor head.

What if time travel is dangerous?

And I don't just mean changing things. I mean the process itself. It could be like X-rays. I feel like I'm coming down with the flu. I wonder if I've given myself radiation poisoning. I'm messing with powers I don't understand here. I'm a time-traveling crash-test dummy. Maybe we don't hear about time travelers because they all die during testing.

Three p.m. My brain freeze reaches a crescendo and the room turns a cobalt blue. I blink and wipe my eyes, but the inky hue remains, like I'm wearing tinted swimming goggles. Just as I convince myself I'm having a stroke, everything changes. In a wonderful rush of normality, I'm released from all my symptoms. The brain freeze, the headache, the blue—all of it gone, instantly. I peer out of the window. The wind has died down, and it's fully dark out there. No more sleet. It's like I blinked and someone turned off the storm and killed the lights.

"What just happened?" I ask the room.

The clock now reads 3:01 a.m. Not allowing myself to panic, I sneak downstairs. All the lights are on, and my kitchen again looks like a crime scene. From the den, I hear a stylus crackling and bumping against the edge of an album on the turntable. Everything, exactly how I left it on Thursday evening.

The big retro clock reads Friday, December 13, 2019—3:04 a.m.

Friday morning . . . Right.

After checking that the Other Joe is gone, I pace my den, working through the timing of my recent jump. After visiting Mum, I arrived home on Thursday evening at five p.m. I listened to *Help!*, fell asleep, and then, at seven p.m., traveled back in time to seven a.m. I then relived some of Thursday and, after a bout of brain freeze, returned to the present in the early hours of Friday morning.

Using my fingers to count, I play it through again. Eight hours in the past, and I get returned eight hours after I left.

A wave of understanding ripples through me.

"While I'm gone, time passes at the same rate in the present," I murmur.

Rules. If that's what they are, rules can be learned, tested, perhaps even mastered, or broken. My traveling this time wasn't deliberate, but so what? I learned something new: the symptoms, the brain freeze, all of this is information. I only have two jumps to compare but, aside from the distance traveled, there is a significant difference between the two. On my first jump I watched myself walk out of my bathroom, turn out the light, and disappear; I witnessed the moment of my departure, a kind of closed loop. Questions pop into my head like coins in a slot machine. Why didn't I remain in the past long enough to see myself come home and travel? Why was it different this time? Why did I only stay eight hours, not the full twelve?

Math is not my strong point, never has been, but facts are facts. I have traveled through time twice now. First, I went back ten minutes, and this time, twelve hours. I have no idea how all the pieces fit together and no clue what I will do next, but I'm smiling. It may have been an accident, but who knows how far I could go? What might happen if I could gain some control?

I see Amy's face, feel her hand slipping from mine, and grit my teeth. *Control.* I get that, and what's to stop me going back weeks, months, even years? Maybe, just maybe, all the way back to 1997.

All the way back to Amy.

PART 2

"YOU ARE THE EXPERT NOW."

Christmas 1989

My little sister was on her way. My grandparents were looking after me at home, and like the presents under the tree, my emotions were all jumbled up and filled with potential. Primarily, I was excited, but I was also a little afraid. Mum had been huge, her swollen tummy a curiosity. Dad was just worried. This was all new. I gazed out of the window, chewing my nails, hoping to see my dad's car. The seconds ticked by slowly. Grandma made me marmalade on toast and told me, "Watched pots never boil."

Grandpa was as excited as I was. "We are getting an extra-special gift this year."

I smiled back at him. "Best present ever."

A baby sister.

It was fashionable back then to cover a Christmas tree with multicolored lights and set them flashing like a nightclub. The room danced with the silhouettes of tinsel and festive ornaments. If my calculations of the box's size were correct, then Father Christmas was bringing me a Sega Mega Drive console. But that was all forgotten when I heard the slamming of car doors outside. I almost burst with joy when I first saw Amy wrapped in a cream blanket, the cold air and chemical smell of a hospital swirling around her.

For a few days, it was one big, exciting blur.

But it didn't take me long to realize that I hadn't thought all of this through. This unexpected gift *sounded* good, until the real impact became clear. My initial excitement faded, replaced by the kind of loss and grief only a seven-year-old can feel.

My parents couldn't see me anymore.

I didn't matter.

Within just a few days, it was confirmed. My life had changed for good. My parents were no longer mine. Three was no longer the magic number. I disappeared into my Sega Mega Drive, and my parents didn't even notice. Their full and undivided attention was on more important matters.

Most kids feel this way, I suppose. A new addition to a family is a huge adjustment. I simply wasn't equipped to cope. In my defense, at this self-centered juncture in my life, I couldn't think much beyond the next hour, let alone consider other people's feelings. As far as I was concerned, I had become second best, forever.

Unable to process these complicated emotions, I regressed, big time. My parents had their hands full, and like anyone with a newborn, they were hardly getting any sleep. I craved attention, stole it wherever I could, because even my parents' bad tempers were better than being ignored. Our house became a bomb, waiting to go off. Selfish? Yes. Absolutely. I was testing them, pushing boundaries, desperate to know if they still loved me.

It came to a head one Sunday afternoon when I deliberately smashed a cup and plate that an aunt had bought for Amy. Dad shouted at me, accused me of acting like a spoiled brat. Mum just told me she was disappointed, which was way worse. I said some horrible things, ran to my room, and slammed the door behind me.

I cried for hours, angry at the world, angry at them for ruining our perfect life.

I chose to ignore the fact that they had tried to prepare me. They included me, asked me to help choose storybooks, tried to let me know I still mattered and they still loved me. Acting like a spoiled, self-obsessed brat is how I repaid them.

Later that evening, Mum paid me a visit in my room. My expectation was another scolding, but she asked me to come and see Amy.

I was still grumpy, but I wasn't stupid.

In Amy's room Mum said, "Let's try this again, shall we?" She held my hand, and we walked to the edge of Amy's slatted wooden crib. My sister was awake, gurgling and punching the air in her pink onesie.

Mum talked to the little home wrecker. "Amy," she said, "this is your big brother, Joe. I hope you will aspire to be like him one day." Mum looked at me and smiled, giving my hand a squeeze, and then addressed Amy again. "Joe is very thoughtful and very kind. He enjoys a giggle." She tickled me as she said this, and I chuckled in delight. "And he loves music too. But you'll get to know him for yourself soon." She turned to me. "Daddy and I love you and Amy both exactly the same. You're very special, and no matter what happens, nothing will ever change that. Do you understand?"

I told her I understood, but I didn't. Not quite, not yet.

Dad joined us. He put his hand on my shoulder. "Amy is so tiny, so delicate, and that means she's going to need some extra help," he said. "Will you help us look after her?"

I was interested in this new role, but I needed more details. "What can I do?"

Dad leaned over the crib and admired his daughter. "Well, we need to make bath time fun for a start. I thought you might have some good ideas." We shared a moment of understanding, a short but fun-filled history of squeezy toys, boats, and bubbles.

"And I was hoping you could read to her and even sing some songs, if you'd like?" Mum added.

Dad fixed me with a serious look. "The thing is, Joe," he said, "you are the expert now."

"Expert? What do you mean?" I asked.

"In life," he said with a smile. "There's so much you can teach Amy. She doesn't know anything yet."

I felt a flush of pride. Looking down on this tiny person, a mind waiting to soak up the world like a sponge, it seemed obvious that I could teach her things.

Amy didn't cry much, but she started then. Mum lifted her up and handed her to me. I was reluctant at first, told Mum I felt better about things, that I didn't *need* to hold her. I was scared, afraid of hurting her, but they persuaded me.

Her soft head smelled of baby powder. I felt her warmth, her breath on my neck. That's when I felt the all-consuming, enveloping focus that would unite us together, our family of four. It felt good, felt right. Suddenly, the years before Amy felt . . . incomplete, as though we had all just been waiting.

We were a sketch. Amy finished the painting.

I patted her back and gently bounced her against my chest, like I'd seen Mum doing. Amy settled, her tiny hand wrapped around my finger, her firm grip melting any remaining worries away.

"She likes it when you hold her," Mum said, her voice soft.

"How do you know?"

Mum smiled. "She's nodding off."

"Does she even know who I am?" I whispered.

"I think she does. You're her big brother."

Amy snuggled into me and fell asleep.

And I realized that I hadn't lost anything. I had gained a little sister, someone to care for, to teach and love. And I knew then, at the tender age of seven, that I would do anything to protect her, anything to keep her safe.

7

In some ways I'm lucky that I don't have a real job. I sleep until eleven a.m., which I haven't done since I was a teenager. I feel refreshed but I'm aware of a new, unique sense of fatigue, energized but also depleted in equal measure. Now that I'm plugged back into the present though, I can feel my body slowly recharging.

Questions tumble around. What if I remain drained, unable to travel again? What if it was like a genie in a bottle, and I've already wasted my chances? I need a plan, one that presumes I *will* be able to travel again. My next trip through time will not be an accident. No, my next jump will be specific, deliberate, and targeted. Controlled.

The house is dark and messy, and to think, I need space. I need light and order.

Time to get to work.

I throw open the curtains and work through the house in a frenzy, tidying, vacuuming, and cleaning. It feels good to be doing something positive. As I finish up, moving a chest of drawers back into position, I see a white piece of card on the floor. It's my entry ticket for the 2005 Cheltenham Gold Cup. Horse racing has never really been my thing, but I went with Dad. It was a good day. As I take hold of the ticket, I feel the latent energy of the past, locked within.

Certain objects are stronger than others, brimming over with depth and clarity. Some, like this one, offer a mere whisper of the past. Psychometry is always a choice though. If I want to see, I must let it in, accepting what the object wants to show me. I decide it's okay. Sometimes my gift can be a comfort, like watching home movies or flicking though family albums. I've viewed this ticket before. It contains a single snapshot, a good memory.

I close my eyes and open my mind. The viewing comes easily, sharp, and clear as day. The past forms a living memory, the heat and noise of a crowded stand. I'm twenty-three years old. Dad is next to me. Hooves thunder in our direction, shaking the ground. My horse was called Take the Stand. I can see it now, coming around the final bend, clearing the last jump, strong and reaching. Twenty-five to one, and it's neck and neck. Next to me Dad is shouting and urging it on. We both laugh and cheer. Take the Stand came in second, but I put thirty pounds each way. It was a big win. Historic for me.

After we lost Amy, I hardly spent any time with Dad, which is why that day was so special, a hint at what could have been. I grab a magnet and stick the ticket to the fridge. One day, perhaps soon, my memories won't be tainted by my family's tragedies. I might be able to change everything.

The landline rings, wrenching me from my thoughts. It's Martin, and by the tone of his voice, it's bad news.

"Is Mum all right?" I ask immediately.

"Yes, as far as I know, she's fine. It's—" He pauses, for a little too long.

"Martin, what is it?"

"They aren't asking anymore," he says heavily. "They're going to repossess your house."

I frown, feeling more than a little déjà vu. "I know, you told me already."

"No, actually," Martin says, "I told you they might use the house as an asset to pay for your mother's care. I was preparing you—preparing myself too, I suppose—for an ongoing battle. This is different though. This is your mortgage lender, the bank. They're forcing you out."

"Can they do that?" I ask, pacing.

"Yes, I'm afraid they can."

"There must be something I can do?"

"We applied for a possession order and received a court hearing."

"A court hearing?" I stop pacing. "So what happens in court?"

"Been and gone. The hearing was two months ago." Martin sounds weary. "When did you last open your mail?"

Guiltily, I turn away from the massive pile of paperwork and unopened envelopes on my kitchen table. I stopped opening them a while back because it was never good news. "I'm a bit behind with my admin," I say.

"Well, I'm sorry, Joe, but there's nothing I can do," Martin says. "The bailiffs have set a date."

"Bailiffs?" A thickness forms in my throat. "When?"

"January seventh." Martin sighs again, heavier. "Joseph, listen. Carol and I talked, and with the girls still at home and my mother-in-law heading our way . . ." He pauses, takes a few breaths, and resets. "You could stay with us for a couple of weeks, but . . . I'm afraid long-term would be difficult."

"I know you can't take me in," I reply. "This isn't your fault. My paperwork has been a car crash waiting to happen. This is no one's fault but my own."

"Joseph," he says, voice cracking a little, "unless there's something you aren't telling me, I have no idea how you're getting out of this one."

There is a lot I'm not telling him. There is a lot I'm not telling anyone. And I'm *definitely* not telling him about the idea forming in my mind, crystal clear, like a shiny gem. I grin, so wide he can probably hear it.

"Joe? Are you okay?"

"I will be," I assure him. "I don't want you to worry about me anymore, everything is going to be just fine. You'll see."

When I woke up this morning, I was gearing up to travel all the way back to 1997 to save Amy. It seemed the obvious thing to do. Now it appears I have a more urgent problem. If I don't do something, I'm going to lose my home, and that is a distraction I could do without. My home is my castle, a refuge in which I will hone my newfound skills. To protect it, I have a new, short-term plan. But I want to get Vinny's thoughts first.

I arrange to meet him for lunch in Imperial Gardens, a small, well-maintained park in the center of town. Cheltenham is busy and vibrant, the sun a brilliant yellow ball against a chalk-blue sky. I breathe in the cool air. It's too cold to sit, so we stroll.

"I was here last week," Vinny says, "and some kids shouted at me, called me 'fatso.'"

"Kids can be horrible, mate," I tell him, knowing the truth of it.

"Do you think I need to lose some weight?"

"No," I say quickly. Vinny is a big guy. He would probably benefit from losing some weight, but now isn't the time to talk about it. "I love you just the way you are, and anyway, all that matters is how you feel."

He scratches his chin and blinks a few times. "I'll tell you how I feel." He grins. "Hungry."

I laugh and pull a couple of full English breakfast baguettes from my bag.

A smile spreads across his face. "Lovely jubbly," he says, patting his tummy.

We walk and eat. People dart across the park, busy as cars at an inter-section. Vinny bites into his huge sandwich, fat and heavy as a wooden club, and groans with pleasure as ketchup oozes from its edges. He talks as he chews. "So, what's up with you?"

"What do you mean?"

He regards me sideways. "I know you . . . something's on your mind."

"Okay. What would you do if you won the lottery?" I ask him.

Vinny laughs loudly. "Oh man, you have that dream too?" His eyes gleam with excitement. "Can you imagine?"

"I can. It would be amazing, wouldn't it?"

"What's going on, Cash? You're a dark horse!" He gives my shoulder a playful nudge. "Is this the part when you tell me you've won the lottery? That you're one of those secret millionaires?"

"I'm afraid not," I smile. "I'm just interested, that's all."

"Too bad," he says. "Well, anyway, I would share it about, chuck some your way, pay off my debts, and then carry on as normal."

"Really? You wouldn't change anything major?"

"Nah . . . I'm happy with my life. I love that old shop."

That must be a nice feeling.

We stroll and eat for a while.

"What if you knew the numbers in advance?" I ask eventually.

"Then I would pick them." He stares at me. "Obviously!"

"But would it be wrong?"

"How do you mean?"

"Would it be theft if you knew the numbers beforehand, if you could find a way to cheat the system?"

"I wouldn't think about it for a second. Anyway, you could always give some to charity if it made you feel better."

"Yeah," I agree. "That would repay the karma, wouldn't it?"

"Totally." Vinny raises his eyebrows. "I never bother with the lottery, but you got me thinking, I might give it a go tonight."

"Why not?" I smile, decision made. "Why the hell not?"

I'M BRITISH, THEREFORE THE FIRST THING I DO when I get home is put the kettle on. I think about Vinny. At heart, he is a conspiracy theorist and all-around sci-fi nut. I suspect he would have believed me if I had told him I'm a time traveler. *No problemo*, I can hear him saying. But there is a lot at stake here, and my idea is already complicated enough. I can't afford to tell him yet.

I run through the plan again, sharpening it like a pencil.

I'm going to travel back to last Tuesday and win the lottery. I've checked, and no one claimed the prize, so it's got my name on it. It's farther than I've been when accidentally slipping back in time, but I have a hunch about how I might make such a deliberate and specific jump, how to gain this level of control. I will never tell Martin this, but it's based on some advice from Alexia Finch, the hypnotherapist. *Objects can sometimes help people focus*, she'd said.

It's a good idea. I just hope it works.

In one of the piles of paperwork scattered around my house, I find a copy of Tuesday's *Gloucestershire Echo*. Close enough? I want to avoid myself during my travels, and Tuesday is the perfect day to do that. I was up early and went to see my bank manager in the morning. He was kind and helpful and realistic. That was annoying, but I'm hoping he's given me my second focus item. I hold it in my hand, his business card, a token, a link to that moment in time. After seeing him I spent the afternoon at my storage unit, pretending that my antiques business wasn't in total meltdown. And after that, I went to see Vinny, and he didn't need much persuading to go out for a couple of pints at his favorite local pub. I returned home around four fifteen p.m., just before Martin arrived. The house was empty most of the day. Like I said, ideal.

I head to the den, take a seat, and sip my tea.

Control.

So far, my jumps have been accidental. This time I'm going to jump with intention. Nice in theory, but I have zero evidence at this point. I lean back in my chair, holding my hands in prayer position and resting my chin on my fingers.

Departure location.

This is also problematic. The process of traveling through time appears to be instantaneous. What if someone is already standing where I land? I get a sudden flashback of my accident in the kitchen, the fruit splattered everywhere, and shudder. And what if I go back and land somewhere that is *different* in the past? We are always changing things; it's what humans do. The slightest difference could make a landing painful, if not deadly.

Time travel is dangerous.

But I am going to try this. I just need somewhere that is quiet, somewhere I can concentrate, that isn't crowded, that isn't my home, and hasn't changed for years.

LATER, I FIND A QUIET BENCH in the corner of Pittville Park. A little plaque informs me that the bench is dedicated to the memory of Ernie. It will be dark soon, and it's peaceful here, wonderfully deserted. I like it, the lake, the space. Plus, it's just a short walk to the nearest lottery-enabled shop. I could have done the lottery online, but I want the paper and my winning ticket. You can't argue with paper. It's proof, it's real. In my pocket I have a printout of all the lottery wins over the last two years. I am also prepared for a misjump. If I go too far, no worries, I can still win. All I have to do is ensure that the numbers don't fall into the wrong hands.

I'm aware of deeper concerns bubbling away in my subconscious, in the area labeled "Morals and Values." It's so easy to convince myself that winning this money is a minor tweak to the past, one that shouldn't really alter anything. But who am I to decide? If this jump is successful, then I am about to alter the past. That comes with inherent risks, doesn't it? For a few minutes I debate with myself, but the outcome is inevitable. How can I fear changing the past when that's actually my goal? This is an opportunity to prove that permanent changes can be made. I decide I am willing to live with the consequences. Whatever happens, it's worth the risk.

Right, come on, Joe, time to get focused.

I have the newspaper and business card. I concentrate and send my mind, just a few days back, to Tuesday morning. I breathe. In and out, slow and steady, just like the hypnotherapist showed me. I begin my countdown, opening and closing my eyes. Each time I open them, I check the date on the newspaper. It's cold in the park, and getting dark now, but I visualize the morning sun, feel it on my skin.

My breath, in and out, like the tide.

I've heard it said that if you sneeze with your eyes open, they can pop out. I'm not sure I believe that, but if you time travel with your eyes open, it's just weird and a little scary. Night becomes day. Suddenly there are cars, people, some walking dogs, a few pushing strollers. The temperature change is rapid, as though someone has just plugged in a heat lamp. I blink, breathing fast. Is it Tuesday? On unsteady legs, I walk toward the road. It's packed full of cars, all modern and familiar. It's morning, seems like rush hour.

I see a gardener on his knees. "Nice day," he says.

I smile. "Yeah, lovely. Er . . ." I hesitate, considering my next question. "Bit of a weird request, but can you just confirm the date for me?"

He checks his watch. "It's the tenth today, be Christmas before you know it."

"And it's 2019, right?"

He arches an eyebrow and nods slowly.

"Excellent," I say, grinning. "That is bloody excellent!"

I'M RELIEVED TO FIND THE SHOP IS QUIET. I nod to the owner and locate the lottery ticket stand. I pull the note out of my pocket and read through the numbers. Most of the lines are useless, they've already happened, but the last row is tonight's draw.

Six correct numbers on the national lottery and you win big. We are talking multiple millions. I don't need that much, and I don't need the publicity either. I thought about doing five numbers, but the discrepancy is huge, the winnings sometimes only a few grand. For my purposes, a better lottery is EuroMillions. In tonight's draw, five specific numbers plus one lucky star will bag me £221,000, enough to take care of Mum and keep the house.

Blank slip in hand, I copy out the numbers, fingers trembling. I can't shake the feeling that the time police might swoop in at any moment. I triple-check my numbers.

"Do you always pick the same ones?" a voice behind me asks.

I jump and almost shout, "Do you always creep up on people?" But I'm glad I don't, because the voice belongs to a sweet, silver-haired elderly lady in a blue raincoat. She smiles, revealing overly white dentures, and waves her ticket at me. "I'm with you," she chuckles, "you look lucky to me."

I study her and grin. "I haven't always been, but I think my luck is about to change."

Outside I inspect my ticket. If I could handcuff it to my wrist, I would. I think through where the other me is now and calculate he's with the bank manager. Poor him.

Time to execute the second part of my plan: binge-watching films at the cinema all day.

Drinking Coke to ensure I stay awake, I half watch whatever's on rotation: a forgettable rom-com, a horror movie, and then some action nonsense with cars and explosions. Around three thirty p.m., I feel the

familiar chill of brain freeze. It slides over the top of my already building headache. I make a quick calculation. Other me is drinking beer with
Vinny, which means I can head home and travel from there.

By the time I get home, we are talking brain freeze to the max. But
it's amazing what you can get used to, especially when you know that it
will come to an abrupt and wonderful end. According to the wall clock,
it's Tuesday at 3:55 p.m. I've been in the past nearly eight hours. I stand
in the middle of my kitchen, winning ticket in hand, and marvel as the
room becomes saturated in blue, like someone popped a cyan gel over a
hidden stage light.

Suddenly, it's like someone turned the sun off. Outside it's pitch black.
The kitchen is cool and dark.

I check the time and laugh.

Ladies and gentlemen, welcome back to the present! Local time is now
1:55 a.m. on Saturday.

I left on Friday evening, spent just under eight hours in the past, and
now I'm back where I belong. I run to my Mac and check the EuroMillions result, half expecting the numbers to be different. They are the same.
I'm holding a winning ticket! But I am not the only winner.

What the hell?

I lean back in my chair and laugh.

"You look lucky to me," the old lady said, and she was right. She
copied my numbers, meaning we are going to share the winnings: just
over £110,000 each. It's easily enough to get the bank off my back and
take care of Mum for a while. Sharing also helps me feel better about what
I've done. Less like a bank robber and more like Robin Hood. All I need
to do now is make a phone call and that money is in the bank. Martin is
not going to believe this.

But cash in the bank is just one ticked box. Now it's back to the main
plan. My first two jumps were accidental, but this one was nothing short of
a triumph. It was deliberate, precise. I was in control. I've learned, too, that
objects help me focus. Of course they do. I've always had a connection.

This is all coming together.

My mind races back to the night I lost Amy. Surely, this will be my next jump. I will solve the mystery of what happened to her, undo all the pain, change everything. I close my eyes and rub my temples. Even after such a successful jump, I know I need to stay alert. I mustn't rush. One step at a time. Traveling a few days back is one thing, but to save Amy, I need to travel back twenty-two years!

When people decided to go to the moon, they didn't just jump in a rocket. They prepared, they theorized, they tested, they calculated, and they tested again. It was dangerous, but they knew it was possible. I can't risk anything going wrong, the stakes are just too high, so I strike a deal with myself. One more controlled jump before I even think about 1997. Get prepared, like a good little Boy Scout. My next jump needs to be brave, ambitious. It needs to move the needle. I think of one of Vinny's favorite sayings, *Play big or go home.*

"Where do I go next?" I murmur, and I smile when I see the answer stuck to the fridge. The Gold Cup ticket I found earlier, an ideal object to help me focus.

It's decided then.

2005, here I come.

8

Saturday, December 14, 2019

I stuff a small rucksack with supplies and head out early. Six a.m., a good time of day. I've been thinking more and more about my landings, both into the past and back to the present. An awful lot can change over the course of fourteen years. Buildings come and go, walkways change, roads and pathways, entire sections of the town and its landscape, almost unrecognizable. Therefore, I've decided that time travel should be like buying a house. Location, location, location. That's why I'm climbing Leckhampton Hill. It's probably been here since the beginning of time, and there's a triangulation point at its peak, which I know has been here for over a hundred years, at least.

It's the best place for departures and arrivals.

It's nearly seven a.m. by the time I reach the top of the hill. The sky is crisp and clear, so I have a panoramic view not only of Cheltenham, but also of a decent slab of Gloucestershire, all the way to the Malvern Hills over twenty miles away. Of course, my focus for today is more local: the racetrack. I glance around. Earlier, I saw a couple of runners, but now, apart from a gray squirrel, I'm alone. I study the Gold Cup ticket. My target. Friday, March 18, 2005. A fourteen-year jump. Can I even go that far? There's only one way to find out.

If this test works, my next jump will be to save Amy.

I hold the ticket. Taking a deep breath, I close my eyes. I imagine the racetrack, buzzing with the excitement before the main event. Flickers of memory cascade into my mind. Dad told me about the jockey, the owners, all the work that goes into making a horse successful. I feel the cool wind on my face and the faintest vibrations beneath my feet. I wonder if I need to go deeper, further inside. I've heard people who meditate talk about searching for a singular moment, a thoughtless kind of peace.

I remember how Dad wanted his business to be successful, to grow so that one day I could join him. When the horse won, he was in such a good mood. We ate steak, and he told me he was proud of me. Life was good then. I felt connected to him.

I feel a subtle shift, and the ground seems to slide sideways an inch. I almost open my eyes, but I remain focused and will myself to the racecourse. I feel the sense of turbulence again, a vibration, and then I dip as though on a roller coaster that has just begun its descent. There's a sense of weightlessness, and then, instant calm. The temperature changes, and the quality of light shifts and becomes brighter. I open my eyes.

It's clearly a different time of year. I guess it could be March. Regardless, that was one smooth landing.

Leckhampton Hill is still quiet, but even from here I can see that the racecourse is busy, light glinting off helicopters as they travel in and out, carrying those rich enough to afford luxury travel. If I'm right, I just traveled fourteen years, first class all the way.

One step at a time, Joe. This is a test, and so far, things look good.

I need confirmation. I grab a small bottle of water from my rucksack and guzzle it down, determined to dodge the headache this time. To avoid someone recognizing me, I don a cap and sunglasses before heading down the hill.

As I navigate the paths, I pass a couple of walkers. Ramblers have dressed the same for decades, so I ask them the time and date. They tell me it's nine a.m. on March 18. I almost ask them the year, but they're already looking at me as though I'm mad, so I decide to find out another way.

Once I confirm the year, I will walk back up the hill and wait.

On the way into town, I see a poster for the Gold Cup and the year . . . 2005. That was a super accurate landing! I remember Vinny saying that he'd opened his shop in 2000. Strange to think that he's now been open for five years, and that he and I haven't even met yet.

I decide that for now, I will just soak in the past for a few minutes, just watch and observe, a time traveler blending in. Everywhere I look, the shops are different, either gone or in the wrong place or a different style, shape, and color. The people, clothes, logos, buses, cars—everything is a little softer and rounder, baggier.

I pause, the sun warming my skin. I overhear someone asking a friend if he's feeling lucky. They're joking around, red-faced, and it seems they've been drinking already. I smile and nod. I'm feeling lucky because I'm one step closer to Amy.

I check the time. Nine fifteen a.m. My father and I got to the race-course sometime before lunch. It's tempting to go and watch us from a distance. The thought scares and excites me in equal measure. I imagine seeing us together, as we were back then, before he went off the rails and left us. I can imagine it, feel it, but it would be dangerous to get too close. That's not why I'm here.

That's when the brain freeze kicks in. I feel the first bite of cold spreading out from the center of my skull like spilled milk. The roof of my mouth feels cold. This is way too early, I've only been here about fifteen minutes. I try not to panic.

My heart races, but I take time to consider my next move. I need to focus. My instinct is to head toward home. I break into a run and it feels good, seems to stave off the tingling and push back the icy chill. I know I'm going roughly in the right direction, but I'm finding it hard to get my bearings. I cut down a side street, and the brain freeze gets worse, confirming that I am not going to make it home in time.

Think Joe, think.

Where I land is critical. I take in my surroundings, wondering what would happen if I just stayed put, waiting for time to shoot me like a cannonball back to the present. But I have no idea how this entire area might have changed. If I get this wrong, I could end up encased in a ton of concrete, halfway through a window, or worse.

There's no way I can make it back to Leckhampton Hill, so I'm thinking maybe a park, but then I have an idea.

Vinny's Vinyl.

It's my best shot, and if I run like the wind, it's about four minutes from here. I break into my best version of a sprint, not pretty to behold, hoping it will be fast enough. Each lurching step shoots a fresh spray of ice inside my head.

I don't have long.

I arrive outside Vinny's Vinyl. The shop's sign, normally battered and flaking, is rich and deep in color. It looks almost new. A chill shivers through me as I descend the narrow stone steps and enter the shop. Music is blasting, the Clash, I think. The shop is like everything else in this version of Cheltenham: oddly familiar, yet somehow new. Posters depict old-school bands and artists—Mary J. Blige, Nickelback, Eminem—all smooth-skinned and impossibly young.

I stagger in and lean against a stone pillar, breathing heavily. I haven't run like that since I was at school. I notice with relief that there are no other customers.

A man approaches. I smell leather boots and body odor. I realize in a mighty flash that the man standing before me is Vinny. Same old Vinny, just a lot less of him. His hair is receding, but after knowing him without any hair at all, he looks like he's wearing a wig.

His expression is a cocktail of confusion and concern. That makes two of us.

"Can I help you, mate?" Thinny Vinny asks.

I catch my breath. "I just needed to be somewhere safe, and this is a place I know, somewhere that hasn't changed in years."

He looks understandably confused. "Do I know you?"

I'm aware I could travel at any moment, so I spill my guts. "I'm from the future. I need your help."

"The future?" He's intrigued.

"Yes, we're friends."

He laughs. "I've never seen you before in my life!"

"But you will, in about five years." I suck in a few breaths. "Please listen, I need to tell you something."

He folds his arms, smiling. "So, you reckon you're a time traveler?"

"Yes, and when I get back you—"

"All right then, Time Boy," he says. "What's my favorite album of all time?"

"Vinny, I don't have time for this," I say desperately. "I'm going back soon and there are some things I need to tell you."

He shakes his head. "No way, you're totally faking it."

Icy waves wash around the edges of my skull. "Okay, you changed your mind recently, but your favorite album is *Violent Femmes*. Best band ever, the Pixies. Gig you wish you'd seen but missed? Stone Roses, Spike Island. Now do you believe me?"

His eyes widen, big as saucers. "Whoa, you *are* a time traveler!" He laughs excitedly. "This is brilliant!"

"Listen, this is important," I say quickly. "When I travel, I land in the same location in the future. It's why I chose your shop, it's somewhere familiar, somewhere safe."

Vinny nods and laughs again. "Wow . . . my shop, in the future."

"I'm going to walk into your shop in 2010," I say, fresh urgency in my voice. "That's when we're supposed to meet for the first time. So you mustn't tell me anything about this, all right?"

"The space-time continuum, butterfly effect, got it!"

I wince in pain.

"What is it?" Vinny asks, mirroring my expression. "Does time travel hurt?"

I shake my head, "Not for long, but I nearly forgot. I come back on Saturday, December 14, 2019, and if my calculations are correct, it will be around seven thirty in the morning. I will land back in your shop, exactly where I am now. Do you understand, Vinny?"

With a determined expression, he says, "Got it. Keep the shop and this area completely clear."

"Exactly." I breathe a huge sigh of relief as a cyan glow descends over my vision, giving Vinny's shop the appearance of a tropical fish tank.

"Wait!" Vinny cries, taking a step toward me. "What's your name?"

"Joe."

"Joe," he echoes in wonder, as though I've just shared some exotic, alien name he could never have imagined.

"But you call me Cash."

9

In a silent rush, the room ages around me. The stone pillars are redecorated with modern artwork and posters. The carpet fades. The light shifts. Everything is rearranged, back to how I remember it, in the present. It smells dusty and stale and wonderfully familiar.

It's cold. My skin ripples with gooseflesh. December. I'm home.

The area around me has been cordoned off with bright yellow sticky tape, the kind of thing police do when isolating a crime scene. Clever. Vinny listened. Where is he, I wonder?

Speakers pop with the vibrant hum of volume gain. This is followed by the familiar sound of a needle hitting vinyl. "Get Back" blasts out, and I imagine Paul McCartney is singing directly to me. Vinny appears from behind a pillar, beaming.

"That was incredible, man!" he shouts over the music, bald head gleaming beneath the lights. "I can't believe it finally happened!"

He snips the tape with a pair of scissors and dances wildly to the music in celebration. I'm shocked by his overexcited welcome, but also from seeing Vinny change so quickly. I've just seen him age fourteen years in a matter of minutes. He is now back to his reassuring big old self, dancing like no one is watching.

My traveling exhaustion is due any minute, but for now I dance with him and catch some of his infectious energy. After the chorus, he turns the music down.

"Sorry about that," he pants, "but I've been so excited!"

"No worries," I tell him. "It's good to see you."

"You too." He shakes his head and whispers to himself. "Time travel. No way, man."

I indicate the flapping pieces of tape. "That was a good idea."

"I listened, did exactly what you said." Vinny shakes his head, smiling, hands on his hips. "All this time I've been waiting for you to come back from that day, and here you are."

I think it through. For me, 2005 is just a few minutes ago, but Vinny's had to wait years for this loop to close.

"When you came in the other day and mentioned the hypnotherapist," he says, "I thought that might be significant. Then, you asked me about the lottery yesterday, and I was like, this is definitely it! Plus, although it's been ages, you've started to look like you did back then, you know, recently."

"Whoa, Vinny, slow down," I say, holding up my hands. "First things first. Can I just check that everything is the same, as in how you and I met?"

"Of course, mate, sorry." Vinny looks a little sheepish. "I didn't mean to bombard you. Come on, we can talk in my office." He shuffles off and I follow him, the sweat from my recent run still cooling on my back.

Vinny's office makes my house seem like the tidiest place on Earth. There are half-filled mugs of tea everywhere, and an ashtray filled with cigarette butts. Vinny switches on two small lamps and collapses loudly into a beaten-up leather chair that looks like a prop from an old movie. I sit opposite him, on a retro machinist stool. "I wanted to check, Vinny. Obviously, you saw me in 2005, but we technically first met in 2010, right?"

He nods thoughtfully. "Yep, you bought four albums and wanted to pay cash."

I bob my finger at him. "And that's why you call me Cash, because I never carry cards." So far, it's all the same. It's a relief. That jump was the first time I actually changed anything major.

Vinny rubs at his ear, looking pensive.

"What is it, mate?" I ask.

He looks a little worried. "I call you Cash because . . . well, you told me to."

"Right," I say. "Yes, I suppose I did." I chew this little paradox over and then ask, "So, I come in the shop all the time?"

"Yeah," Vinny says easily. "All the time. We talk rubbish."

"That's a relief." I realize I've been clenched, hardly breathing. I try to relax.

Vinny looks eager to please. "When I met you, I pretended I'd never seen you before," he says, "just like you told me to."

"You did really well, Vinny, and I appreciate you keeping this a secret for so long."

He smiles, visibly pleased with my praise. "It's okay. No biggie."

It is though, and it's good to know I can trust him. He puts the kettle on and while it boils, grabs a pouch from his shirt pocket. He rolls tobacco deftly into a cigarette paper. Its dark, rich aroma hits me, and I almost ask if he can roll me one, but I know it would just send me into a coughing fit. He licks the paper quickly, lights it with a match, and puffs aggressively to get it going. He exhales blue smoke. "Do you want a coffee?"

"Yes, please."

He tugs open a drawer and pulls out a bottle. "We should celebrate your triumphant return. Spot of brandy in yours?"

"Go on then," I tell him. "Why not."

Vinny points to a packet of chocolate cookies. "You want one?" I take two of them.

He sits back down with a *humph*, sees my expression, and asks, "What's up, Cash?"

"2005 is the furthest I've been so far. It was a test."

"Right," Vinny nods. "I remember when you came into the shop, you were really worried, you told me that you needed somewhere safe. You were scared. What happened?"

"Initially, when I landed, I thought it went really well," I tell him. "I thought I would have hours in the past, but I didn't get very long at all, and brain freeze kicked in way earlier than I was expecting."

"Brain freeze?"

"It happens before I return."

He nods, as though this makes total sense. "So why didn't you get very long?"

"That's the thing, I don't know." I chew my nails for a few seconds, thinking. "This was only my fourth jump, but if I think about it, it seems like every time I travel back, I get less time."

Vinny sips his coffee. "It's almost like time is running out."

"Maybe." Hearing it out loud sends a ball of dread rolling through me.

"So what's next, are you going to go back and save Amy?"

"Actually, I was wondering how much you know."

"About her?" he asks.

"About my plans."

"Well," he shrugs, munching a cookie, "we haven't discussed it, if that's what you mean, but I know that if you've figured out you can time travel, then that's the plan. Save her. Right?"

I let out a little laugh. Vinny has a way of keeping things wonderfully simple. "Yes, that is the plan, but I think I'm going to need to recharge first."

"Recharge?"

I lean back in my chair. "I'm working on hunches and feelings, but 2005 took a lot out of me. It feels like if I jump that far, I can't just do it again immediately. I'm going to need some time between the jumps." I sip my coffee and devour both cookies.

"What does it feel like?" he asks. "Time traveling, I mean."

"It's quick. The brain freeze hurts, but the time traveling part is instantaneous."

He smiles to himself. "This is so cool, Cash. It's just the best, most awesome thing that ever happened to me."

"It is pretty awesome," I admit. "The rules are weird though, and I really need to understand them."

Vinny munches his way through another cookie, deep in thought. "There are always rules," he agrees. He slurps more coffee. "I wonder if you only have a certain number of jumps in you."

"What do you mean?"

"Like a gun with bullets. Once you've shot 'em, that's it. Game over."

"I hadn't really thought about it that way," I tell him. "I hope that's not the case."

Vinny puts down his half-eaten cookie. "Or maybe it's like a genie in a lamp, and you've been given a certain number of wishes!" he says excitedly, obviously proud to be coming up with ideas. That is, until he notices my expression. He visibly deflates, chewing his lip, guiltily. "Ahh, sorry. Not very helpful."

"Vinny, to be honest, you probably understand this more than I do," I say. "It's just, I'm worried I'm messing things up."

He shakes his head. "No way, Cash. You're going to save her. I know it. And actually, there is one positive you've totally ignored."

"Oh yeah, what's that?"

"You came back."

"How do you mean?"

"Think about it!" he says earnestly. "You don't know how this works. If this was a movie, you might have been trapped in 2005 for good!"

Vinny brings total optimism to any conversation, but there's often a dark angle. "I hadn't even considered that I could get stuck in the past, that I might never come back," I say.

"Well you did, and that's all that matters. I'm just so glad we can finally talk about this!" he exclaims, opening another packet of chocolate cookies. "It's been a long time coming. It's such a relief."

"I owe you one, Vinny."

"Yes, you do," he says, face lit up. "So let's talk about all the gigs I missed, and how you're going to go back, film them, and make Uncle Vincent very happy."

10

I shower, shave, and get dressed. On the sleep front, things are looking up. I got a decent amount of shut-eye, and it makes a world of difference to my mood. However, there's no point feeling refreshed if I then starve to death. My fridge is woefully bare. At some point, I really do need to go shopping. In the freezer I find half a loaf of bread. As I sip coffee and munch through my fourth slice of dry toast, I become increasingly convinced that I only have a specific number of jumps in me. There are rules to this, and I need to understand them fully.

That leads my thinking to Mark D'Stellar, my old friend from uni. He always knew what to do, always saw the angles. He lives and works in Bristol now, which is an easy enough trip to make, geographically at least. Do I go and see him? Maybe, but I will need to think about my approach. If I do, all I can do is hope that because it's about Amy, Mark will talk to me.

My thoughts are interrupted by a niggling sense that I'm supposed to be somewhere else. It's the same feeling I've had for a few weeks now, a whispering energy, emanating from upstairs in Amy's room. It's been calling me, and I've been ignoring it. Perhaps it's time to start listening.

Rooms have power, they contain energy. You don't have to be tuned into psychometry to know that. We've all felt it at some point, an undeniable and unique sensation when you enter a space—a sense of joy, or unease—that can send your skin creeping or heart soaring. Some people explain it away with stories of ghosts, blaming benign or malignant spirits with talk of good and evil. What is it really? It's us, I think. We pour our souls into the very fabric of our buildings, our homes, our sanctuaries. It's only us that instills them with meaning. These walls, these boundaries give the past a safe place in which to grow. And then our minds add fertile soil, helping the past establish roots. You don't have to be a time traveler to step into the past; sometimes it's right here in the present.

I take my courage in both hands and open the door to Amy's room.

It's neat and tidy, exactly how Amy left it. The air is still and faintly dusty, like in a museum. Her bedroom wasn't the biggest in the house, but it was always the brightest, situated on the corner of the house and getting natural light throughout the day. Sun streams in through one of the windows, and the pale-yellow walls glow warmly. I can see Amy now, staring wistfully out over the back garden. I caught her like this once, singing a song, a mixture of lyrics she'd heard and some of her own. I just listened for a while and then slipped away. It was an impossibly cute moment.

I feel like I shouldn't even be here, that if someone caught me, they would accuse me of snooping or a lack of respect. I walk in slowly, the pale-blue carpet soft underfoot. Amy's posters remain on the walls, like a shrine dedicated to the 1990s, along with some of her sketches and paintings. Her bed, with its bronze metal frame fit for a princess, is covered in scatter cushions and toys. They look lonely.

Part of one wall is a chimney breast, replete with a beautiful ornate fireplace, typical of a period property like this, and thankfully not ripped out when my parents bought it. To its right is a wooden chest crammed with Amy's clothes and personal belongings. On the other side is Amy's favorite piece of furniture, a kidney-shaped dressing table with matching stool. She loved hearing the story of where this came from, how it belonged to a little girl in a French château, a long time ago.

"How do you know that?" she would ask me.

I would smile and tell her, "I just know."

I sit gently on the little bed, afraid I might break it with my weight. I remember now why I don't come in here, why I stopped connecting with the objects. This room is a portal, a connection to Amy, and reliving the past is a perfect way to never move forward. My parents argued about what to do with the room in the years following Amy's disappearance. It was Mum who first accepted that Amy wasn't coming back. Time passed quickly in some ways and slowly in others. At some point Mum suggested it was time to redecorate, to go through some of Amy's things, to begin the process of moving on, but my father wasn't having any of it. I remember once catching him, sitting where I am now, crying. He never cried in front of me or Mum, in front of anyone. Like all of us, at various points, he was asking whatever God he believed in where Amy had gone. I wasn't sure what to say.

I tried to console him.

"This is Amy's room. Get out!" he shouted.

I froze. I wanted to help him, but the hatred in his face shocked me into silence.

"You lost her," he snarled. "You cursed our family!"

Tears streaming down my face, I told him that I was sorry, told him that I didn't mean it, that if I could take it back, I would.

"That's impossible," he said, bitterness in his voice. "But you could find out what happened to her."

"What do you mean?" I asked.

But I knew what he meant. My father knew what I could do, my connection to objects. He accused me of not using my gift. "You could find her, but you won't do it!"

I pleaded with him, tried to explain that it didn't work like that, that I had no control over it. He didn't want to listen. It was fair enough. All the blame in the world was on my shoulders. The loss of a child sends shock waves through a family, cracks the foundations, exposes weakness, and eventually, if left unchecked, it can bring the whole house down.

Here, in Amy's room, there are so many tokens of her life. Polaroid photographs. Sketches, awards, and badges from school. A shelf of fairy-tale books. Her jewelry. I've connected with all of them over the years, and they all contain stories, little vignettes, memories.

So why am I in here today? Because an object is calling me, a new one that wants to be found.

I open drawers, peer under the bed, even crack open a few photograph frames. Nothing. For the next few minutes, I turn the place over. It's frustrating. I close my eyes and exhale, trying to quiet my mind. "What?" I ask the room. "What is it that you want me to find?"

The answer comes not in words but in the language of psychometry.

A feeling. Magnetic. Powerful.

My eyes snap open, focused on the wooden chest in the corner of the room. I open it, and the sad, musty odor of unworn clothes washes over me. I rummage through shoes and scarves and then feel the tingle of connection. I pull out a small satin jewelry box and place it on Amy's dressing table. She received it for Christmas from our aunt one year, I forget exactly when. When you open it, a little ballerina mouse spins to the music. You have to turn the key to make it play, but I stopped winding it years ago because the music made me cry.

I'm afraid to open it, scared of the answers contained within, but it's a bit late for that now. Tentatively, I open the box. The pink velvet interior is still colorful and bright. I feel a pinch of grief squeeze my heart.

The object that has been calling me is Amy's hair ribbon, the one I found in the dirt the night she went missing. I don't remember when I last saw it. I remember bringing it home, my mum taking it from me. I remember the tears, the endless crying. I didn't know she'd kept it, and I wonder if perhaps I closed my mind to it, like I did so many of Amy's things.

I run it through my fingers, feeling the potent strength of the past laced within its overlapping fibers. "Have you been calling me the whole time? Should I have listened?"

If I'm going to get back to Amy, then surely this is the object to help me do it. I can hear Vinny warning me: *It's dangerous, you could get hurt.* He's right, of course, but who am I kidding? I'm not going to wait anymore. It's time to do this.

For the next few hours, holding the ribbon, I try and travel. I'm not sure what I expected, but I'm forced to admit that my batteries are dead. It feels counterintuitive to rest when I want to just run at the problem, but I need to.

So that's exactly what I do. I go shopping. I eat good food, juice some vegetables, doze, and listen to music, all the while holding the ribbon, connecting to the past. I think of Amy, of reaching the fair, finding out what happened, and finally, saving her. I relax. I stay calm. I recharge.

BY THE TIME MONDAY COMES AROUND, I'm feeling refreshed, buzzing in fact. I can practically feel the fizz of potential time travel tingling at the end of my fingers. I've decided that my destination should be near the fair. Somewhere I can focus, really feel the geography and the connection. It's midmorning. Just as I'm leaving the house, the phone rings. Martin and pushy salespeople are the only ones who use the landline these days, so I leave it to go to voicemail.

It's Martin. It doesn't sound important, a short message about a party at his place next week. Yeah. No. I'm not going to be there, because if this works, I'll be having my own party. Every day, for the rest of my life.

Cox's Meadow, the site of the fair, was just a great big field back in 1997. Now it's part of Cheltenham's flood defenses. Completely excavated and relandscaped, it's now a huge basin surrounded by trees and pathways. I explore for a while, trying to find a jump location that will avoid me landing in the middle of a stall or one of the hellish rides they had back then. In the end I decide it's best to avoid the fairground completely and choose a nearby field, one that looked identical in the past. It's quiet, has been recently mown, and is surrounded by a well-established hedgerow. In other words, ideal for a bit of discreet traveling. I walk to a large oak tree in the corner of the field and look back toward Cox's Meadow, imagining the fair in full swing. I have a sudden attack of nerves as I hold the ribbon. I feel its power. It seems to be ready, even if I'm not.

Come on, Joe. You can do this.

I think of Alexia Finch and feel instantly more relaxed. Time to practice my breathing exercises, to find my inner peace and calm, as much as I'm able. I take long, deep breaths, and within a few minutes, I sense the fabric of my location moving, the thin veil of reality fluttering gently, as if caught on a breeze. This field is just an illusion, and I can move through and beyond it if I wish. I close my eyes and think of Amy, of the fair, and the night she disappeared.

Amy. Here I come.

My heart beats faster but I command it to steady itself. I feel a shifting of the earth beneath me, and the sudden cool air of a winter evening. I open my eyes. It's dark. What the hell? Where am I? My surroundings appear to be phasing between different times. Day becomes night, grass becomes soil and grass again, tall stems that sway in a summer breeze followed by wet stubble and mud. The seasons accelerate around me. People flicker into life, but then are shadows, gone before I can make out any detail. Time cascades around me. Panic sinks into me. My mind spins. I drop to my knees. The skin on my hands is pearlescent, like fish scales shining under moonlight. As the sun returns, they become translucent, the blood within pulsing and coursing like an angry river.

"What's happening to me?" I whimper. I cry out for it to stop, but it won't.

Time accelerates, faster and more aggressive, spinning and swirling around me. Impossibly, I find myself floating, thirty feet above a building. I scream but there's no sound. Colors and shapes blur, and I'm instantly transported into the middle of a road, traffic thundering past me, a huge truck about to smash me to pieces. Then it, too, is gone. I'm in and out of time and space, and for one horrible moment I feel as though I'm going to explode.

And then, it all stops.

I feel the security of solid ground beneath me, and in the distance I see the fairground, but all my senses are overridden by a blinding surge of pain. When I look down, it all makes horrifying sense. I've made it to 1997 but I've managed to land right in the middle of a barbed wire fence. Sections of it protrude from my clothing at sickening angles, pinning my left arm and midsection. I try to haul myself up, but I'm stuck. I scream out in pain and frustration as brain freeze builds to a crescendo and the world fades to black.

PART 3

"OH, I THINK YOU CAPTURED IT PERFECTLY."

October 1995

It was the era of Blockbuster Video, rack after rack of entertainment just waiting to be consumed in the comfort of your own home. It was the best reason to have older friends. I watched films then that still scare me now. Amy, on the other hand, was obsessed with the film *Pretty Woman*. It had been out for a while, and Amy was still too young to watch it, but that didn't stand in the way of her obsession. Mum knew someone who worked at the local cinema and, after much pestering from Amy, persuaded them to get her a copy of the film poster. Up it went on Amy's wall. She would look at it wistfully, talking about how Richard Gere was so handsome, and Julia Roberts was so pretty. I couldn't disagree, but as far as I was concerned, it was a girl's film and not high on my early nineties priority list. I mean, how could it compete with *Terminator 2, Jurassic Park*, and *Die Hard*?

Finally, *Pretty Woman* was released on VHS. Amy begged to watch it, but my parents kept telling her the same thing. "When you're older, you can watch it as much as you like." Amy would get cross, complaining that she would never get to see it.

That is how *Prettier Woman: The Musical* was born.

I pleaded to be spared, but my parents insisted I should be nice to my sister and play the part of Richard Gere. I was forced to endure an entire Saturday of near-pointless rehearsals. Amy bragged that she'd written the whole thing from scratch, but there wasn't a script in sight. "Don't worry, it's all in my head," she kept saying.

Handwritten invites landed on the breakfast table the following morning. The stage was set, my embarrassment secured.

The previous year I had begged for and received some disco lights for my birthday. In my usual style, I had announced that I would be a famous DJ one day. Within weeks that dream had been forgotten, and the lights were shoved under my bed. Amy had fished the lights out though, along with a long-forgotten Casio keyboard. She had also liberated some costumes, courtesy of Mum, I presume. My school uniform was jazzed up with one of Dad's ties and an old hat. Amy, in way too much makeup, wore jeans and a crop top, and she tottered around in a pair of Mum's high heels.

Our parents sat down to watch the performance. They smiled at Amy but looked a bit sorry for me. They had, after all, sacrificed me to the whims of a five-year-old girl. The lights flashed. I pressed the auto accompaniment button on the keyboard and spent the first half of the show (oh yes, there was an intermission) doing little more than pressing single keys to change chords, while Amy danced. She made up the story as she went along, dragging me onstage occasionally and then escorting me off when the scene imploded.

One thing was crystal clear. Unlike me, Amy had not managed to sneak in a secret viewing of the film at a friend's house. She had absolutely no idea what *Pretty Woman* was about. Her version was a random patchwork of her influences to this point, a half-baked story about a princess and a man who worked at a bank. It turned out that my character was secretly a painter or sculptor, but the story changed as it went along and petered out quickly near the end. Amy got angry with me because I wasn't keeping up with her on-the-fly alterations. I remember my parents laughing quite a bit. Mum even clapped along at one point. I expected Amy's musical to invoke groans, some laughter, and eventually mild boredom, but there was a subtle sadness in my father's expression that I didn't understand back then. With the benefit of hindsight, I wonder if he felt the pain of time, the sense of a life split into parts and intervals, one that—no matter how magnificent, crazy, and filled with wonder—must eventually come to an end. I guess I will never know.

Amy shuffled on in yet another new outfit, wobbling on high heels. She nearly fell over during an overenthusiastic pirouette. Mum and Dad were both in tears, and whatever it was that consumed my father's thoughts, it appeared to leave as quickly as it had arrived. Dad was always careful to tell us that he was proud of us both, that he loved us equally, but I knew Amy was special to him. I accepted it, because I think it's true what they say about fathers and daughters. There is no love more powerful in the world. It is a bond that cannot be broken. He blinked away tears and announced that while the show was incredible, it was definitely time for dinner. Amy and I held hands and bowed.

While we ate, perhaps sensing her audience's confusion about some key points in the story, Amy asked what the film version of *Pretty Woman* was about. My father considered this and, after a long pause, said, "Oh, I think you captured it perfectly."

11

Monday, December 16, 2019

"Mr. Bridgeman?" A woman's voice echoes softly through the void.

I try to answer, but my throat is a dry riverbed. My eyes won't open. I try to move, but my body isn't playing either. More voices, muffled by the sound of machines whirring and beeping their self-important tunes. I'm in a hospital.

I'm alive.

A man's voice, off to my left, slow and serious. "We've just received the X-rays," he says. I hear the acetate being manipulated. "Sections of a wire fence, one piece embedded in his thigh, another through his side, and one through his abdomen." He inhales thoughtfully. "He's lucky it didn't pierce any major organs."

With what feels like superhuman will, I force open my eyes, and a dazzling golden world floods into view. I tense my abdomen, wincing at a flash of brilliant white pain, hot as a grill. I groan, shifting my weight slightly.

"He's awake," a nurse says.

A short pale man with a thick beard leans close to me. "Mr. Bridgeman. You are in Cheltenham General Hospital, you've been in an accident. Do you remember what happened?"

Unfortunately, I remember only too well.

"How are you feeling?" he asks. "How is your pain?"

Something sore and sticky rattles in the back of my throat. "Hurts,"

I say, my voice a pathetic croak. The doctor presses a red button attached to a drip and the pain slips away in a warm, albeit queasy, rush. "Thank you," I say, lips numb.

"Can you tell me what happened to you?"

I decide that honesty would be a bad policy now, but I'm too drugged to be clever. "I was, er, walking and I fell over. Into a fence."

He nods, clearly concerned but also confused. "Mr. Bridgeman, you were found and brought here with three pieces of wire running *through* your body. This wire has been cut neatly at the edges." His tone is uncertain, like he doesn't believe what he's saying. He examines an X-ray intently, holding it up against the light. "There are no signs of entry, no ripping or dragging, no torn flesh. If this was an *accident*, it makes no sense." He looks at me questioningly.

I clear my throat. "Just one of those things," I say nonchalantly.

"Sure." I can tell he's frustrated by the fact that he can't work out what happened, and I won't tell him. "You're very lucky that you managed to miss all your vital organs, and you didn't hit any arteries either. Some of the wire is embedded into the muscle, but it's so clean, it should be comparatively straightforward to remove."

I swallow. "Remove?"

"Yes," he says. "We're prepping you for surgery."

A nurse removes the bandages on the right side of my abdomen. There are three stubs of shining metal, like tiny rivets protruding from my skin. I start to work out when I last had a tetanus injection, but my thoughts are interrupted. A tray of instruments crashes to the floor, coinciding with a rush and a wonderful release from pain. I let out a long, deep exhalation and begin breathing normally. Only now do I realize how tense I've been.

The nurse inches away from me, "Doctor, I think you need to see this."

The doctor steps forward. "That's impossible." He presses my side gently, leaning in for a closer look. "It's steel, it can't just . . ."

"What?" I ask.

He stares back at me, confused. "It can't just *disappear*."

Over a few hours of prodding and a couple more X-rays, a parade of medics ignores me completely as they discuss my bizarre injuries. Finally the room empties, the throng of doctors and consultants no doubt decamping for a more private discussion. Gingerly, I move my body, and I'm surprised by how little pain I feel. As I shift my weight and lift myself up in the bed, I actually feel okay. Bruised and aching, but otherwise all right.

"That might just be the world's weirdest form of acupuncture." It's a voice I recognize.

"Vinny!" I laugh as he enters the room. "Good to see you."

"I was worried there for a bit." He flashes me a pained smile.

"Yeah, I'm sorry."

"I'm just glad you're feeling better," he says. "What happened?"

"I had a bad landing and brought some fence back with me, but then it disappeared," I say. "Guess it didn't belong here."

"Does it hurt?"

"It just feels sore now, like after you've had a tooth removed and the anesthetic has worn off."

Vinny glances around, leans in, and whispers, "How far did you go?"

"I reached the fair, Vinny. I made it back to 1997."

He looks at me, incredulous. "Sheesh madeesh! You didn't!"

"I found Amy's hair ribbon," I tell him, "the one she was wearing the night she went missing. It helped me, I think." I hold it tightly. The energy is still there, but it feels less insistent now, weaker.

"What is it?" he asks, noticing my expression. "What's wrong?"

"I was so close, but I only stayed for a few seconds."

"Why?"

"I don't know." Vinny's expression mirrors my own worry and concern. "What if I'm like a battery, and I've used up all my juice? What if I should have tried this years ago and now it's too late?"

"What do you mean?"

It's an idea that's been brewing in my subconscious. "I probably could have traveled before, but I didn't." Anger and regret fill me. "I've wasted so much time. All these years, with this potential ability . . ." My eyes sting, my chest tightens. "I know I could be imagining this, but it feels like my opportunity is fading, like a light bulb dimming."

Vinny winces in empathy. "It might *feel* like that, but you don't know how this works."

"That's why I need to try again, Vinny. Before it's too late."

"Joe," he says, firmly. "If you carry on like this, you're going to end up killing yourself, and then where will Amy be?" He sits on the edge of the bed. "I believe you've been given this gift for a reason, but you need to understand it. Is there anyone else who can help you figure out what's going on?"

I let out a long, slow breath while I consider whether to say the name out loud. I decide there's nothing to lose. "Mark D'Stellar."

"Who's he?"

"He's an old friend from school, a real megabrain. He's got letters after his name and everything."

"Sounds perfect!"

"I'm not sure. Mark's clever, but we fell out, and we haven't spoken in a long time."

Vinny considers this. "Whatever happened between the two of you, this is about Amy. That changes everything. Go and see Mark. Ask him for help."

I place my hand on his shoulder. "Thanks, Vin, I appreciate it."

We sit in silence, listening to the beeping of machines and distant voices in the corridors. At some point I think I must drift off to sleep, because when I open my eyes again Vinny's gone and I'm alone. I peer down and gingerly prod my abdomen. The wire may have disappeared, but the pain still throbs, hot in my side. I sniff the air, strong disinfectant masking everything, and hear the squeak of rubber-soled shoes in the corridor outside. It's strange to be here. Hospitals always make me think of my dad. I remember slipping in the bath when I was about nine years old, him passing out when they stitched up my eyebrow.

My solitude is broken by a friendly nurse who asks me to grade my pain from one to ten, which is such a relative question. I consider what it would be like to be burned alive and tell her seven, hoping that will bring out the good stuff. Finally, a decision is made to pump me with morphine, which isn't as much fun as I was hoping. It makes me feel nauseous, and at one point illustrated animals dance across the privacy curtain. An elephant in a tutu, a monkey crashing cymbals together frantically. I know they're hallucinations, but they're also fascinating. I'm relieved that the animated circus doesn't last long or access the darker part of my mind. In the drug-fueled haze, my sense of self drifts sideways a little. As I fall into a restless sleep, thoughts of my father in the hospital, combined with the morphine, trigger a painful memory in the form of a detailed dream, a day I wish I could forget but often haunts me.

I'M THE PASSENGER IN A BATTERED FORD FIESTA, hurtling down the motorway. My feet are pinned on either side of a rusting hole in the floor, through which I can see the surface of the road whizzing past at sickening speed. It's summer, 2005, the windows are down and the White Stripes' *Elephant* blasts out from the underpowered stereo. Mark D'Stellar is driving, singing along at full volume, fighting the whine of the engine. "Twenty minutes to Cheltenham," he barks, "if I keep my foot flat down!"

I nod and smile. Cheltenham. Home. I haven't been back for months and feel bad about that; not terrible, but I know there will be some emotional bridges to cross, some awkward unseen membrane to break through before Mum and Dad will welcome me back fully.

"How do you get on with your folks these days?" Mark asks, as if he's reading my mind.

"Oh, not so bad I guess," and then, without thinking, I add, "Mum and I get along fine."

He smiles, knowingly. "Me and my old man haven't spoken in years. Separation. It's part of life, you know? I reckon we might get along one day, when he's old and I've grown tired of having fun." He nods his head enthusiastically to the music, which has just reached a crescendo.

I watch the patchwork of fields flashing past the car window. Since losing Amy, Dad and I have been drifting. We've talked on the phone, but only pleasantries, nothing of any substance. I want to see if I can change that, make more effort, break through his barriers. We all lost, we all hurt. Dad is bottling that up, and it's not healthy.

After more smoking and singing, Mark and I arrive in Cheltenham, not far from my parents' house. I want to walk the rest of the way, take in the place, reset my bearings, and adjust to the calmness of home. "Thanks for the lift, mate," I say, offering him some cash. He frowns and shakes his head. "Take it easy, man. See you after the summer for some more deviant behavior."

I drag my suitcase along the tree-lined street. The last time I spoke to Mum, she said Dad was worried about losing control of the business, that he had been at home more often. This was unlike him. Mum described things as "difficult." That could mean anything though. My mum is tough. She would probably describe being eaten alive as an "inconvenience." Whatever's going on, I decide, if possible, to connect with Dad again and who knows, maybe even lift his spirits. Take him fishing like we used to do, or just drink a beer together.

I'm home two weeks earlier than expected and plan to surprise them, but when I walk up the driveway, I'm disappointed to see it's empty. Maybe they're out? I notice Dad's workshop door is open. Originally a stone double garage, he partitioned it, one side a garage, the other a workshop to accommodate his woodworking hobby. He's actually very good at it and could, in my opinion, run a handmade furniture business on the side.

I knock on the door but don't hear an answer, so I walk in. The radio is chatting away to itself. The workshop is empty, absolutely immaculate. Dad is very particular about cleanliness, a quality that he claims skipped me on God's production line, but I can't remember ever seeing his workshop so organized. His workbench has been cleared and his tools are back in their slots in the rack he built to house them. Each has its place, each one angled the same way. I feel an unexpected lump of dread land in my gut. I've never seen it looking so . . . ordered. Like he was expecting visitors.

"Dad?" I call out. I hear machinery next door and smile. He's working on one of his projects after all, a wreck of a classic car that only he is convinced will ever be roadworthy again.

I walk toward the sound of the engine and pause. The internal door that separates the workshop and garage is closed, but through the large glass panel I see movement, swirling. I step forward, my hand hovering over the handle for a moment. When I finally open the door, I'm hit by a cloud of foul-smelling fumes that covers me like a duvet. I step back, coughing and gagging. Inside the garage I make out the cherry-red paintwork of Dad's project car and, through the mustard haze of smoke, the shape of him slumped at the wheel. My scream arrives, the weight of the truth pulling me to the floor. I fight the building panic and shock, and stagger into the smoke.

He can't be gone. Not Dad. Not him too.

I'M ALONE WHEN I WAKE. The hospital smells of bleach but there is a familiar undertone of exhaust fumes, a sour odor that stains my memory and often lingers when I dream of that awful day. Sometimes I hate my dad for what he did, for checking out of this world, but I can't blame him. He just couldn't do it anymore.

THE FOLLOWING DAY I am feeling a bit better. Amazing how the body heals, especially after the interesting acupuncture I subjected mine to. The hospital staff nuke me with a course of antibiotics, and two days later, on Thursday, I'm finally discharged and limping home. The metal caused some scarring of the muscle on the inside of my right thigh. It aches, but apart from that, the only evidence of my torture is the circular scabs left by the exit wounds. They itch, which means they're healing.

It's raining heavily when I get home. The house is dark and cold. It smells musty and sour, probably some fruit and vegetables gone bad. The phone rings. It's Martin.

"Where have you been?" His voice is a mix of frustration and a hint of concern. "I've been trying to get hold of you."

"I was away. Forgot to take my phone, sorry."

"Where did the money come from?"

"What money?" Then I remember: the lottery. In all the pain and excitement, I'd almost forgotten about winning. "I robbed a bank," I tell him cheerily. Then I tell him the truth, a version of it anyway. Martin can't believe my luck. He isn't the only one.

"I know things are tough right now," he says, "but we're having some people over to the house on Monday evening, a bit of a pre-Christmas party. You're welcome to come along." After a pause, he adds, "Carol would be happy to see you."

Martin's second wife thinks I'm a pain in the arse. She's right. I thank Martin for the invite and tell him I will think about it. We both know I won't be there.

Over the next few days, I do very little but heal and rest. Vinny calls a couple of times to help me plan. He also makes me promise not to travel again until I understand the rules. He's right. I need help.

On Sunday morning, I find a recent article online, entitled "A Numbers Game: Considering the Role of Infinity in Our Understanding of the Universe," by Mark D'Stellar. Sounds boring, but in Mark's words, it's an interesting read. He writes of Aristotle, infinity, and multiple dimensions, and I succeed in following the gist. The illustrations help.

I stare at Mark's picture at the end of the article. Mark D'Stellar, Professor of Mathematical Sciences, Bristol University. I call the campus and explain that I'm an old friend who would like to surprise the professor. They advise me to drop in at the end of his last lecture tomorrow.

I haven't seen Mark in years. We were good friends for a long time, but my psychometry created a dilemma for me that opened a rift between us, which eventually grew into an almighty chasm. Sometimes my gift for seeing the hidden past with objects can also be a curse.

I couldn't tell Mark what I had seen because some secrets are best left buried.

But tomorrow I'm going to dig mine up.

12

Monday, December 23, 2019

Bristol University. When I read that article, I knew it was time. I also knew it had to be face-to-face. Sometimes it's the only way. I'm nervous about seeing him again, about his reaction to me just turning up like this, but I remind myself that whenever I needed to understand the impossible, Mark D'Stellar was always the man.

I check a nearby campus map and head in the direction of the lecture theater. It's been a week since the accident. I'm still limping, but my body has healed quickly. The building is modern, framed by a neat lawn. Students roam around. It's weird being here, reminds me of when I was in school, where Mark was by far the coolest kid: good-looking and mature for his age, rugby captain, and lead guitarist in a rock band. After what happened to Amy, I had withdrawn. School became a prison sentence for me, until one day when Mark asked me, "You play keyboard, right?"

It was a pivotal moment in my life, a moment so blessed and perfect I still can't quite believe it happened. After an audition in which I was so nervous I could hardly play, I became the first and last keyboard player in the Dark Angels. I suddenly had friends, girlfriends, and kudos. I even grew a few inches, as if the weight of the universe that had stunted me was suddenly lifted. I often wonder how different my life would have been if Mark hadn't come along, or if we hadn't followed each other to university. Luck shines on everyone at some point. Even me.

Eleven a.m. A bell rings. My heart rate increases, and I steady my nerves.

Then I see Mark walking in my direction, tall, striking, with an air of easy confidence. His black hair is shorter now, flecked with gray, and he's stockier, but it's him all right. He sees me and stops a few feet away, shaking his head. "Well, well," he says, "Joseph Bridgeman."

"Hi, Mark," I say. "It's good to see you."

"You too," he says. "What are you doing here?"

"I know it's unfair of me to just drop in like this, but I really need your help."

"Why didn't you call?"

"I did. They said you would be here."

"I don't mean now, today." His face wears a pained expression. "I mean ever."

"I'm sorry, Mark."

"Right," he says. "I'm sorry too. It's the last day of term. It's nearly Christmas, Joe. I've got stuff going on."

"I do appreciate that, and I wouldn't ask if this wasn't urgent."

"I can't believe this," he says. "You just turn up out of the blue, asking for my help, like nothing happened, like everything's fine."

He's angry, has every right to be. All my planning and now I'm struggling to find the right words. The silence between us, all these years, returns heavier than ever.

Mark folds his arms. "Are you ill?"

"No, it's nothing like that." I pause. "It's Amy."

His expression softens and his defenses melt away. "Oh," he says. "I'm sorry, did they find her?"

"No, it's not that," I say. A group of students walks past us, giggling. "I can't really tell you here. Can we go somewhere and talk?"

"Joe . . ."

"*Please*, Mark. All I'm asking is that you hear me out, and then, if you want, I'll disappear. I won't bother you again."

He laughs. "Yeah, you're good at that." I deserve that. Mark shakes his head and sighs heavily, the first chink in his armor. "If we go to my office, we will probably get locked in. I'm due at a friend's house this afternoon and I have dinner plans this evening." He pauses. "But if this is about Amy, then of course I want to help."

"Thank you."

"On one condition." He points a finger at me. "I want a favor from you in return."

"Of course," I say. "Anything."

"I want a full explanation." He fixes me with a familiar, determined glare. "Why you cut me out, why I haven't heard from you for all these years. The truth."

My throat clicks as I swallow. "Mark, I can't do that."

"Fine," he says, expression cold and blank. "Well, it was good to see you again." He turns and starts to walk away.

"All right," I tell him. "You win."

He turns back. "Sian is away with the kids until tomorrow, so we can go to my house and talk there. I need to get ready anyway."

Mark's wife is the same Sian I had a crush on all those years ago, the girl from the fair. They got together in the last year of university and were married four years later. I was happy for them, but when my psychometry revealed Sian's secrets to me, it was the end of my friendship with Mark. It was just too difficult to pretend I didn't know.

Mark drives. We head to his house in silence. There's a lot of water under the bridge of our friendship. I gaze out of the window of his expensive BMW at the bustling suburbs of Bristol. People race around like ants, most of them either talking on or playing with their phones, connecting with loved ones, friends, work colleagues. It highlights the distance between us.

At midday we arrive at Mark's house, a large Victorian property with a sweeping gravel driveway surrounded by a walled garden. It's peaceful, idyllic, and no doubt cost a fortune. In the center of the driveway is an ancient oak tree. He parks beneath its canopy and we get out.

I pause for a few seconds, basking in a rare moment of sunshine, the welcome warmth on my face. In the distance are the raucous cries of children on their afternoon break, a plane overhead, a dog barking.

Mark turns to me. "Are you all right?"

I nod and tell him I'm fine. If my plan goes well, he will understand soon enough.

"Come in," he says. "I'll put the kettle on."

The hallway is covered in glossy family photos. I admire one with his two daughters wearing smart, matching uniforms.

"They're beautiful," I say.

"Thank you," he says, a hint of pride in his voice. Another photograph is of Mark and Sian. They are seated at a small wooden dining table on a white beach, palm trees in the background. Paradise. From their age and lack of bags under their eyes, this one is before they had children. They look happy. Perhaps they were. I follow Mark into the kitchen, which looks like the set of a cooking show. There are more family photographs here. Mark makes tea, and we sit opposite each other at the kitchen table.

"So," he says, leaning back in his chair. "Here we are."

Questions swirl around my head at speed. I'm desperate to ask Mark about my time traveling, but I know I need to pace my delivery. Mark is a man of science. He will want me to build the story logically, piece by piece. I wonder where to start.

"I went to see a hypnotherapist," I tell him, "to see if she could help me sleep."

He shakes his head. "We can talk about that in a minute. First, I want you to tell me why I haven't heard from you. What happened?"

My heart sinks. What happened was I saw things I didn't want to see. My psychometric viewings sometimes reveal things I wish they didn't. On this occasion, it was a house party at my place, a good one if I remember, a kind of reunion a few years after our university days ended. Sian and Mark had been together a while by then. She dropped a silver earring at the party. When I found it a few weeks later, it had a story to tell.

And that tiny piece of jewelry was all it took to bring down a solid friendship.

"Joe?" Mark says. "Are you going to tell me or not?"

He always was persistent. I stare at him, his thoughts not yet tainted with knowledge of his wife's infidelity. The earring was given to Sian by

Chris Tomlinson, one of our so-called mates. They were embroiled in a long-term affair. I considered telling Mark so many times, but whenever I played the scenario through in my mind, it never ended well. Mark wouldn't stand for cheating. I would be forever known as the one with the weird gift, the one responsible for breaking up his marriage.

"This isn't fair," I tell him. "I don't want to judge anyone."

"You saw something, didn't you?" He leans forward. "You saw something you shouldn't have."

"Mark," I say nervously, "it isn't straightforward."

"When is it ever?" He sounds bitter, defeated even.

The earring had one more secret to share with me. Sian was thinking about leaving Mark, but there was a deep river of uncertainty, pain, and regret. I saw this, and as with so much else in my life, it held me in limbo.

Mark exhales loudly. "I can see you're struggling, Joe," he says. "So, I'm going to make this easy on you. I think I know what happened." I say nothing, afraid to move a single muscle in my face. "It all came out last year. Sian told me everything."

"She did? Everything?"

He stands and looks out over the garden. "I know about her affair with Chris." He turns to me, offers a weak smile. "Do you want to know the saddest part? It came out because *I* had an affair."

He stops talking. "Go on," I say.

He looks embarrassed. "After we had the kids, things weren't great between us." He shakes his head. "I'm not making excuses. I was an idiot. A student showed me some attention. She was attractive, but she was smart and interesting too. I actually *liked* her . . ." He trails off, as if silently berating himself for his enthusiasm. "I messed up. It didn't last of course, but the guilt . . ." He lets out a hollow laugh. "I ended up telling Sian, and it opened the floodgates. All our problems spilled out."

I swirl my mug of tea, feeling suddenly awkward. "I'm sorry."

"No," he says, "don't be. It was a good thing. It was a year ago now, and we've been working on our relationship. We've stuck with the counseling, and honestly, it's better now. More genuine, I think. Who knows, we might still make a go of it."

The relief is huge. The air feels clearer already.

Mark studies me. "That was it, wasn't it? Chris and Sian, that's what you saw?"

I nod.

"And you didn't tell me."

"I couldn't."

A year or so after the party, Mark came to see me and suspected Sian was seeing someone. He was drunk, and in the end he accused me, said I had always wanted to steal her from him. That hurt, on so many levels. Part of me always blamed Sian for Amy's disappearance. Stupid and unfair, I know, but I couldn't help it. When she got together with Mark, I suppose there was a tension between us that could easily have been mistaken for suppressed attraction. The truth was, I had to dig deep to accept Sian, to spend time with her in a group, but I did it because Mark was a friend.

He places both hands behind his head. "I feel bad about the night I came to see you, about what I said."

"It's all forgotten," I tell him. "It doesn't matter now."

He glances at me, because we both know it does.

"I understand why you didn't tell me." Mark pauses and then reluctantly says, "I would have done the same."

"Really?"

He nods, and for a few minutes, we adjust to our new world. It continues to spin. The clock ticks. "You know, we could have done this sooner if you'd answered your phone," Mark says eventually, "or my emails."

"I don't really do any of that answering stuff anymore," I say apologetically. "I've become a bit of a hermit."

He laughs. "No kidding."

The air settles for a while longer as I plan my next move. I know Mark. Once I start he will become a question machine, and I want to give him the answers he deserves. Also, now I'm here, I realize that every step on this journey needs to be a deliberate one. Each decision will either move me closer to saving Amy or further away. Coming here today was the right move. Now, I just need to win him over and gain not only his wisdom, but his support. I believe he is the key to unlocking full understanding of my abilities.

"So what's this all about?" Mark asks. "You said it had something to do with Amy."

"It has everything to do with her."

"Okay then," he says. "I'm listening."

And so I begin to tell him. I get as far as "hypnotherapy led to accidental time travel" when he raises a hand and stops me, a deep frown etched into his forehead. "Sorry, you mean, you lost track of time and had some kind of episode?"

"No, I mean I time traveled."

Mark takes a sip of tea and nods calmly. "You time traveled," he says slowly, with the cautious demeanor of a scientist listening to an interesting theory. "You mean, in your mind."

I knew this would be harder than Vinny, because Mark's so utterly convinced that he understands how the world works. It isn't his fault, but he has an air of superiority. He looks as though he's deciding who to call on my behalf. I press on regardless, explaining that after the accidental jumps, I managed to do some specific and surprisingly controlled ones. Well, before the wire incident, at least.

"So, you see, I need your help," I tell him, "to make sense of all this, to understand the rules."

"Joe," he says soberly.

"For example, why did I only stay for a few seconds at the fair?"

"That's enough," he says, placing his cup down. "Why are you doing this to yourself?"

"I know it's hard to believe, Mark, but it's real."

"Real? Let me tell you what I know for sure. I'm sorry, but it isn't *my* help you need." He stands and paces the room. "Is this what you came all this way to tell me?"

I hold his gaze and my nerve. "You told me once that you believed my viewings were given to me for a reason."

"Your psychometry is one thing," Mark counters, "but this is completely different."

"No," I reply. "I believe they're linked."

"Right." Mark folds his arms. "You seriously expect me to believe this?"

"I don't, actually, which is why I'm going to prove it to you."

"Amy died, Joe," Mark says, "a long time ago."

"Maybe that's true, but I can save her."

"Listen to me," he says, "if you carry on like this, you're going to end up like your dad."

The air freezes between us, a thousand possible replies clambering at my throat.

Mark sits down again. "Yet another problem you haven't dealt with. You need therapy, Joe. You need to face the truth, accept what's lost, and move on."

"But what if I can *prove* it to you?" I say, more firmly this time. "What then?"

He smiles. "Prove that you can time travel?" I nod, and he points to a fedora hanging on a row of hooks. "If you can prove it, beyond any reasonable doubt, I will eat my hat."

I grin. "Then I hope you're hungry."

At 12:25 p.m. we head back out to the driveway. It's quiet and private. Mark stares at me dubiously. My plan is to go back just a few minutes in time. I'm confident I can do a short jump like this now, without the need for a focus object. And it should be a safe landing because nothing has changed out here since our arrival. Compared to my recent jumps, this should be simple enough. It's weird with Mark watching me, but I focus and breathe, and it isn't long before I feel the familiar sensation of weightlessness. I leave the present and slip back in time. Mark mumbles some unsavory words, and then I am alone, just the wash of trees above me, the sound of a bell ringing in the distance.

No Mark and no car. Otherwise, the driveway looks the same. I hear kids spilling out of school, screaming like it's the most exciting thing in the world. A plane buzzes overhead, a dog barks and yaps. I hear the rumble of a car approaching. Just in time, I dart behind the old oak tree in the center of the drive. I was aiming for a short jump . . . turns out I slipped a little farther, and it's midday again. From behind the tree, I watch as Mark and I arrive and enter the house, the air thick with our secrets. With a headache and brain freeze for company, I wait outside, and then hide again when

Mark and I emerge at 12:25 p.m. My world turns cyan. I see myself disappear, and then, along with the blue sheen and some pretty blue language, Mark disappears too. I check the time. It's one p.m. The loop is complete.

Right. Time for a debrief.

I knock on the door. "Mark, it's me," I say. "Are you all right?"

He cries out. I hear heavy breathing and shuffling, then silence.

"Can I come in?"

The letterbox flicks open. "Wha . . . Wha . . . you . . . you disappeared, you teleported!"

"Actually, I time traveled," I correct him. "Can you open the door?"

Eventually, he does. His eyes shine like wet marbles, and his mouth hangs open, lips trembling, as he attempts to speak. His head ticks left and right in tiny motions, the world's smallest pendulum of denial. He swallows, then collapses.

Checking behind me to make sure no one's seen us, I step over Mark, grab his arms, and drag him a few inches at a time into the hallway, just enough to close the door. He's breathing softly. I roll him into the recovery position, which makes him look like a murder victim. I grab a cushion from the lounge and place it under his head, which only slightly improves matters.

Perhaps it was too much in one go. Should I have gone easier on him? Maybe, but I know Mark, and his need for absolute proof. He stirs and mumbles, voice thick with fear. "Joe? What happened?"

"You're fine," I tell him. "You just passed out."

He jerks suddenly, as if hit by an invisible cattle prod. He scrambles to his feet and points at me, finger shaking. "No, I mean what happened to *you*? You vanished, right in front of me!"

"Technically, I didn't vanish—"

"Yes, you did, you disappeared!" He snaps his fingers. "Gone, just like that!"

"I time traveled," I correct him again, part of me enjoying the role reversal.

"What? No. Are you sure?" His mind is clearly overheating. "Where did you go?"

"Just back to before we arrived at your house."

He laughs, a manic kind of giggle. "Sure, you just slipped back in time because that's totally possible." His eyes search mine for answers. "I locked myself in the house, I was scared rigid. I thought you might be dead! You were gone for half an hour!"

I place a hand on his shoulder. "Why don't we sit down and have a drink?"

"This is messed up," he murmurs. "Whatever trick you just performed, you're going to need to explain it to me, and I mean in *extreme* detail. I need to know why you *think* time travel is what's happening here."

"I understand," I assure him. "I'll explain everything and it will all make sense to you soon, I hope."

We walk into the kitchen, where I find some whiskey. We take a generous shot each and over the next twenty minutes or so, I fill him in on the basics. I'm not sure Mark will believe that I just time traveled, but as I tell him the story, I can see that he's beginning to trust me.

"I'm sorry I didn't believe you," he murmurs when I've finished, "but this is about the most unbelievable event I could possibly imagine. You understand that, right?"

"I do," I say honestly. "Sometimes I can hardly believe it myself." I grab the fedora off the rack and hand it to him. "But a deal is a deal, Mark. Come on, eat up."

13

Mark has his own version of a man cave, a Norwegian-style log cabin situated at the bottom of his garden. It smells of fresh pine and wood-smoke. At the gable end, three tall windows bathe the pale-wood interior in golden sunlight. Mark stokes a wood burning stove to life, its silver flue clicking as it expands. The walls are lined with books, more than I will read in my lifetime.

"This is where I come to think," Mark says, "when I need a bit of head space. You know what I'm like."

"I do," I say, recalling Mark's obsessive studying and songwriting. He would sometimes go all night to make sure a certain section of a tune was done properly. "I'm sorry about earlier," I add. "I knew you would need proof, but I didn't mean to scare you."

Mark waves a hand. "It was a shock, that's for sure, but that's wearing off now. It's been replaced with many, many questions." His expression softens. "I wanted to say sorry as well."

"For what?"

"For mentioning your dad. It was out of order."

I tell him it's okay, and it is. More than ever I feel the weight of unsorted junk in my mind and know that it's *my* problem to fix. "What about your plans tonight?" I say. "You said you were meeting people."

"That doesn't matter now," Mark replies. "Not anymore." His

expression darkens a little. "Although, tomorrow morning, unless I want to kiss my marriage goodbye, I have to be at Heathrow Airport. I'm telling you this because you might need to help me out the door."

"I understand," I assure him, knowing that when Mark attaches himself to a problem, he is a limpet against the tide.

"Good," he says. "For now, I'm all yours." He gestures to a large floral sofa piled with cushions. I take a seat and he drags over a whiteboard, wheels clicking on the wooden floor. The board is covered in mathematical equations, all hieroglyphics to me. "So. How does it work?" he asks. "You said you hypnotize yourself?"

"Yes. That's how this all began."

"And how far have you been?"

I lean forward. "I made it all the way back to the fair, Mark. I made it to 1997."

His face is a picture. "My God," he whispers. "Did you find out what happened to Amy?"

"No." I shake my head, remembering the pain and sense of hopelessness. "I was only there for a few seconds before I got dragged back."

He frowns, blinking. "Hang on—so you don't decide when you come back?"

"No."

"Why not?"

"I don't know," I tell him, "that's why I need your help. It seems like the farther I go, the less time I get. I just get pinged back after a while. But I need to find a way to stay longer."

"Have you changed anything?" he asks. "Altered the past in any way?"

"Yes," I tell him, a little reluctantly. "I won some money on the lottery."

Mark laughs. "Good for you. So it's possible to change the course of things?"

"Seems that way."

"But what about the chronology protection conjecture?"

"The what?"

"Stephen Hawking. The laws of physics prevent time travel . . . on all but a submicroscopic scale." Marks speaks quickly, staring unseeingly at the ceiling, his voice only just above a murmur. "The semiclassical calculations? Didn't they indicate that the pileup would only drive the energy density to infinity . . ."

"Mark, I don't know about any of that." I shrug. "But it doesn't seem to matter. It just happens."

He snaps out of his daze. "Have you told anyone else about this?"

"Just one person," I tell him, "but I trust him completely."

"You know what I'm going to say, don't you?" he asks.

"That we need to test and validate?"

"Exactly," he nods. "But I'm not sure we should be doing this alone."

"No! We can't tell anyone else, Mark," I say vehemently. "I trust you, but other people . . . they'll complicate things, slow us down."

"I understand."

"I have proven that I can reach her," I say. "I just need enough time in the past to find out what happened and hopefully change it."

Mark rolls up his sleeves and goes to work erasing the board. He checks over his shoulder. "All my work, all my thinking, in fact everything that happened before today has just become irrelevant." With the board clear, he adds, "Now, start again at the beginning, the first time you traveled. Tell me everything."

As I talk him through my first couple of accidental jumps, he writes, nodding and recording the basics like location and duration. It feels good to work this through, finally to have Mark's considerable brain engaged. When I explain that the Gold Cup tickets helped me focus, he nods. "I knew your weird ability would come into its own someday."

"Weird ability?"

"No offense," he replies, smiling. "Interesting though, that objects help you focus."

"Yes, and when I found Amy's ribbon, the one she lost on the night she went missing, I thought I had everything I needed." I tell him about my last jump, about landing through the fence and my stay in the hospital.

"Christ," he says, suitably horrified, "are you all right now?"

"Fine. I was lucky."

"You were," he agrees, and then in typical Mark fashion, he gets right back to the facts. "Interesting that the wire disappeared once you were back in the present. It's almost as if it knew it belonged in the past and went back there again. And the brain freeze . . . that's a consistent indicator of your return?"

"Seems to be," I tell him. "First I get a headache, then about fifteen minutes before I'm due to return, it really kicks in."

"Hmm, right." He rubs his face. "And time spent in the past is accrued in the present?"

I grimace, feeling like I'm back at school and wishing I had studied more. "Sorry?"

He tries again, patient as always. "If you spend five hours in the past, you return to the present five hours after you left? Correct?"

"Yes."

"Good. Let's call that temporal adjustment." Mark writes an equation, seems to rethink it, scrubs it out, and tries again. As I watch him work, I realize how much I've missed him. He always was a ball of energy, and it's good to feel his drive and focus again. Using different colored pens for some scarily complicated formulas, Mark gets things down. When he's done, the board is a mess, but in the center is a simple log of my progress, which I can follow.

Jump 1: Traveled back 10 minutes, watched yourself travel, completed the loop—Instant relocation forward in time, 10 minutes.

Jump 2: Traveled back 12 hours, remained in the past 8 hours—Early relocation? Why?

Jump 3: Lottery win. Traveled back 4 days, remained in the past just under 8 hours—Slightly less time in the past than previous jump. Why?

Jump 4: Gold Cup. Traveled back 14 years, remained in past 30 minutes—A pattern?

Jump 5: The Fairground. Traveled back 22 years (!), remained in past a few seconds—???

Jump 6: Driveway. Traveled back 30 minutes—relocated 30 minutes after departure. Internal clock keeping time?

WE PORE OVER THE BOARD for a while, fire crackling, the room warm and pleasant.

"What are you thinking?" I ask him.

He rubs his jaw, deep in thought. "You have to understand, this is limited data. These are rough approximations. None of this would stand up to even the most basic scrutiny. We need controlled tests." He peruses the board, deep in thought.

"Mark," I say, "what is it?"

He takes a long, deep breath, grabs a pen, and draws an axis. He writes *duration* on the left hand side and *distance* below it. Then he draws a curve from the top left to bottom right; a sloping line that flattens out to almost nothing.

I don't know what I'm looking at. "What does that mean exactly?"

"It's a logarithmic curve," he explains. "It's a kind of graph. If we map each time you traveled onto it, the data fits pretty much exactly." He plots my various jumps onto the curve using dots, writing the year of my arrival and duration spent in the past next to them. He rummages through his desk drawer and fishes out a red elastic band, placing it on opposing forefingers like a fan belt. He wiggles his right finger. "This is you, in the present." Then he moves his left finger away, tightening the band. "This is you in the past." He stretches it to near breaking point. "The farther back you go, the tighter the band."

I stare at him. "And the less time I get in the past."

"Correct. The tighter the band, the sooner you snap back to where you're supposed to be."

That makes sense. But my heart sinks because the facts all point to one simple truth, a sobering reality. The farther back I go, the less time I can stay. If 1997 is my limit, there is no way to save Amy. I think somewhere deep down I already knew this. I've been in denial. All that inner chatter about running out of fuel, of using up my chances. Each jump was giving me information, I just didn't want to listen.

Mark taps his pen against his board. "Have you tried jumping twice?"

"What do you mean?"

"Jumping back just a few years, then jumping back again, from there?"

"No, but I don't think I can."

He tilts his head. "Why?"

"It's hard to explain," I say. "When I jump back a few days, it's not too bad, but if I go back years, then I feel drained. It's almost like I need to recharge my internal battery."

"That makes sense, I suppose," Mark says. "Well, as much as any of this makes sense. Nothing is free."

"Longer jumps take more out of me, use up more energy." I search his face, desperately hoping for a sign that he can see an angle, how to beat time at its own game. "I need to reach Amy with enough time on the clock to make a difference."

"I get it, Joe," Mark says thoughtfully. "It's a hunch, but we need to try that second jump. You need to reach 1997 . . . we need to try and split that into two achievable jumps and see if it changes anything." He's obviously struggling, and he flips between confidence and deep confusion as his brain tries to process the destruction and reconstruction of everything he's ever known in the space of one afternoon. "Seems the universe knows where you are supposed to be and the farther back you go, the faster it evicts you. I'm wondering if a second jump might not accrue the same amount of"—he searches for the right word—"resistance . . . from whatever forces are at work here. To be sure, we need to try it. It's the only way to know."

"All right, what do we do?"

He smiles. "We make a plan."

And over about a gallon of tea, we do just that. An hour later the Double Jump Test is born. Using the deeds from Mark's house as a focus object, I will attempt to jump to 2010. Departure location: an empty barn adjacent to the main house, a renovation project that never happened. The barn has been locked up and left undisturbed since they bought the place over a decade ago. So far, so possible. Once there, according to Mark's theory, I should have about an hour to attempt a second jump.

The barn is dusty and smells of oil and mold. We run through the plan again, and Mark hands me a digital stopwatch. "Do you mind if I film this?"

"Better not."

I can tell he would prefer to be in a lab somewhere, surrounded by a large, dedicated team, documenting and recording everything. His obvious excitement fades. "What if something goes wrong?" he asks. "What if you don't come back?"

"That's my job."

He looks confused. "What do you mean?"

"Worrying!" I offer him a wry smile. "Leave that part to me."

He gives me the deeds to his house. I hold the documents in both hands and commence my breathing exercises. I think about the space around me. All things are connected. It's like vinyl, I think. I'm the stylus, and if time has been recorded—if it's happened already—then I can select the track and jump wherever I like. This visualization does the trick, and I feel myself rising up and away. It's getting easier to do this, but I'm not celebrating yet. This gift is only useful if I can harness it.

When I open my eyes, the barn is almost identical. The change in the light outside is the only visual indication that I've traveled at all. As instructed, I set the stopwatch running and peer through the gap in the barn doors. It's warm, summer maybe. On the drive is a battered old Peugeot that has seen better days and a VW Camper Van, hand painted in a sickening green color. The house looks tired, in need of repair, and the garden is overgrown. I spot a tall bald man seated beneath a well-established pagoda. My headache arrives almost immediately, but so far, no brain freeze. Assuming this is 2010, Mark estimates that I will have an hour before being dragged back. Plenty of time to try a second jump. I pull Amy's ribbon from my pocket, gently rotate it in my fingers, and feel a growing sense of unease. The ribbon feels weaker than ever, its story fading.

What if it's not me that's running out of energy?

It takes some effort, but I banish these negative thoughts and focus on the memory of Mark's graph. I can beat that curve at its own game, I tell myself, and close my eyes. Time to try a second jump. I count down, breathe, focus. For twenty minutes I try, and nothing happens. I sit on the cold, dusty floor, cross my legs, and focus again, desperately seeking that feeling of impending travel, the lifting of the veil of reality. But it's gone. I feel like I'm watching a pan of cold water and willing it to boil. A lesson in futility. I continue to try, but when the stopwatch hits forty-five minutes, as expected, brain freeze bites at the base of my skull. Just before the hour, the barn turns an electric shade of blue. In a rushing snap, I return to the present.

Mark appears from nowhere. It's darker now. A lamp illuminates the barn. "Wow," he says, shaking his head and laughing. "That was incredible." He sees my expression and shifts quickly from scientist back to friend. "What happened?"

I stand and brush myself down. "The house looked pretty rough," I tell him. "There was a green camper van, a bald guy in the garden."

"Yes! That was the previous owner. He was a pain in the arse, only lived here for two years. He bought the camper van just after he sold the house to us. So the date is confirmed, you landed in 2010. Did you manage to jump again?"

"I had an hour, just like you said, but there was no way I could travel again, absolutely no way. And I couldn't now either."

"How do you know?"

"It's a feeling as strong as thirst or hunger. You just know." I pick at my fingernails, mind burning with frustration. "I can go back in time, but what's the point if I can't save her?"

"We need to stay focused," he says. "It's too soon to draw any conclusions. We just need to keep testing, trying things, experimenting."

"No," I say, voice wavering with fear. "I could have acted sooner, Mark. If I had, maybe I would have been able to reach her. But now, I think it's too late."

After more tea and frustrated discussion, we end up back in the house. I clench my jaw and stare out of the kitchen window. The late evening December sky is cherry pink, quite beautiful and totally incongruous with how I'm feeling.

"I finally understand how to time travel, but I can't reach Amy," I say, exasperated. "This is horrible, it's like torture."

"And you are absolutely sure you couldn't travel again?"

"Yes. It's like pressing the accelerator of a car when it's turned off," I insist. "There is literally nothing, not even a vague sense of power. It's like I'm drained, empty."

"Maybe you can recharge?"

"But that takes time, and the farther back I go, the less time I get." I shake my head. "It's no use, I'm miles out."

It's obvious Mark feels guilty. His brilliant brain has honed in on the details—as I knew it would—and burst my bubble. "I really appreciate you helping me, Mark, but this is your Heathrow reminder."

He nods. "I need to leave around three a.m."

"Where are you going?"

"Austria, skiing," he says. "I'm meeting Sian and the kids at the airport. I do have to go."

"Yes, you do," I agree. "We can pick this up when you get back."

He nods enthusiastically. "In the meantime, you can stay for dinner and we can talk some more. Okay?"

My stomach growls its answer. Mark prepares spaghetti carbonara, from an apparently autonomous section of his brain, while he talks to me.

"This was just the first test," he says. "There's more we can do. I would like to go over all your jumps again. Let's make sure we have all the details down. Also, I'm thinking I should create a jump calculator, so we know exactly how long you'll have in the past, before you head off. It might help you plan."

He opens an expensive-looking bottle of red wine, pours a healthy glass, and hands it to me. "Cheers! It's been a bit of a day."

I thank him, spinning the wine around inside the glass. "Yeah, it certainly has," I say.

"What will you do now?" Mark asks.

"I'm not sure." I focus on my wine glass, processing the past, my regrets, new possibilities, and then look at him, eyes narrowed in thought.

"What is it?" he asks.

"I just had an idea. What if I was to go back in time and persuade myself to start traveling earlier?"

Mark considers this and then shakes his head. "It's an interesting thought, but you need to be really careful with what you try and change."

"Why?"

"What you've been through is a process, albeit a painful one." He licks his bottom lip, clearly trying to find the right way of saying this.

"Just tell me what you're thinking," I reassure him.

After some thought, he says, "It's hard, Joe, but that pain could be essential. The whole process could be . . . critical, in fact."

"How do you mean?"

"Think about me and Sian," he says, taking a slug of wine. "We had lessons to learn, both of us. It wasn't easy, but it was a process." He switches into teacher mode, I've seen it many times. He is animated, thinking on the fly. "Life is sometimes like an experiment. It takes us a while to learn things. We build on each event, each experience. We grow. Think of it like a plant. For it to become stronger, you prune it, cut it back. Your pain might have encouraged growth, your determination eventually leading you to your gift. Do you see what I mean?"

"Yes, but if I have no other options, it could still be worth a go."

"I don't think so," he says, "because if you go back and tell yourself, that's a shortcut, and once you've done it, how can you be sure it will work? You could go back in time and make it worse. You might even change it so that you don't develop your gift. Then you might not be able to travel at all."

As Mark combines steaming pasta with the creamy sauce, I consider this. He's probably right, changing my course now could be dangerous. We sit and eat the meal, which tastes as good as any top Italian restaurant. But even I know that company is the true spice of life. We chat about the old days a little, band members and what they are doing now. I tell him about Vinny, and Mark insists I take him through all my jumps again, while he makes notes on his laptop. Mark tops up my wine glass and, after a brief silence, navigates his next question soberly.

"Joe, I know we've talked about it a lot, but what do you think happened to Amy?"

"I honestly don't know. I can only *view* what I saw that night, and it's not enough. I don't see her go, or where she went." I clench my jaw. "Honestly, my heart tells me that someone took her, that she was abducted." I let out a shuddering breath. "Why would I have been given this ability, Mark, if I can't stay long enough to change things?" I sink my head into my hands.

"Come on, Joe," he says. "You need to stay positive, for Amy. If there's a way, I know you will find it." He waits until I look up at him. "Listen to me now. It's early days. You've uncovered an amazing ability, but this is likely to be just the beginning."

"The beginning?"

"Yes!" Mark's eyes glisten with excitement. "Breakthroughs come from the strangest places. Scientific epiphanies are all like this. Just think about penicillin. It always comes from left field, always unexpected." He reaches across the table and gently punches my shoulder. "Something will happen, I'm sure of it. You will have your Eureka moment."

"Thanks, Mark."

"Hey, what about the hypnotherapist?"

"Alexia Finch?"

He nods. "That's where it started, right?"

"I guess," I tell him. "Although maybe it was always there, waiting."

"Maybe," he shrugs, "but it seems to me she's the one who unlocked it. Either way, I think it's worth pursuing."

I'm not totally convinced.

Mark pushes his empty bowl away and interlaces his fingers, "So much of this is in your mind. All of it, in fact. Your psychometry, and now this. It *must* be connected."

"I know what you mean."

We talk and drink for a while. It's true what they say: a good friendship should be easy to slot back into, even if it's been years. We could easily carry on like this for hours.

"Listen, Mark, I need to let you pack. I should probably head off."

He offers me a warm, genuine smile. "How on earth am I supposed to carry on as normal, knowing all of this?"

"You have to," I say firmly. "And you can't tell anyone."

"I know," he says, clearly frustrated but thankfully resigned to my request.

He drives me to the station, and as we say goodbye, he hugs me. I hug him back. "It's good to see you again, Mark."

"You too," he says. "You can call me anytime, okay? If I can't talk, I'll call you back. You are not alone in this."

"Thanks," I say.

"And go and see the hypnotherapist," he says.

"I will."

"And don't do anything stupid while I'm gone, will you?"

I laugh. "Okay, Dad!"

Mark smiles, shaking his head. "Seriously, you need to keep your wits about you," he says. "Look what happened with the wire fence. It's not worth dying for."

"Says the man who's about to hurl himself down a mountain."

"Yeah, good point."

It's nearly Christmas. The train is packed, the mood buoyant. People are excited, heading home to see family and friends. Not my favorite time of year, as you can imagine. During my journey home, I wonder if Mark and I will stay connected, if—like his plant analogy—our broken friendship could grow and sustain itself now that we've pruned away the dead leaves. We are both older now, and he—for one—is wiser. I suppose only time will tell.

When I get home, the house is cold, dark, and empty. I'm exhausted. I head upstairs and collapse, fully clothed, onto the bed. I didn't make a big deal out of it with Mark, but I'm still aching from my altercation with the wire fence. I guess having the festive break to recuperate is just what the doctor ordered, but it feels as though time is a constant pressure against me. As I drift from consciousness, I think again about saving Amy and changing the entire course of my life, but I'm asleep before I can plan anything else.

14

I wake suddenly, my senses bright and raw. Moonlight cuts the room in half. The house is quiet, just the sound of my breath and heartbeat pulsing in my ears. My imagination often plays tricks on me, but this time I can tell for sure I'm not alone. For a while, there's nothing, just a vague sense of unease. I'm about to lie back down when a girl's voice cuts the silence, a playful laugh.

My nerves screech. It sounded like Amy. She's outside.

From my bedroom window, I look down onto the garden and see my sister, wearing her blue dress. She's the same age as when I last saw her. Shock bursts over me, along with a complicated wave of pain, love, and panic. "Amy, stay there!" I shout. She looks up at me, her pale skin luminescent in the moonlight.

She waves. "Come outside and play!"

I try to open the window, but it's locked. I don't have the key. Without hesitation, I break into a lurching run, descending the stairs quickly. The front door is open. The hallway is familiar but lined with mirrors of various shapes and sizes. As I cross the hallway, I'm aware of how the mirrors stretch and distort my body.

Outside the air is frigid, deathly still. A brightly lit stall has been set up in the garden, filled with stuffed toys. Their glassy, expressionless faces stare at me. Beyond that, I see Amy. She's gazing up at a blazing neon

Ferris wheel that dominates the skyline. I call her name. She doesn't turn. I run silently, my bare feet on cold grass.

The Artful Dodger appears, blocking my path.

"Going to give it a go, sir?" His voice is modulated, squeezed through time. "Win the little lady a prize?"

"Amy!" I cry, trying to run but feeling sluggish, as though my pajamas are soaked in cold mud and my feet are stuck to the earth.

The Dodger folds his arms and sneers at me. It takes a Herculean effort to push him aside. As my hands connect with his chest, the world explodes into light. A camera flash off to my left obscures a lone figure in the blackness. I remain focused on Amy. I'm close, but my bare feet slide on the wet ground, slowed by an invisible wall of pressure. I cry out in frustration.

Slowly, Amy turns. Fear grips me. What horrors will my mind conjure up now? When I finally see her face, it's a relief. She's exactly as I remember her. She's perfect.

"Amy," I gasp, tears streaming down my face, "tell me where you are, tell me what happened!"

She folds her arms, expression calm and determined. "If we're going to play the game, you have to play it properly."

"I don't understand," I tell her. "What do you want me to do?"

"I want to play hide-and-seek," she says with a playful frown. "You have to count down, silly."

"Please, Amy, just tell me where you are. I will find you."

"Shut your eyes and count to ten," she insists. "Then you can come and find me."

I do as she asks. When I'm done, she chastises me. "You have to say the words too!"

Fighting back tears, voice trembling, I clear my throat and say them. "Ready or not, here I come."

Amy takes a step toward me, her pale skin ghostly in the moonlight, her expression fearful. "You must come soon. Time is running out. Do you see?"

She points to the Ferris wheel. It's old and rusted now, some of its carriages missing. Its fractured lights flicker and die. It moves away from us in jerking motions, as though the world is made up of Polaroid photographs, hastily discarded by unseen hands. The lawn is a boat, and we are adrift. I scan the scene around me. The edges of this place are fading.

An old man steps from the shadows. His clothes are rags, and his lifeless, milky eyes roll in their sockets. It's the Artful Dodger. Time is eating him alive.

"That's weird," he says, voice thin and raspy. "She was right here."

When I turn back to Amy, she is translucent. She, too, is fading.

"No!" I cry, falling to my knees.

The frayed world becomes an all-consuming blackness.

I LURCH AWAKE WITH A SORROWFUL MOAN. Outside the wind howls in response. My back is hot with sweat, and tears burn my face. Amy's words echo from my dream into the present.

You must come soon. Time is running out.

I swing my legs out of bed and walk to the window. The moon is full, but there's no Amy. I turn on my bedside light, lie back in my bed, and stare up at the ceiling. The dream was also a warning. The distance between us grows with every second. I hold Amy's ribbon. It feels cold and weak, and I wonder if its story is fading and soon—like the Ferris wheel— its lights might go out for good.

Questions dance in the shadows. Who took the photograph? I've seen it in one of my viewings, but I never see the face. Could it be the person who took Amy too?

I'm convinced I won't sleep, but I do, and when I wake again, it's light outside and the ground is covered in a pristine layer of snow. Christmas Eve. Another year nearly gone.

What am I going to do? Keep traveling, keep jumping to the same moment? If I'm going to save Amy, then I need to change my methods. But how?

I get up and shower. As the water runs over me, I become convinced that if I leave this until the New Year, it's going to be too late. I think about what Mark said. He told me that something would come up, my eureka moment. Well if there's one thing I know, it's that if you do nothing, nothing happens.

This leads me to Alexia. She was the catalyst for all of this. Perhaps she could help me to improve, hone my skills, sharpen my mind.

After coffee and toast, it's decided. I need to ask Alexia to help me, and that will require some planning. I wonder if the best thing I could do is just time travel in front of her, like I did with Mark. It's certainly a fast track. When you evaporate in front of someone, it's difficult for them to argue.

However, there are issues with this plan. I will be more nervous in front of Alexia because I don't know her. It will probably take more time to focus and slip back, and I would like to avoid asking her to "Watch this!" and then failing. The ideal situation would be during a hypnotherapy session at her office. It's private and she would be a captive audience. I can take my time, talk to her, prepare her, and get her on my side.

I call her office and get the answering machine.

"Thank you for calling the office of Alexia Finch, solution-focused hypnotherapy." It isn't Alexia, it's an older woman, equally professional. "Unfortunately, our offices are now closed and will reopen on January eighth. If you would like to make an appointment, please leave your name, your—"

I hang up. I can't wait that long. I could go to her house I suppose, but I imagine myself, desperately trying to time travel on her doorstep, melting under her pitying expression. No, I need a better plan.

In need of cheering up, I call Vinny.

"Cash!" he says. "You're lucky you caught me. I was just heading out the door."

"Where are you off to?"

"I'm going on a seasonal yoga retreat."

"Really?"

After a pause, I hear a hearty burst of laughter. "Just kidding! Man, I get you every single time . . . I'm going to see my family, to binge on Christmas telly, and eat my own body weight in meat and gravy. Lovely jubbly."

Just the thought makes me feel a little queasy. Vinny demands a full update, so I tell him about Mark, my attempted second jump, and my frustration that I can't get hold of Alexia.

"I'm worried about wasting all this time, Vinny."

"I understand, but it's not a waste," he says, doing his best to reassure me. "Take some time to recuperate, then go and see Alexia in the new year. It'll be okay. But listen, I gotta go. Call me anytime, yeah?"

"Thanks, Vin."

"Adios!" He hangs up. I stare at the phone for a while. I'm lucky to have him, and Mark too, but in some ways, it makes it harder. Gaining support and then losing it again makes me feel even more alone. They might be right about Alexia, but I have no idea where or how to find her. The sense of loneliness reminds me that I should go and see Mum again. She might not realize that I haven't been around much, but I know, and that's all that matters.

I ARRIVE AT THE CARE HOME just after lunch. Mum is up, dressed, and watching the news silently with subtitles. I lean into her sight line and she smiles, fiddling with the remote. "Hello, darling," she says. She gestures for me to sit next to her. Her cheeks—often pale and drawn—have a little color, and someone has cut her hair.

"How are you feeling, Mum?" I ask. "You look well."

"Oh, you know, I can't complain."

"You can if you like."

She glances around her room and curls her lip, "It isn't so bad, but it's not really . . ."

"Not really what?"

"Not what your father and I had in mind." She finds a smile, but it's haunted. "He's gone, you know. He died."

"I know," I say softly.

Her face crumples. "I want him and Amy to come home. I want to cook a meal, to laugh and joke like we used to."

"Me too," I tell her, voice wavering on the edge of tears. "I would give anything to have them back."

"You're a good boy, Joseph." She tuts and inhales quickly, pulling out a book she has tucked down the side of her chair.

"What are you reading?" I ask.

"Your father's diary," she says, patting the cover. "He wrote some nice things, and I like to read it sometimes." Her expression clouds over. "He wrote some bad things too. He was in pain, your father. He wasn't well."

"What do you mean?"

"In his mind." She taps her temple.

She hands me the heavy leather-bound book. I'm intrigued but also fearful. In the space of a few seconds, I go from certainty that I don't want to read it, to opening and fanning though the pages. Instinctively, I go to the last few entries. My father's handwriting carries his voice back through time.

Every day I wake and it's the same: a few blissful seconds of life before the dark wave pulls me under and reminds me that my beautiful daughter is gone. Eight years. It feels like a thousand, and still so many unanswerable questions repeat in my mind. They gnaw and burrow into my brain, day and night. Especially at night.

Memories of happiness haunt me. How am I supposed to cope with this? I built a family. When things went wrong, I fixed them. But I can't this time. Our life . . . my life is broken. Permanently. And the worst thing of all, the thing that scares me, is that my grief has used me up so much, I can't feel enough to even care.

I first heard it around six months ago. It was just a whisper at first, calling my name. I searched the house, convinced I'd find someone playing a nasty trick on me. I never did, of course, because the voice isn't real, but that doesn't matter. It keeps going now, a whispering voice in the darkness, asking me the same question.

"Do you know?"

I have no idea who it is. I call out, asking what it wants from me. And then the voice laughs and disappears for a while, leaving me alone again.

Judy asked me to go to the doctor, and I did. I took their drugs, and for a while, all was quiet. But then it started again.

"Do you know?"

"Know what, for God's sake?" I cry out, and then I'm left with the echo of my own voice for company. I realize now that the voice is trying to help me. All the questions I've had since Amy disappeared, and in the end they boil down to just one.

"Do you know?"

Finally, I figured out what it means. It's asking if I know whether she's alive.

"I think I do know," I told the voice.

"Good," it whispered. "Tell me."

"She's dead."

"Yes," came the slow reply, "and you know what you must do."

I cried for days, finally accepting that Amy was gone. I have no idea how I knew, or whether she was kidnapped or murdered, but either way she's dead, and the "how" makes no difference. She's never coming back. I don't expect anyone to comprehend why this knowledge brings me peace. Only those who have been through what I have could possibly understand. But it does.

The voice is calling me again.
I cannot remain here.
It's time to be with Amy.
My life here had a purpose, once.
But not anymore.
Forgive me.

I HOLD MY FATHER'S DIARY, this written record of his pain, his loss, and I wonder if I could have done anything to help. Should I have talked to him more? How did we miss the signs?

"Your father's gone," Mum announces. "Killed himself, the idiot."

"I know."

My father was a good man. He looked after us, cared for us, but in the end he went mad. Voices told him to kill himself, and he listened, because he felt the world was against him. As I lower the book, I'm aware of the lie I let myself believe nearly every day. Dad didn't die, I tell myself, he left us. Denial is clever, it's smart, it wants to be listened to and rewards your attention.

"He shouldn't have done that," Mum says, angrily. "It's a sin."

"I know," I say, automatically. Tears threaten to spill down my cheeks. I wipe them away.

We marinate in our thoughts for a while. Mum picks up the remote, scans the channels, then turns the television off.

"Do you remember that time in Wales?" she asks. "It's there, somewhere in his diary. Amy was about five, I think, and we stayed at a caravan park."

I have a vague recollection of this, but it's fading. "I do remember, I think, but tell me anyway."

"Amy met a girl her age, and they played beautifully, but her friend left a new doll outside overnight, and in the morning we found it all smashed up." Mum's face drops. "Why would anyone do that?"

"The world can be a cruel place," I tell her, remembering the scene better now.

"Yes. It can." She finds a thin smile. "But do you remember what Amy did then?"

"I do." I smile back at her, thankful of a little light. "She dragged you into town to buy the girl a new doll, didn't she?"

"Yes, but not one—two, and the most expensive she could find." Mum laughs and stares out the window at the courtyard garden, the same view every day. "Amy was determined that this girl's holiday wouldn't be ruined, desperate to make it right."

"Yes. She was good like that."

"Was?" she snaps at me. "Why do you say *was*?"

I don't answer, I've learned to wait. Mum frowns at me for a few seconds, and then she turns on a beaming smile like a light switch. "She hasn't gone far, she'll be back soon."

I've followed Mum down these conversational dead ends many times, and all roads lead to confusion.

"Amy has gone to the fair with Joseph," Mum explains, the fog of her cruel disease descending further. "They'll be back soon."

Grief spreads in my chest like an ink stain. I clench my fists, and when my words come, they are for my benefit only. "If there is any way I can change this . . . I will."

Mum takes my hand, a look of clarity in her eyes. "It's not easy, Joseph," she says softly, "but anything worth doing rarely is."

By the time I get home, it's early afternoon. The snow is falling heavily, blanketing the ground. The white flakes dance and swirl, coming together occasionally in strange little vortexes. I make tea and settle on the sofa, sighing heavily as I lean back. What am I going to do? I think about my dream. Time is running out. If Alexia is the key, I need to talk to her sooner. The Christmas break is going to be torture.

Mark sends an email, practically bubbling over with ideas. He explains that he is in a bar on a mountain, with crappy Wi-Fi. He wishes me a happy Christmas, reminds me again to take care of myself, and assures me that it's all going to be okay. He attaches a spreadsheet entitled "jump_calculator.xls." He is such a nerd, but I can't deny, this could be quite useful.

On my way to microwave a decidedly unfestive meal, I notice my answering machine flashing. I press play.

"One message, received Monday, December twenty-third." A piercing beep. "Joseph, it's Martin, are you there?" Long pause. "I guess not. It's just a quick message to remind you about the party at my place tonight."

"You're a day too late," I tell the machine.

Martin's voice continues. "I understand you won't know that many people, but they are a nice crowd . . . And actually, there is one person in the same boat as you. Alexia Finch just confirmed she's coming, and she doesn't know many people either." An even longer pause. "She asked after you. So, if you can . . . do come along. Hope to see you later. Bye for now."

Why didn't I think of this before?

Instead of trying to figure out how to time travel in front of Alexia, why don't I just travel *back*? I can locate Alexia and then return to the present, while she looks on in total amazement! A different approach, but it creates the same visual impact. And thanks to Martin's voicemail, I know exactly where Alexia was yesterday. I don't need to wait for the Christmas break to be over. I can time travel!

"Martin," I say, smiling, "it seems I'm going to make your party after all."

PART 4

"DON'T TAKE YOUR EYES OFF HER"

August 1996

Amy was six years old. We were on holiday in the Dordogne, France. Dad had inherited some money from an elderly uncle and decided to splurge on a special holiday that year. We got the early evening car ferry from Portsmouth. Mum and Dad shared the driving overnight while Amy and I slept in the back. The following day we arrived at our villa around lunchtime.

When we got there, I helped Mum and Dad unload everything from the car while Amy explored. She ran from room to room, admiring the shutters, the cold polished flagstone floor, the ornate ceiling lamps, and rainbow patchwork quilt on her little single bed.

"Come up here, Joe!" she called to me, her voice shrill with excitement. "You've got to come and see!"

I climbed the creaky stairs to a loft room and found Amy, bathed in brilliant sunlight, peering out of the window.

"Careful, Pip-squeak," I said. "You might fall."

"I won't!" she said indignantly. "But come and look, Joe!"

I went over to the window and followed her gaze.

"There's a swimming pool," she said breathlessly, her eyes shining with delight. "Can you see? It's all wiggly, like a banana. Can we go in it?"

"We can," I said. "As much as you like."

My parents had told me about the pool, but we'd kept it secret, a surprise for Amy. She adored swimming. In the summer months, we took her Winnie-the-Pooh water wings with us wherever we went, just in case there was an opportunity to get in a pool or go for a paddle.

"Can we go now?" Amy asked.

She didn't wait for an answer.

We were hardly out of the pool that holiday. Amy learned to swim without any flotation aids. She was determined. At first, she would get one of us to support her tummy with both arms as she dog-paddled along. She progressed quickly, and by the end of the first week she could swim the entire width of the pool all on her own. Rules were rules though. No swimming without someone watching.

One evening, as the sun set on another perfect day and we were all about to go back inside to get ready for dinner, Amy refused to get out of the pool. Her hair was up in a cute little bun she called a "bam-bam," but straggles of damp hair had escaped, and she pushed them impatiently out of her eyes. "Please, Mummy, please can I stay in? *Please*, Daddy?" she implored.

"Well . . ." Dad said, thinking. Although the pool was close to the house, it was shielded from view on three sides by a tall hedge, which granted us privacy all day, but meant that it was impossible to see from the kitchen. Amy waited, bobbing up and down, sunlight dancing under her chin.

"I can look after her," I offered.

"Yes! Joe can look after me!" Amy shouted excitedly.

Dad's gaze flickered from Amy to me and back again. After what felt like an hour, he said, "Okay, yes, you can, as long as you call out every five minutes and tell us you're all right." Amy squealed in delight and started splashing around on the inflatable dolphin.

Then he called me over to him. We sat together on the sun loungers beneath an impossibly red sky, the lavender-scented air hot and still, the song of the crickets all around us.

"Joe, I need you to listen to me," he said sternly.

"What?" I said gruffly.

He eyeballed me. "Your mum and I are very proud of you. You know that, don't you?"

"Yeah," I said, kicking a stone with my toe.

"So I know you're going to do a fantastic job of looking after your sister," he continued.

"I will."

"Look at me, Joe," he said. I looked up at his face, lines of worry highlighted by his tan. "It's a big responsibility."

"I know," I said with the worldly tone of a thirteen-year-old desperate to be a man. "I've looked after her before."

"You have, but not like this." He leaned in and locked his gaze on mine, the way that only fathers can. "Amy is precious, and water can be dangerous. I want you to promise me you won't take your eyes off her for a second. I need to be sure you *fully* understand."

I did, but I was enjoying the man-to-man nature of our chat, so I paused for effect and then said, "Don't worry, Dad, I'll make sure she's safe."

He placed his hand on my shoulder. It was strong, supportive. "You're a good boy, Joe. You have fun now, enjoy your swim."

AMY AND I SWAM TOGETHER, the water pleasantly warmed by weeks of sunshine. "This is where I want to live," Amy said at one point, apparently completely serious. "I don't want to go home. I want to stay here forever."

"I know, but we have nearly a whole week left." I said. "Try not to think about it."

That seemed to work. She made her way over to me, her little legs kicking under the surface. "Joe," she whispered, "I saw Mummy and Daddy holding hands."

"That's nice, isn't it?" I said, leaning back in the cool water, wafting my arms.

"Yes," she replied, and then screwed up her face. "I saw them kissing too!" We both laughed, bobbing in the water.

"How long can you hold your breath under water?" Amy asked.

"About an hour."

She considered this. "Will you throw me in again?"

We climbed out of the pool, and I lifted her, swaying her easily in my arms like a tiny pendulum, over the water and back again. She trusted me completely. I counted down from ten, and when I reached zero said, "Hold your breath. Ready?"

Amy nodded, cheeks bulging, and I threw her.

She screamed in delight as she hit the water, sinking in a cloud of bubbles. I guess it was only a few seconds, but it felt like minutes. Panic burst over me, but when she broke the surface, Amy was laughing. She looked up at me, wiping water from her eyes. "Don't worry, I'm all right."

"Don't just tell *me*," I said, heart still racing. "You need to shout it, remember?"

"Oh yeah," she said. She took a deep breath and yelled, "I'm all right!" at the top of her lungs.

From the house Mum called back, confirming she had heard. Amy stuck both thumbs up at me, grinning, then kicked her way back to the edge of the pool, ready for another go.

All families have their traditions; this became one of ours. Whenever any of us said those immortal words, the rest of us would chant it back in unison.

"I'm all right!"

And then we'd fall about, laughing.

15

I plug the dates and times into the jump calculator spreadsheet Mark made for me. It informs me that I if I travel back to December twenty-third, then I will spend seven hours in the past before being relocated to the present. The party was due to kick off at seven p.m., so I figure nine p.m. would be a good time for Alexia to not only be there but to witness my return. This means I need to land at two p.m. The twenty-third was also the day I visited Mark in Bristol, so there is no chance of bumping into myself; my house will be empty, making it an ideal landing location. I find a newspaper from Christmas Eve—I plan to give this to Alexia as a form of proof—and at four a.m., I head to my den.

I focus, drawing calm, strengthening breaths. When I close my eyes, I visualize the day, the afternoon, two p.m. I feel the connections between the past and the present, each moment like a pin in a rock face, established routes that can be navigated, traversed, mastered. Perhaps shorter jumps are easier, or maybe I'm gaining confidence in my ability. Whatever this alchemy is, it's working, and I'm not surprised when I open my eyes again and see the retro clock in my den.

Monday, December 23, 2019—1:59 p.m.

It flashes once and changes to two p.m. I'm getting good at this. Now all I need to do is ensure I'm at the party at nine p.m. when nature takes its course and returns me to the present. In town, I find a quiet coffee shop and hide myself away, running through what I'm going to say to Alexia. My headache builds reassuringly, and at eight fifteen p.m., I set off for Martin's house. Cheltenham is beautiful this time of year. The lights of the Christmas market shimmer, and couples and families meander, hand in hand.

I arrive outside Martin's house at eight forty p.m., twenty minutes before relocation. His front door is cut with stained glass, which casts a multicolored glow over me. I pause outside, feeling quietly optimistic, until I hear the raucous laughter and chatter of a house party in full flow. When I planned this, I didn't really consider other people.

I take a deep breath and press the doorbell. In a wash of heat, booze, and chatter, the door opens. It's Martin. He looks surprised. "Joe, you came! Great!"

"I wouldn't miss it," I say, offering him a wry smile. I follow him into the hallway, the first hint of brain freeze nibbling at my shoulders. Martin asks if he can take my coat.

"I really appreciate the invite, but I'm afraid I'm not able to stay very long."

He looks genuinely disappointed. "Oh, that's a real shame, but it's good to see you anyway."

"You too," I tell him, plucking up my courage. "Is Alexia here?"

"Yes," he says cheerfully. "She's in the kitchen, I think."

I work my way quietly past people I don't know. Once upon a life, I used to enjoy this sort of thing, but you get out of the habit and it becomes difficult. I see a girl in her midtwenties. She looks a little like I imagine Amy might, with a similar energy, a positive vibe. This happens occasionally. Imagining what Amy would be like now is both comforting and painful.

I reach the kitchen, and there are at least ten people in here, all talking loudly. I spot Alexia in a small group over by the sink. She looks to be enjoying herself, easy and confident. I remember Martin saying that she had her reasons for getting into therapy, that she has her own tough story. Looking at her now, you would never guess. But what do we really know about people?

I check my watch. Seventeen minutes to go. I head across the kitchen to a table filled with nibbles. A good spread, as my mum used to say. I pour myself some red wine, take a deep breath, and remind myself why I'm here. I drink the entire glass and steel my resolve.

"Hello, Joseph," Alexia says, suddenly appearing right next to me.

I swallow the wine, demanding my cheeks not to flush. Too late. Damn. "Alexia," I mumble. "Hi, good to see you. You look great." And she does. She's wearing a classic black cocktail dress with an interesting green-and-purple scarf. Her hair is down, almost to her shoulders, and she's wearing makeup that really accentuates her smoky, gray eyes. Her expression is one of easy-going confidence. The professional edges seem to have been smoothed over a little. It's the party atmosphere, the time of year, I suppose.

"Martin said you might be coming," she says with a smile. "I've been looking forward to seeing you. I'm keen to hear how you're getting on with your sleep routine."

"Oh yes, of course." My cheeks flush again. "I've actually been sleeping really well."

"Good." She grabs a couple of peanuts from a bowl on the table next to us. "It's really decent of Martin to do this, don't you think? To get people together." She leans forward conspiratorially. "I don't know about you, but I never seem to be organized enough."

"Er, yes, he does seem to know a lot of people," I say, choosing the most boring answer possible. I blame the ice pinching at my neck.

"Are you not staying?" Alexia asks.

"Sorry?"

She takes a sip of wine and smiles. "You still have your coat on."

"I'm not going to be here long." I lower my voice. "I just came to see you, actually."

"Ah, intriguing," she says playfully. "Well, here I am."

"Is there any chance we could talk in private? Outside? It won't take long." I'm desperately trying not to sound weird, but failing miserably. "Is that all right?"

"Sure," she says. "Let me grab my coat."

The night is still and calm, the moon a silver coin. Martin lives on a quiet road, and the street is thankfully deserted. Brain freeze is kicking in nicely. I estimate I will be traveling back to the present in just a few minutes. We walk away from the house, Alexia's heels clicking on the pavement.

"I'm not a big fan of Christmas, you know," she says, pulling her coat more tightly around her in the cool night air.

"Why not?"

She sighs. "I don't mean to sound *bah humbug*, but it can feel a bit forced, like we're supposed to be happy. There's a lot of pressure around this time of year, you know?"

Brain freeze squeezes at my temples. "Yes, I do," I tell her. "I'm not keen on any of the days we're supposed to act a certain way. Mother's Day, Valentine's Day, World Peace Day. All those things matter, but we should do them because we want to, not because today's the day."

"Very true." Alexia stops and looks at me, her face pale in the moonlight. "So what's on your mind?"

Turns out, quite a lot. I asked Alexia to come outside, and now it's just the two of us, and she's nice to be around. She's fun and interesting. Part of me would just love to be normal, to enjoy this moment, and I realize, standing here in the moonlight, that even something as simple as having a drink with Alexia feels alien to me. I'm so out of practice. And now, here I am, just me and this stupid plan. Come on, Joe, get on with it.

"I don't have much time," I tell her. "This is about my sister, Amy. She went missing."

Alexia nods sympathetically. "I know, Martin mentioned it to me." She places a hand to her chest. "I hope you don't mind that he told me. He wanted to try and help you."

"Not at all," I say. "That's why I'm here, because I do need help . . . specifically, your help." I pull a copy of *The Times* from the inside pocket of my jacket and hand it to her. It's dated December twenty-fourth. "This is tomorrow's newspaper."

She studies it and laughs. "Wow, that's really good. It looks real."

"It is real."

She frowns, her cheekbones accentuated beneath the orange glow of a streetlamp. "Is this a joke?"

"No," I tell her. "I've come here to prove something to you."

"That you're good at Photoshop?" She holds up the paper. "This isn't *that* difficult."

"I may have a chance to save Amy."

Alexia is very still. "Martin told me she went missing a long time ago."

"She did, and I think I may have found her, but I need to act quickly. I don't have time to wait for an appointment, to try and persuade you to help me."

Alexia looks worried. "Listen, it's cold, why don't we go back inside? We can talk more, if you like." I feel like someone just poured an ice bucket down my back, and I wince.

"Are you all right?" she asks.

"It's all part of the process," I tell her. "I've come here from Christmas Day to prove to you that I can time travel."

She looks troubled. "Joseph, I don't really know what to say. I do want to try and help, but maybe you need to talk to someone with more experience."

"Once you see this, you will believe me." The world changes color, leaving Alexia and me alone under a blue moon. "Don't be afraid, okay?"

She looks more like she feels sorry for me.

"Will you just take this?" I hand her the newspaper. "Please."

She looks dubiously at my outstretched hand, but apparently decides it can do no harm. As she takes the paper, our fingers touch, and a spark of connection travels between us. I close my eyes and travel.

Whatever happens now, she's seen what I can do. For better or worse, this mission is complete.

I open my eyes. It's midmorning, Christmas Day, and everywhere is white. I'm back in the present, outside Martin's house.

"What just happened?" asks a trembling voice beside me.

I let out a stifled gasp. "Alexia? What are you doing here?"

She stares at me, horrified, searching our surroundings frantically. She stumbles back into the road, away from me, the madman who just . . . who just what?

A car horn blasts through the fog in my brain, and when I turn, I see a large SUV heading straight for us. I grab Alexia by the arm, dragging her back to the pavement. The car slows to a crawl, pulling up next to us. Inside is a young couple with two small kids, strapped into the rear seats, swamped in layers of clothing. The entire family stares at us, wide-eyed with concern.

The smartly dressed driver winds down the window. "What on earth were you doing in the road?" he says furiously. "I could have killed you! That would have ruined Christmas Day, wouldn't it!" He looks at Alexia and his brow narrows. "Is everything all right?"

Alexia nods. "I'm fine," she says, her voice thin and unconvincing. "Just a bit cold, that's all."

"I'm not surprised," the man says. "It's freezing." He doesn't say it, but I can tell that he disapproves of her clothing. A black cocktail dress and high-heeled patent leather shoes aren't exactly ideal for a Siberian Christmas stroll. "Well, if you're sure you're all right," the man says stiffly, "you both have a good Christmas." His tinted window whirs up automatically, offering a perfect reflection of Alexia and myself, looking perplexed.

The car pulls away, sliding a little. Thick white clumps of snow fall around us, already filling our footprints. I turn to Alexia and attempt a reassuring smile.

"Christmas Day?" she says. "That man said it was Christmas Day."

"He did," I tell her, "and it is."

She swallows and looks around. "It's daytime. It's *snowing*." Her breathing begins to settle, and she regards me with a focused look that I recognize. She tugs her coat inward and looks at me, bewildered. "What just happened? What have you done to me?"

It's a good question. "This has never happened to me before, but I think when you touched my hand at the exact moment I traveled, you came with me."

"Traveled? With you, to Christmas Day?" she says again, processing the madness.

"Yes."

She folds her arms. "You're telling me that this is the future?"

I blink, considering it from her perspective. "For you, I suppose, yes, but for me this is the present. I'm back where I came from."

"What?" Anger and disbelief build in her voice. "And you expect me to believe you? Night has just become day. And I'm absolutely frozen," she says, her hands blue now and her teeth chattering. "What's going on? What happened to the party? Is this some kind of trick?"

"I assure you, it isn't a trick." I take a breath and speak slowly. "I wasn't expecting this. I've only ever traveled alone. I never thought about trying to bring anyone with me."

"Just stop." Her voice trembles and I think she might cry. "This isn't happening," she murmurs to herself, rubbing her temples and taking deep breaths.

New possibilities fall into my mind like the thick flakes of snow around us. There was a reason I sought Alexia's help, even if I didn't fully understand it until now. She unlocked my ability to time travel, but the fact she traveled with me is exciting beyond words. I could never have imagined that. Mark's words return to me and I grin. I think Alexia might just be my eureka moment.

"Are you smiling?" Alexia says incredulously, interrupting my reverie. "Do you actually think this is *funny*?" Her expression slackens a little, then she looks confused, blinks a few times, and begins to sway. Based on Mark's recent collapse, I read the signs and slide forward, steadying her as best I can. Thankfully, she doesn't pass out. Her breath is warm against my neck. After a few seconds, I pull away a little.

"Are you okay?" I ask gently.

She looks back at me, her face pale. "No, not really."

We can't stay out here. It's bitterly cold. I consider my options. There aren't many that don't involve a hypothermic hypnotherapist. Decision made, I guide her by the arm across the road, toward Martin's house.

How on earth am I going to explain this?

MARTIN'S WEARING A FEROCIOUSLY PINK SWEATER. It looks brand new, not a bobble in sight. A Christmas present, probably. I imagine it'll go to the back of the drawer tonight and never see the light of day again. His face is flushed, and he's wearing a silver Christmas hat. It's too big, and only his eyebrows are stopping it from falling over his face.

He opens the sitting room door and stands back. "Why don't you guys have a seat in here for minute?" he says. "The fire's going. I'll put the kettle on." Obediently, we go in. Christmas music spills out of the kitchen as Martin opens the door, then fades again.

The room is warm, and there's a stumpy little Christmas tree in the corner by the bay window, adorned with fairy lights and colorful decorations. Alexia collapses onto the green velvet sofa and rests her head in her hands.

The fire crackles comfortingly. Through the wall I hear muffled voices, questioning intonation, calming tones.

"Alexia?"

"Don't!" she snaps. "Don't try and make this okay, don't try and smooth things over and pretend everything's fine!"

I pause. "But—"

"No," she shuts me down. "I don't want to hear it right now."

Well, this is awkward. Through the wall, I hear Martin's wife guffaw. I like Carol well enough, but she's prone to sudden bursts of crazed laughter at things that just aren't that funny, and when alcohol's involved, she gets even louder. I wonder what she's laughing at. I hope it isn't me and Alexia, turning up on Christmas Day looking worse for wear in our party gear.

I decide to help Martin with the drinks, but I meet him in the doorway carrying a tray.

"Here you go," he says to Alexia, handing her a mug and putting a plate of mince pies down on the coffee table. "Joe?" He offers the other mug to me, and I take the hot sweet tea gratefully.

"Alexia," he continues, "I thought you should know your father called me last night. He was worried he hadn't heard from you."

She smiles up at him wanly. "I was supposed to be there last night, but . . . I couldn't get there. What did he say?"

"He was concerned," says Martin, "but I said I was sure you'd be in touch soon. Shall I give him a call and let him know you're here?"

"You're very kind," she says, "but I'll call him in a bit." She takes a sip of tea and leans back into the sofa. She takes a deep breath, visibly relaxes her shoulders, then stares, unblinking, out of the window.

Martin looks at me, then back at Alexia, then at me again. I make a series of faces at him and hope I've managed to convey, "Sorry, Martin, and thanks for being so nice and everything, but could you go away again now?"

It seems to do the trick. "Er . . . I'll just leave you two with your tea for a bit," he says. "I'll be in the kitchen if you need anything."

"Thanks, Martin," I say. He leaves the room and closes the door quietly.

I wait.

"Okay," Alexia says wearily, still gazing out of the window at the wintry street beyond. "I'm listening."

I shift forward in my seat. "Alexia," I say earnestly, "I am so, so sorry. I promise you, none of this was supposed to happen. Well, not like this."

"Not like this?" she says, finally turning to look at me. "What does that mean?"

I wipe my sweaty hands on my thighs. This is my moment, and I am terrified of blowing it. I clear my throat, but nothing comes out. Where do I start?

"Shall I kick things off?" Alexia offers, with a hint of sarcasm. "Did you or did you not drug me at Martin's party?" She looks at me unwaveringly. "Tell me the truth."

"No! Absolutely no way! I would never do that!"

"Shh!" she warns me in a low voice. "You'll have Martin back in here."

"Sorry," I mutter, dropping my voice. "But no, of course I didn't drug you. Who do you think I am?"

She looks at me and shakes her head. I can't blame her. She barely knows me at all.

Warily, I say, "I've found out that I can travel back in time."

Alexia says nothing. I take this as a sign that it's safe to continue.

"I traveled back to 1997," I continue, "to the night my sister, Amy, went missing. But for some reason I could only stay there a few seconds. I came home again almost straight away. I need to find a way to stay there longer. And because I only discovered I could time travel after my hypnotherapy session with you, it seems obvious to me that you're the best person to help me."

Still, she's silent.

"So on Christmas Day, I traveled back in time to Martin's party."

Alexia lets out an incredulous snort. "My plan was to prove to you that I can time travel by disappearing in front of you, and then ask for your help. But because we were touching, I . . . somehow brought you back to the present with me."

We fall into a long silence, broken only by the occasional pop of wood in the burner. Alexia drinks the last of her tea and places her mug on the coffee table.

"I don't know what to think about any of this," she finally says. She stands up and goes to the window. She stares out for a moment, as if gathering her thoughts, then turns to face me. "One thing's for sure—you've completely ruined Christmas for me. And for my parents." She stops and winces, massaging her forehead.

"Are you okay?" I ask.

"My head is splitting," she says.

"Your head?" Then I remember temporal adjustment, how I always get a headache before I travel home. This could be bad.

"Listen to me, Alexia," I say, "this is serious. I don't think you are where you're supposed to be."

"Tell me something I don't know!" she retorts.

"No, I mean—having a headache is a possible sign of—" I struggle to think clearly. I decide I have to speak to Mark D'Stellar now, and I mean *right now*, because if this means what I think it does—

"Wait there," I say, yanking my phone out of my pocket. She flinches as if I've just pulled a gun. "Just give me two minutes, okay?"

"Sure, whatever you need," she says, unnervingly calm. "Take your time."

I step out into the hall and look for somewhere quiet. I try the door under the stairs, which opens into a small downstairs toilet. I lock the door and call Mark. Christmas morning, 11:21 a.m.—I cross my fingers he picks up.

"Joe?" It's a relief to hear Mark's voice. "Happy Christmas! This is a surprise."

"Yeah, happy Christmas, mate. Listen, have you got a few minutes?"

"Sure," Mark says.

I explain to him as quickly and quietly as I can about the party, how I seem to have accidentally brought Alexia back with me. "So, what do you think's going to happen to her now?" I ask.

"Talk me through the jump again?" he says.

"I jumped back to the twenty-third of December. I arrived at two p.m., and I was due to return to the present at nine p.m. I dragged Alexia with me and arrived here, in the present, at eleven a.m. on Christmas Day, about twenty minutes ago."

"You spent seven hours in the past?"

"Yes, that's right."

"Well, based on the evidence so far, I suspect Alexia will relocate seven hours after you dragged her."

"At six p.m.?"

"Correct," he says, "and I presume the hours will be added on at her end. So, she'll get home seven hours after you left the party . . . four a.m. on the twenty-fourth."

"This hurts my brain," I tell him.

"Well, I'm already halfway through a bottle of prosecco . . . it helps."

Someone tries the toilet door. I freeze, but after they've wiggled the handle a couple of times I hear their footsteps walking away again.

"And you know what else? It's pretty amazing," Mark carries on, "that you can take people with you."

What a mess I seem to have created. Then a thought occurs to me. "Mark, what if I travel back again and warn myself not to drag Alexia? Or maybe even tell myself not to go back to the party at all?"

I hear him sucking air through pursed lips. "Don't do that, Joe. If you keep going back and trying to change the past, I don't know what'll happen. But you could definitely make things worse."

I don't have time to imagine how much worse things could be.

"Okay, I won't do anything stupid," I tell him. "Well, more stupid anyway."

"Good," he says. "The main thing is you need to warn Alexia. Explain what's going to happen, and ensure she knows how critical it is to be somewhere that hasn't changed, so she can land safely."

That stops me in my tracks. Without all this knowledge, Alexia can't plan, she has no idea what's going on. She could be seriously injured or even killed when she relocates. I need to warn her, to make her listen to me. I have to.

"Gotta go," I tell Mark.

"Good luck, Joe. Keep me updated?"

I assure him I will, hang up, flush the toilet for authenticity, and peer cautiously out into the hall. There's no one there. I walk down the hallway and head back into the lounge. Martin's sitting alone on the sofa.

"Joe, I think we should talk," he says.

"Where's Alexia?"

"She's gone home."

"I need to go after her," I say, turning to leave.

Martin stands up. "Joe." He holds my elbow. "I don't know Alexia that well, and I'm not going to ask what's going on between you, but I really think you should give her some space." He lets go of me, but his expression is serious.

Reluctantly, I say, "Sure." But I'm just buying some time.

"Why don't you spend the day with us?" Martin asks. "The family are all keen to see you." I bet they are. Especially Carol. I bet she can't wait to ply me with wine, pump me for details of what Alexia and I have been up to, and then laugh in my face like a manic jack-in-the-box.

"I think I'll head home," I say. "I'm pretty tired. Thanks though. Can I just use your bathroom before I go?"

"Again? Are you all right?"

I nod. "Er, yes, but not feeling too well, so I won't say hello to everyone."

"I'm worried about you."

"Thanks," I tell him. "But don't be. I'm fighting fit. Just ate one too many mince pies, probably." I fake a stomach cramp, and on my way to the toilet, I pick up Martin's address book that I'd noticed on a table in the hall earlier. In there, thank the stars, are Alexia's contact details. Maybe the world isn't totally against me.

Successfully avoiding any guests, I head back outside. It's stopped snowing, and the streets are eerily quiet.

Once I'm around the corner and out of sight of Martin's front window, I call Alexia. She doesn't pick up, so I text her.

> Sorry I upset you. I need to talk to you urgently. I'm worried about you. Please call me back.

It takes me fifteen minutes to get home, and she doesn't call. I'm going to seem like a stalker if I text her again, but how else can I get through to her that she's in danger? I send one more message.

> IMPORTANT. Your headache means you're probably going to travel again soon, to the night of Martin's party. Please make sure you're somewhere that hasn't changed in the last few days—a spare bedroom, maybe? And stay there till you travel.

I don't know what else I can do, so I lie back down on the bed, wrap myself in my duvet, and cross my fingers, hoping that Alexia's going to be okay.

After all, she's completely innocent. It's me who dragged her into all this. Literally.

16

Wednesday, December 25, 2019
5:47 p.m.

I jolt awake and sit upright in bed, my heart hammering. It's pitch-black, apart from my phone, which is about to buzz itself off the bedside table. I grab it and press the answer button.

"Hello?" I say, sounding high and panicky.

"Hello," says a small voice on the other end. "It's me. Alexia."

I nod to the heavens in silent thanks. "Hi, Alexia," I say, trying to relax my quivering vocal cords. "I'm glad you called. How are you feeling?"

There's a click as she swallows and clears her throat. "You said I was going to travel back soon."

"Yes, I think you are."

"So you're still persisting with this time-travel story?"

"It's not a story, Alexia. It's the truth. This is all happening because time wants to relocate you, wants you back where you should be, and that causes . . . well, it's the reason you're feeling like this."

"How do you know how I'm feeling?" She sounds more curious than annoyed.

"Because I've done it too. For a little while before you travel back, you feel weird. Bad headache, a bit shivery, that kind of thing. Then everything turns blue, and you travel." She doesn't reply, but she's still there, listening. "And about fifteen minutes before you go, you get brain freeze, you know—"

"—like when you eat ice cream too fast," she finishes. "It just started a couple of minutes ago. It's why I called." She sounds scared.

"I'm so sorry," I say. "I honestly didn't mean to bring you with me when I traveled. This feeling won't last long though. You'll travel back soon, and then you'll be fine."

"Fine?" she snaps, suddenly sounding angry. "I'll never be the same again!"

I don't know what to say. I listen to her breathing, fast and shallow. At least she hasn't hung up on me.

"Look, Alexia," I say gently. "I know this is weird and frightening and impossible to believe, but soon it'll be over, and then you'll never have to speak to me again. I can get you through this safely, but I just need you to do what I say for the next few minutes. Okay?"

"Why should I listen to you?" she says. She sounds like she actually wants me to give her a reason.

"Because I've been in your position, and I know how to help. And because I want to do the right thing. I got you into this mess, and it's my responsibility to get you out of it."

There's another long pause, followed by some crackling on the line.

"Look, you're going to be fine," I assure her. "Time travel has predictable rules, and as long as we stick to them, you'll be completely safe." I could add, "I hope," but that isn't going to instill confidence in either of us.

"I was perfectly safe until you came along."

"I know. You're right. I'm sorry." I'll apologize a thousand times if I need to. "All we need now is to make sure you're in the right place when you go back."

"What do you mean, the right place?" Before I can answer, she lets out a frustrated, painful moan. "It's getting worse."

"Okay, don't panic," I assure her. "But we need to move fast. Is there a room in your house that hasn't changed in the last week? Somewhere nobody's been? A spare room, maybe?"

"I don't know," she says. "I've had friends to stay, and they could've been anywhere. Why?"

"You need to be somewhere that hasn't changed at all, so that when you get back, the space you land in will be clear and safe, so you don't hurt yourself."

"The conservatory," she says weakly. "I don't use it in the winter."

"Perfect," I reassure her. "Go there now."

"Okay," she mumbles. "I'll call you back in a minute."

"No, don't hang—"

The line goes dead.

"Up," I say to myself.

Alexia said her brain freeze began a few minutes before she called me. That means she will relocate soon, in ten minutes, maybe less. I pace the bedroom, willing her to call me back. A terrible thought grips me: what if she travels before she gets to the conservatory, and ends up stuck through the middle of the kitchen table, or worse?

The phone vibrates in my hand. It's a video call.

"Alexia," I breathe in relief.

"I'm in the conservatory," she says quietly. I can just about make out her features in the ghostly blue light of the phone screen. Her eyes sit deep in their sockets, dark shadows beneath them, and the fine lines across her brow have turned into deep furrows. "There's no heating in here. It's freezing." She draws her coat collar closer around her neck. "What's going to happen to me?"

I choose my words carefully, condensing what I've already told her into digestible facts. "You're going to travel through time, back to where you're supposed to be."

"Back to Martin's party?"

"No, the seven hours you've spent here will be added back on. So you'll arrive seven hours after we left, at about four a.m. on the twenty-fourth of December."

"How do you know all of this?" She winces again and rubs her forehead. Her rings glint in the half-light.

"I've traveled a few times already. And I have a friend who's a physics lecturer. He's much smarter than I am. He figured out how it all works."

She considers me, still for a moment. "You really believe you're telling me the truth, don't you?"

"I am," I say, returning her gaze. I hope she can sense my honesty.

"So where will I be when I get back?" she asks.

"You'll be right where you are now. You'll feel fine again, and you can carry on life as normal. Oh—except that on Christmas Day and night, you should avoid your house and Martin's house. There'll be two of you knocking around for a few hours, and you don't want to bump into the other you. That could be weird."

Like this isn't.

"Okay," she says wearily.

Suddenly the screen turns black. I wonder if she's hung up on me again, but I can still hear her, groaning.

"Alexia?" I say. "Are you okay?"

I hear scratching noises, then her pale blue face appears again.

"Sorry, I dropped the phone," she says. "This is awful. What's it like when you actually . . . when you . . . Does it hurt? I'd rather know, so I can prepare myself."

I have a momentary out-of-body experience as I metaphorically stand back and wait for myself to give time-travel advice to a professional hypnotherapist I barely know.

"The brain freeze does get pretty bad," I explain, "and it's at its worst just before you go. The traveling itself though, it's nothing. It's instantaneous."

"That's strange," Alexia murmurs, her eyes moving as if following imaginary butterflies.

"What is?" I ask.

"It's all blue in here," she says. "Everything's blue."

"That's normal," I assure her. "You're about to go back."

"If anything goes wrong, tell my parents I love them."

"It won't go wrong," I assure her.

A tear rolls down her cheek. "Just try and explain it to them."

"I won't need to," I insist. "You can tell them yourself. You're going to be fine."

She doesn't seem to hear me. She's become unexpectedly calm, as if she's passing into the eye of some terrible storm.

"You know, I was glad when you came to the party . . ." I can see her lips moving, but her voice is barely audible now, and her face is shimmering like reflections in a moonlit pond. "Are you there?"

"I'm here, Alexia."

But I realize that she isn't. Not anymore.

My phone beeps. Connection lost, it tells me impassively. I stare at the blank screen. Alexia disappeared in an instant, but the world takes a moment to adjust. Like me, it needs time.

"If there is anyone up there who cares about good people," I say to the ceiling, "please let Alexia Finch get back safely."

My head swims. I feel like I'm going to pass out. The room pinches in my vision, as though it's a painting and someone is pulling the canvas from behind. Then it snaps back quickly, making my temples throb. I stagger, lean down, and place my hands on my thighs, drawing long shaking breaths that chill my chest. A creeping, almost euphoric sensation moves over me, like déjà vu. "It's a head rush," I tell myself, voice weak. Whatever just happened, my world has been changed. I just hope she's okay.

There's a loud knock at the front door. I consider not answering—my default position—but I know I shouldn't ignore it. I walk in a daze to the door, take another deep breath, and open it. Standing there, beneath the cover of a large umbrella, is Alexia Finch.

17

With the exception of Martin, it's been a while since I've had any visitors, and a long time since I've had a woman in my house. It always amazes me how shirts, jeans, and underwear seem to find their way into every room. What do they do? Crawl in there on their own?

"I'm afraid the place is a bit of a mess," I tell Alexia as we enter the kitchen. Unfortunately, it's not much better in here. I still haven't cleaned up after my blender incident.

Alexia eyes the fruit splatter with concern. "Gosh, what happened?"

"Oh, I had an argument with some fruit," I tell her, filling the kettle. "I haven't exactly been here much lately, so I haven't had a chance to tidy up."

Alexia works her gaze over the kitchen like she's trying to memorize it, as if she's here to gather facts and data. I find a couple of mugs that are clean and not too chipped. I make tea, and we sit opposite each other at the kitchen table. From my perspective, Alexia just left, angry and afraid. But she's had time to adjust and to plan her questions.

"I need to talk about what happened," she says. "I need to work it through, to process it all."

"That's understandable," I say.

She regards me with a thoughtful, calm expression. "I've been home for a few days now. It happened exactly as you said it would. I arrived seven hours after the party, early morning on the twenty-fourth." She takes a sip of tea. "I need you to tell me again, what you were *thinking* when you came to the party?"

I draw in a breath. "I thought that if I could prove to you that I could time travel, then you might agree to help me."

"But why do it like that?" she says. "Why didn't you just talk to me?"

"I considered that," I tell her, "but with Christmas and the whole New Year break . . . I couldn't wait. I feel like time is slipping away. It's hard to explain, but I don't think I have long to reach Amy, and I knew that if I just talked to you, you wouldn't believe me. You would think I was mad . . . probably still do."

"Actually," she says quietly, "I don't think you're mad."

"So you accept that I can time travel?"

She regards me coolly. "I still can't quite believe I'm saying this, but yes, I do accept what happened."

Alexia seems like a practical person, someone who rationalizes the world, sees things for what they are. But I don't know if that makes this easier for her than it was for Mark or Vinny. She studies me, and when she speaks again, her tone is sharp. "You put me in danger."

"I know, and I'm sorry," I tell her. "But I didn't know I would drag you with me. It wasn't deliberate. You know that, don't you?"

Her lips set in a thin line, she blinks, then nods. "I understand you didn't plan for it to happen that way." Her expression softens a little. "I actually wanted to thank you for being kind . . . I was panicking."

I lean forward. "It was me that put you in that situation."

"Yes," she says, "you did, but I was scared, and you were patient with me, and I'm grateful for that."

"Well," I say, "it won't happen again, I promise."

We drink tea and sit in silence for a while.

Eventually she asks, "Why do you think I can help you?"

I hold her gaze and do my best to sound confident and clear. "My time travel started after my first session with you. Accidentally at first, but then deliberately, I began to slip back in time. When I found my sister's ribbon, the one she dropped the night she went missing, it gave me a deeper connection. I thought, 'This is it, all the pieces have fallen into place.'"

"The ribbon helped in some way?"

"Yes, but not enough."

"What happened?"

"I jumped all the way back to 1997." Alexia's eyes widen in shock. I almost tell her about the barbed wire but decide not to. If I'm going to get her on board, then talking about the dangers of time travel probably isn't the best idea. I focus on the basics. "I reached the fairground, but I only stayed for a few seconds."

"Why?"

"The rules, as I understand them, mean that the farther back I go, the less time I stay in the past. It's like an elastic band. I snap back."

Alexia absorbs this in silence. Then she says, "I still don't understand what you think I can do?"

"Whatever you did unlocked something in me."

"But I didn't do anything," she replies, confused.

"You did, because now I can time travel, and it doesn't involve machines or complicated equations." I lean forward slightly. "It's all in my mind," I say softly. "That's why I believe you can help me."

"But how, Joe?"

"I need to improve," I say, thinking over all the ideas I've had since leaving Mark. "Maybe you can help me stay longer, or jump a second time once I'm in the past. Perhaps you can help me to go back through my memories and see if I missed something that night." I hold up my hands, palms up. "I don't know exactly, but I only started to time travel after my first session with you."

Her brow furrows. "Are you saying that this is my fault?"

"Not your *fault*, but without you, it would never have happened."

She regards me for a moment. "Look, I'm sorry about your sister, really I am. But I don't think it's me you need."

"It is," I tell her. "Because *you* unlocked me."

"That could have been anyone," she argues. "I'm nothing special."

"You are though. It *has* to be you."

As the words leave my mouth, I realize it's true. I was clutching at reasons why Alexia is the only one that can help me, but those are my rational, conscious thoughts. My heart knows exactly what it's doing. Alexia is hope, a connection, a lantern flickering on a dark sea.

"I trust you," I tell her, and before I can think it through, I add, "and I believe this is supposed to happen."

She glowers at me. "*Supposed* to happen?" Her voice is laced with skepticism. "What, you mean like destiny?"

I'm not sure where I'm going with this whole fate-brought-us-together speech of mine, but I'm telling the truth. When things are right, it's like a tuning fork, it rings true, and I'm listening, now more than ever. I can feel primal, powerful forces are at work. They're hidden from view and, perhaps, my understanding, but they are there. A sense of magnetism. My psychometry. All forms of attraction, of energy. If you had asked me a week ago if time travel were possible, I would have laughed in your face. But I'm learning that there is so much in our world that we cannot see, waiting to be discovered.

"It's hard to explain," I say, "but when I saw you at the party . . . I felt something."

Her neck and cheeks flush slightly. "What do you mean?"

"I felt as though someone was pulling strings in the background," I say, offering a gentle, almost apologetic smile. "I don't really believe in all that stuff, but yes, I suppose it felt like destiny, or something equally powerful."

There's a long pause. I listen to Alexia's breathing. She finishes her tea and looks ready to leave, but then she says, "Look, maybe I felt it too, but I hardly know you, and you put me in danger, scared the absolute hell out of me, not to mention my parents, and now here you are asking me to help you travel back through time. It's not fair."

"I know it's a lot to ask," I tell her, "but this is about saving my sister."

Alexia stands up and walks slowly over to a set of double doors that overlook the garden. She has her back to me. Without turning she says, "There's something I need to say, and I'm sorry if it hurts you to hear it."

"I'm listening," I reply.

She turns to face me, and when she speaks, her voice is softer, calming, like when I first met her. "I understand your desire to save your sister. Of course I do . . . but I have some serious concerns about the morality of changing the past."

"Morality?"

"You're talking about changing history," she says, her expression pained. "That may have serious repercussions, things that you can't foresee. How can you be sure that what you're attempting to do is right?"

It's a fair question. Alexia's concerns are valid, and she has a right to them, as we all do, but to question saving Amy? It's almost incomprehensible to me. I bow my head and take a long steadying breath. "I understand why you might feel that way, Alexia. Really, I do. But this is my sister we're talking about."

"And I'm a therapist, Joe," she says firmly. "I've spent my entire career teaching acceptance, helping people to accept the past, to embrace the future."

"I'm not altering time to suit *me*," I say, frustration spilling over in my voice. "I'm not planning to change what happened just because it didn't go the way I wanted it to." I stand up and walk over to her. "I believe someone took Amy, that someone abducted my sister, and that's just wrong."

Her expression is flat. "Sometimes, terrible things happen," she says, her voice clipped, "and they're often very hard to accept, but this is too much. I didn't come around here for you to persuade me."

"Why did you come then?"

She thinks for a moment. "I came here because I wanted to talk about what happened. I had to process what you did to me, try to understand it. I couldn't talk to anyone else. It's not exactly the sort of thing you drop into conversation. I had to be sure I wasn't going mad. And even though it was your fault, I wanted to thank you for being kind to me." She draws a breath and appears to reset herself. "I also came to tell you that I can't help you."

"Alexia, listen, I—"

"Joe, you need to listen to *me* now." Her face flashes with kindness, or perhaps pity, then her expression flattens back to the same calm determination. She's made her mind up. "I believe you will save her," she says, "but I can't be a part of it. I'm sorry."

I look up at Alexia, unsure what to say. She offers me another brief smile and heads to the door. I follow her, knowing that I can't let her leave, but unsure what to do or what to say. Amy's words echo in my mind.

You must come soon. Time is running out. Do you see?

Alexia reaches the front door.

"Wait, please." She turns, and I hand her a photograph. She looks at it briefly then back up at me, her lips a thin line.

"I need you to understand why I have to do this, Alexia."

She glowers back at me. "This isn't fair."

"Amy was seven years old when she disappeared," I say. "She was never seen again. Is that fair?" I'm not proud of myself for the guilt trip, but I have no choice. It's all I have left.

"This is emotional blackmail, Joseph, and I don't appreciate it." Alexia steps away from me. "Who do you think you are?"

"That's what I'm trying to show you, Alexia: who I am." The words fall from my mouth faster than I can think. "I'm a brother who let go of his sister's hand. I took my eye off her for a second, and she vanished, and I have lived with that my whole life . . . It was my fault." My voice wavers. "I'm also a son who failed his family, and I'm desperately trying to right a wrong here. I believe that you can help me save her. That's why I can't give up, that's why I'm begging you to help." I hold out the photograph again. "Please, see Amy in all of this."

Alexia's shoulders drop a little. Finally, she takes the photograph. It's from Amy's fifth birthday. As always, she looks impossibly cute, wearing a yellow dress with her hair in pigtails. Surrounded by friends, she blows out the candles on a cake, completely unaware of the camera. Pure joy is in her eyes.

Alexia looks at it for a while, then murmurs, "She's beautiful." She hands the photo back to me. Then she is Alexia Finch, the therapist, again, immune to empathy for all the right reasons, detached from this, from me. She lets out an apologetic sigh. "I'm sorry, Joseph, really I am, but I meant what I said. I can't be involved in this." She leaves the house and walks away without looking back. This time, I don't call after her.

In the kitchen, I stare at the photograph of Amy. The edges are frayed, the color desaturated. My world has darkened again. Suddenly, the clock in here is way too loud. Or perhaps the kitchen is too quiet. Either way, I'm alone. All my talk of destiny, of feeling invisible strings being pulled, it was all true, but it amounted to nothing. I was convinced Alexia was going to help me. And now she's gone. Her perfume lingers, but like all things, it too will soon fade.

Time is running out. Do you see?

PART 5

"EVERYTHING WE NEED IS RIGHT HERE."

October 1996

Amy had a lot of friends at primary school. Her sunny disposition and irrepressible giggle were appealing, and she was never short of invitations. One of Amy's friends, Lucy Brookes, was going to have a treasure hunt for her birthday party. The anticipation lasted weeks. Lucy churned through new best friends as girls clamored to make the cut, and invitations were proudly paraded at break time by the favored few. Amy was thrilled when she was handed an invitation and talked of little else until, two days before the party, Lucy got chicken pox, and the whole thing was called off.

Amy was gutted. She wasn't a spoiled child, and she didn't complain, but her disappointment was almost harder to watch. The sheen had gone from her, and we all felt it.

So, with the blessing of Mum and Dad, I hatched a plan. If Amy couldn't go out and hunt treasure, then the treasure would come to her.

On the day of the would-be party, while Mum and Dad distracted Amy with a jigsaw puzzle, I transformed the garden with candles in glass jars, a ring of bricks surrounding a campfire, and a tent. At teatime, I called her into the kitchen. "Come on, Pip-squeak! We're off on an adventure," I told her. "Here's your kit bag." I gave Amy a mini backpack with a headlamp and a plastic trowel inside. My bag held a box of matches, a water bottle, and a ton of snacks.

"We have to go to the meeting point," I said.

"Where's the meeting point?"

I leaned down to whisper to her. "It's inside the tent. I'll meet you there in a minute."

As it got dark, I lit the fire. We ate hot dogs, grapes, Kit Kats, and bags of popcorn. After the excitement of not cleaning our teeth or washing our faces, we climbed into our tent, chatting by flashlight.

"This is fun," Amy said. "But when are we going to search for the treasure?"

I opened my backpack and pulled out a treasure map. I'd made it from an old piece of wallpaper lining and aged it by singeing the edges and dabbing the paper with wet teabags. I covered the map with little pictures of different parts of the garden, with a big red X in the middle of the vegetable patch.

Amy's eyes were big as saucers.

"Where did you get the map?" she asked.

"I bought it off a pirate in the park."

"What's the red X for?"

"X marks the spot!" I said. "It's where the treasure is!"

"Can we go and find it?" she said, eyes gleaming. Without waiting for me to answer, she put on her wellies and her dressing gown, pulled swimming goggles out of her pocket, and put them on.

"What are the goggles for?" I asked her.

"To stop stuff from getting in my eyes, of course," she said.

Of course.

We entered the garden, which was a maze of mysterious shapes in the beam of our flashlight, the lawn a blanket of golden leaves. We followed the map to a spot just next to "Rhubarb Forest."

Amy handed me the trowel. "You do it, Joe," she said. "I can hold the flashlight."

She held the light while I dug. I went slowly, to prolong the excitement, her breath clouding in the beam.

Then . . .

The trowel struck metal. Our quarry.

"I've found something!" I gasped. If my drama teacher could see me now . . .

"What is it?" Amy asked breathlessly.

Digging with my fingers, I eased a small metal tin from the cloying earth, wiped away most of the mud and handed it to her. "I don't know!" I whispered, "You should open it and see."

Inside the tin were two packets of jelly beans.

"Oh," she said, obviously a little underwhelmed. "Jelly beans? I thought it would be real treasure."

After studying them for a few seconds I said, "They're not ordinary beans . . . they're *magic* beans."

Amy picked up on the game immediately. "And if we eat them, we turn into fairies!"

"Er—exactly," I said.

We took the beans back to the tent and ate most of them while I read Amy fairy stories from her favorite book. Eventually she dropped off. I was convinced that she would bail before morning, but it was me who lay awake in the garden, listening. I was thirteen, sleep was my religion, but I didn't get much that night.

The birds woke me up. I turned to see if Amy had heard them too, but she wasn't there. Had she gone back inside after all? I scrambled out of the tent and found her anointing daisies with her very last jellybean. She said she was blessing them.

"Did the birds wake you up?" I asked.

"Yes, they were so loud!" She giggled, with her hands over her ears. Then her hands went to her tummy. "I'm hungry."

I lit the fire again, and we rummaged around in the bottom of the rucksack to see what snacks were left.

"Just marshmallows," I showed her.

"That's okay. Fairies *always* eat marshmallows for breakfast," she said.

While we ate, Amy picked up the treasure map again. "You didn't really get this off a pirate," she said. "Did you make it?"

I wasn't sure what to say. I didn't want to spoil the magic.

"I don't mind if you did," she said, looking up at me. "Actually, it's even better."

I confessed.

She grinned. "You're clever."

"So you don't mind that you missed Lucy's party?"

She wrinkled up her face. "No! This has been the best adventure ever!"

Mum and Dad looked out at us from the kitchen window. Mum waved and Dad gave me a thumbs-up. I felt proud. I'd taken care of Amy all night, and she'd had fun.

Dad was right. I was becoming an expert, passing knowledge on.

"Amy . . . *we* made this happen."

She looked at me blankly.

"If things don't go your way, you can change the way you feel about it."

She narrowed her eyes. "What do you mean?"

"I made the map, but you made it fun . . . You danced with the fairies!"

She laughed. "I *am* a fairy, silly! So are you!"

"You see?" I smiled, tapping the side of my head. "Everything we need is right here. In our imagination."

And it was.

18

Saturday, December 28, 2019

I punch the bed in frustration. Once again, I have failed to time travel. I tried on Boxing Day and then again yesterday. I've been trying to travel from Amy's room. I thought I'd give myself the best chance by sitting on her bed, holding the ribbon, surrounded by her toys. But my tanks are totally empty. I've completely run out of gas.

It's eleven thirty a.m. I've been trying for an hour, concentrating so hard that I've almost been forgetting to breathe. Enough. I fold Amy's hair ribbon and put it back in her precious jewelry box—here, safe, so I don't lose it. A part of me hopes that keeping it in here will give it more power or maybe slow down its fading.

I go downstairs to the kitchen, make a rocket-fuel coffee, and turn the radio on. They're playing the usual end-of-year, best-of dross, hosted by some tired old DJ from the 1960s, trying to be cool. I hate this time of year.

Through the window I notice a robin in the garden. He's scuffing the snow with his little beak, looking for—what, worms? He digs away, determined, at the frozen earth. His feet must feel like blocks of ice.

I think back to Alexia's words on Christmas night. "I have some serious concerns about the morality of changing the past," she said. I feel a surge of frustrated anger. I understand why she decided to distance herself from me. She's a therapist, and therefore an expert at empathy avoidance. You have to be, otherwise you can't do your job, and whatever it is I'm asking of her is way outside her sphere. Still, it annoys the hell out of me.

"Bloody integrity," I mutter out loud. I feel immediately ashamed. I think back over our conversation and wonder if there's anything I could have said or done differently to change her mind. Probably not. Alexia Finch is a woman who knows her own mind very well.

I look back out the window, just in time to spot the robin flutter onto the wall, then disappear over the side, into my neighbor's garden. At the end of the day, I'm on my own. And there's nothing to be gained by picking apart what I should or shouldn't have done. Alexia Finch made her choice.

I spend the afternoon reorganizing my record collection. I have 422 LPs, 71 twelve-inches, and 311 singles. Luckily, I also have a lot of shelf space. I'm standing back, admiring my work, when I hear it. It's only a whisper, barely discernible in the thick silence of the winter afternoon, but it's definitely there.

I run up the stairs, two at a time, and into Amy's bedroom. I hold my breath and listen. My heart beats in my chest, my ears throb. I carefully open the jewelry box and lift out the little blue ribbon. I can feel it has something it wants to tell me. It's happened to me before. Sometimes objects talk to me, and sometimes they don't. They have phases. I thought the ribbon had given me everything already, but there's an extra untold chapter it wants to share. "What is it?" I ask quietly. "What is it that you still need me to know?"

Kneeling on the floor beside Amy's bed, I hold the ribbon and focus on creating a space for it to share its tale. I slow my breathing, sinking away from reality and into the night I lost Amy.

I've relived this scene a hundred times. Everywhere is gray and silent, like thick fog. No sound except the steady thrum of my heartbeat, that is, until a single object falls into my vision, descending like scenery onto a stage. It shines with a dull luster, like the hub at the center of a giant bicycle wheel. Metal spokes push from it, growing and forming into a huge steel snowflake. Carriages appear at its edges and lights break through the darkness. The massive Ferris wheel, now complete, stands stock-still, holding its own breath.

Next come the stalls. At first, they're just blocks of color, outlined with rough childlike strokes, but then layers of detail begin to resolve. People appear, like raindrops on dry soil. Initially just a few here and there, but more appear, then more, until the fairground is filled with them, colorful but still motionless.

The sky bleeds up from behind this world, a canvas of grassy earth unfurls beneath my feet, and then it comes—a gust of wind, warm and alive, rushes over me, and with it, time becomes motion. It moves slowly at first, like a hand-cranked camera, one frame at a time. I hear the slow sound of laughter and excited cries, followed by a distant pipe organ. They mesh, gaining speed, then the fairground bursts into life. I smell rich dark toasted chestnuts, sweet pink cotton candy, the oil and smoke from the rides, and, weaving through it all, the fresh green scent of summer grass.

So far, everything is as it always is. What can I have missed? I will only ever see this night through young Joe's eyes. I know from past experience I won't really be able to see anything new or from a different angle, but maybe I'll notice a detail I didn't spot before.

This time, though, I'm already in the middle of the action.

Amy has gone already. I've lost her. I find myself running toward the gaudy, brightly lit carousel. The painted wooden horses mock me, mouths pulled back in evil grins, and the children's screams torment me. Every shape is a possible clue, every figure a potential kidnapper.

People turn their heads toward me, and I feel a familiar mixture of pity, curiosity, and suspicion. To my left is the Hall of Mirrors. Signs read Lots of Laughs! and Fun for Everyone! At the corner of the building, next to a cartoon of a thin bespectacled man laughing at a fat version of himself in an undulating mirror, stands a stunningly pretty young woman. She has a short, wavy blond bob pushed behind her ears, and she's wearing dangly pearl earrings. Her cream-colored knee-length dress is cinched at the waist with a wide pink belt. She carries a leopard-print handbag, and her cherry-red lipstick matches her stiletto heels. Sunglasses sit atop her head like a hairband, and she's posing with an ice cream. She stands out in the sea of faces, but they're all faces I've seen before.

"Like this?" she calls. She's looking at someone to my right.

I glance over and see the photographer. He's a young lad in a white shirt with the sleeves rolled up to the elbow, brown trousers, and shiny leather shoes. His mouth twists into a grin and he raises his thumb.

"Perfect," he says, voice deep and gravelly. He has huge sideburns that come down to his jawline, and he's holding an old-fashioned camera to his face. I've convinced myself over the years that if I could only see him, I would know him, but the camera always blocks my view. "Hold it there, baby."

His finger presses down to release the shutter, and suddenly everything switches to slow motion and turns hyperreal, colors screaming at me, so vivid I have to squint. The camera flash slowly explodes into blinding light. I blink, and as I open my eyes again, the light fades. Then, agonizingly slowly, the photographer inches the camera away from his face.

As I watch, mesmerized, waiting for it to reveal the photographer's face, I notice for the first time that the camera is an antique Leica, probably from the '60s, with a black body and a small telephoto lens. The flash is attached on an arm like a mini–satellite dish with a bulb at its center. The photographer's hands are young and smooth, the flat round fingernails short and clean, and he's wearing a large gold signet ring.

Something chimes deep within me, like a silent bell. Young Joe has already started to turn his head away from the photographer, and my eyes are still suffering from the searing flash, but I can make out his basic features. He's about twenty, with thick black eyebrows and a strong nose. He has bright-pink lips, unusually full, and he licks them lasciviously as he watches his girlfriend take a bite of her ice cream. I desperately want to recognize him. I scan him up and down, wildly, as I move past, but I'm forced to accept that I don't know who he is. My heart sinks as I work desperately to commit his features to memory.

The viewing continues. I move toward the carousel, but the fairground starts to collapse around me, falling away to nothing and leaving me surrounded by the dark gray fog I arrived into. The last thing to disappear is the carousel, straight in front of me, and as it drops away, my vision is filled with burning orange light. But slabs of detail resolve into a shape that looks like a building. I open my eyes and shut them again. The brief flash of fresh light exposes new detail, an old black-and-white timber building, like the Tudor houses in Stratford-upon-Avon, and there's a sign on the front of it. As the image fades, I just make out the word *Seabrook*. The letters are fuzzy and indistinct, each runs into the next. As I strain to see, the image fades away completely, and I'm left in a timeless void.

I strain my ears for the sound of distant voices, for another glimpse, another clue. Nothing comes. I open my eyes and run the ribbon through my hands. The whispering has stopped.

The winter sun shines weakly through Amy's window. Watery rainbows flicker on the back wall. As I watch them dance, I digest what I've just experienced. Finally, I've seen the face of the photographer. I always thought I'd recognize him. I'm good with faces, but I know I've never seen him, before or since. I didn't recognize the girl either. A chilling thought strikes me. Did this couple abduct Amy? Have I just viewed the faces of the last people to see her alive? Is this what she wanted me to see?

Seabrook. As the word spins around my head, the bell inside me chimes again. Could it be the name of the photographer? The outline of the timber building dances on my retina. Is it the name of a hotel? Is it where they kept her, before . . . ?

Horrific images play out in my mind's eye, but I cut them short. This won't get me anywhere.

I need another coffee, then I'm going to turn the internet inside out.

19

Tonight, I'm at Curry Club in Vinny's fabulous kitchen. The rest of the house is chaos. Records cover every surface. Shoes, old beer-making kits, and roller skates clutter the living room—and hats, which Vinny collects but only ever wears when he's performing with his band. But the kitchen is pristine. One wall is exposed brick and covered floor to ceiling with shelves full of clear glass jars filled with a panoply of ingredients. The kitchen units are pure steel, and the fridge is one of those gigantic American ones with a built-in ice maker. Vinny knew the owners of a restaurant in town that was shutting down, and he got the fridge for a song. In fact, if he ever gave up Vinny's Vinyl, he could probably set up Vinny's Vindaloo—although the risk is that he'd eat most of the food himself. The room is nothing if not practical, with polished concrete floors that could be jet-washed clean in less than a minute.

Vinny and I started Curry Club a couple of years ago. The original idea was that we'd take turns preparing a new curry each month, but Vinny's such a brilliant cook that we agreed we'd stick to our strengths: I would buy the ingredients, and he would do the cooking. We've shared some weird and memorable dishes over the years, from vegan chocolate curry to fermented fish phall. I had to keep the windows open for days after that one.

I'm sitting at the solid wooden island, on one of the carved oak barstools, sipping a beer and watching Vinny speed-chopping onions in a pool of bright white light.

He sniffs loudly.

"Don't cry, Vin," I say.

"Silly bugger," he says, flicking me a grin. "It's just the onions." He wipes his eyes on his red-striped apron, which clashes horribly with his pink-and-green Hawaiian shirt and yellow shorts. He gets so hot cooking that he always wears summer gear on Club nights. "So Seabrook," he says. "Sounds like a racehorse."

"Wasn't that Sea Biscuit?" I take a sip of beer. "Could be so many things. I spent most of the day on the internet, searching for leads. I thought because it's written on the front of this old building, it might be a hotel, but I couldn't find a similar-looking Seabrook Hotel anywhere on the planet."

Vinny sips sauce from a wooden spoon, opens a jar of dried chilies, and throws in a huge handful. The curry smells fantastic—earthy, pungent, and aromatic. I'm sweating in anticipation.

"You said the building reminded you of Stratford," Vinny says, coughing a little to clear the remnants of volcanic sauce from his throat. "Any luck there?"

"Not really," I reply. "There were a few similar buildings, but none with the three roof ridges and the chimneys. I also looked for other towns and villages called Seabrook with similar buildings, but nothing."

Vinny reaches up to the magnificent spice rack. It runs the length of the wall to the left of the cast-iron oven, and holds a dazzling collection of spices, all neatly labeled and dated. He pulls down a little jar of small black seeds and puts seven of them into the pan.

"Always seven, no more, no less—" he begins.

"—that's what Sanjeev says," we finish together and chuckle. Sanjeev runs the curry house around the corner. We've never invited him to Club nights because we're too intimidated, but Vinny often calls him for advice.

Vinny stirs the curry. "Do you think you need to travel deeper into the past?" He turns to me. "You know, go back to medieval times or something?" He says this nonchalantly, but I can tell he's excited at the thought.

"No, I think it's a clue to finding Amy. I just don't know what it means."

"And you got all this from the ribbon?" Vinny asks.

"Yep," I confirm. Vinny knows about my gift, that objects tell me stories sometimes. "This was different though. I knew it had something to tell me, but I almost had to coax it out."

Vinny pulls a tray of huge puffy naan from the oven. He splatters it with melted butter and takes it to the little dining table behind me. "Grub's up!" he says.

I move to the table and take a seat. It's right by the French windows, which look out over Vinny's backyard, just a small patio with a single flowerpot filled with cigarette stubs.

Vinny brings the huge pan of bubbling curry to the table, and we help ourselves.

"What's this one then?" I ask.

"Madagascan chicken and vanilla curry," he tells me. "Hot and sweet. I quite like it. See what you think." He piles a great mound of curry onto a hot piece of naan and takes a huge mouthful. As he chews, his cheeks turn even more red, and his mouth spreads into a wide grin. He gives the thumbs-up.

I tuck in and I'm relieved to discover I like it too. It gets a bit tetchy sometimes when we disagree.

We're silent for a couple of minutes, focused on our meal.

"So you said the viewing was different from the other times," says Vinny, leaning back in his chair and mopping his bald head with his handkerchief. "How?"

"Well, it usually starts at the shooting range. This time though it began halfway through, when I was running toward the carousel, just as I got to the photographer and his girlfriend. And then time slowed down, like a super slo-mo on your phone, like it wanted me to focus. I saw them both in a level of detail I hadn't seen before."

"What did you see?" Vinny asks. "What did they look like?"

"Well, the girl was really pretty. Young, blond bob, nice dress—basically a young Marilyn Monroe. And the photographer had huge sideburns and an old-fashioned Leica camera."

Vinny puts down his fork. He's staring at me like he's seen a ghost.

"It wasn't actually Marilyn Monroe," I tell him.

"No, I know," he says. "It was Debbie Sharpe."

"Who's Debbie Sharpe?"

"It has to be her. She thought she was really special, she did. Always dressed like Marilyn, hoity-toitying about like she was better than everyone else. Actually she was rough as a badger's arse. She'd do pretty much anything for the boys, if you get my drift, as long as there was something in it for her."

Vinny's always lived in Cheltenham, and he's a couple of years older than me—just old enough to have joined the Cheltenham dating scene at the time Amy went missing. He wasn't at the fair that night so he's never thought he could help, but now my heart is beating at a million miles an hour.

"And what about the guy then, the photographer?"

"That's the bloke she was seeing at the time. Now what the bloody hell was his name?"

I wait for the rusty cogs to connect in Vinny's brain.

"Brian? No, that wasn't it. Harry? No, no, come on . . ." He rubs his chin, and I hear his stubble rasping.

"Barry!" He slams his hand on the table, triumphant. "Barry Powell! He was really into photography, liked old-fashioned stuff. They both did. They used to strut around town like a couple of peacocks. She dumped him a few weeks later, once she'd got her glamour shots, I guess. Ended up with a chap called Malcolm. Shagged him, had three kids, then dumped him too." Vinny downs his beer and surveys me. "So what do we do?" he asks. "Now we know who they are?"

"Well, if you're sure, then we need to find him," I say.

"Malcolm?"

"No, not Malcolm. *Barry*. The photographer. Maybe he saw something."

"Or maybe he had something to do with it . . ." says Vinny soberly, echoing my own thoughts. "We all thought he was a couple of cans short of a six-pack at the time. There's a problem though."

"What's that?"

"I have no idea how we'd find him. After Debbie dumped him, no one saw him for a while. Last I heard, his family emigrated to Australia."

That sounds a lot like the behavior of a guilty man. What chance do I have of tracking him down now, after all this time? And what could I prove if I did? What's the point if I still can't get to Amy?

"You're looking discombobulated," Vinny says. "It'll all make sense in the end." He goes to the fridge to get another couple of beers and puts his hand on my shoulder as he squeezes past me. "All this stuff is happening for a reason, Cash. When the time is right, you'll figure it out."

I LEAVE VINNY'S EARLIER THAN USUAL. My heart's just not in it. Walking usually helps me think, but tonight, every step I take toward home seems to lead to a dead end. My brain aches with the effort of trying to decipher the meaning of Seabrook, and I just want to climb into bed and sink into oblivion.

It's just gone eight p.m. when I round the corner onto my road. The porch light looks like a welcome harbor in a storm. Sometimes home is the hardest place to be, but tonight I just want to be surrounded by my own four walls.

My phone buzzes. I ignore it. It's probably Vinny, with some new theory, but it'll wait until tomorrow. A few seconds later, it buzzes again. That's not like Vinny; if I don't pick up he knows not to hassle me. I pull my phone out of my jacket pocket.

Two missed calls—Alexia Hypno.

I press the call-back button and wait. Alexia picks up after three rings. "Joe?" She sounds a little breathless, and I can hear footsteps in the background.

"Yeah, hi," I say. "I missed a couple of calls from you."

"Where are you?" she asks.

"Nearly home. I've been out with a friend," I say. There's a half second of silence. "Er—with a mate. I've been to a mate's house for a curry."

"Sounds nice," Alexia says breezily. "After four days straight of turkey, I fancy a curry myself!"

I chuckle politely. "So what can I do for you?"

"I wanted to talk to you again," she says, then hesitates. "About Amy."

"Okay," I say carefully, determined to keep my cool this time. "Go on."

"I've been thinking a lot. I found myself questioning how I really felt about your situation, about what I said to you, about accepting the past, moving on, and focusing on the future. There are times in life when acceptance is right. Perhaps we have a lesson to learn. It's how we grow. Sometimes there is loss and sometimes there's gain. It's the way of life."

Mark said a similar thing. Pain helps us grow stronger. But what happens when there's too much? Do we instead grow sad and twisted, internalizing the pain in permanent ways?

"Joe?"

"I'm still here." I'm home now, but I sit on the wall outside my front door, cross my legs, and pull the flaps of Vinny's deerstalker hat down lower, to keep my ears warm.

"I went to see Martin," she says. "I asked him about what happened with Amy, what happened to your family." Her voice is gentler. "I'm so sorry, Joe. It's terribly sad. Not only losing Amy, but the impact it had on your father, your mother. And you . . ."

"Thank you," I say. "I appreciate that." Her empathy feels genuine.

"Joe, listen." Alexia's voice gets louder as, I imagine, she pulls the phone closer to her mouth. "Everything I talked about . . . my values, my approach, were all from the perspective of a therapist. I still believe what I said is right. When we can't change things, we need to adapt, and I help people to look inward at their beliefs, their attitudes. But that's the thing. My outlook was based on the fact that the past can't be altered. With you, the rules of the game are completely different. For some reason, you've been given the chance to change what happened. And that changes everything!"

She stops talking.

"Are you offering to help me?" I finally ask.

"Yes. If I can. What happened to your sister and your family is wrong. This is yours to fix, but if I can help you, I will."

"Thank you," I say gratefully. "That means a lot. I've been trying to travel again on my own for the last few days, with absolutely no luck."

"Maybe that's something I can help you with."

"Well, if anyone can, it's you."

"There is just one thing. Time travel wasn't covered in my training course"—she laughs—"and you and I are going to need to work this out together, a step at a time. So I don't feel it's right to offer you therapy on a professional basis. I just want to help you as a friend."

"That's fine." I'm so euphoric that I think I'd agree to almost anything. "You are officially relinquished of therapist duties. So how do we do this?"

20

I sleep fitfully. I dream that Alexia and I set up a stall on George Street in Cheltenham, selling tickets for one-way trips to the moon. We sell out in a couple of hours. At midday we hand out lunchboxes to our twelve travelers and pack them into the hull of a bright-red rocket ship. I climb into the driver's seat, and Alexia climbs in beside me.

"Ready?" she asks, smiling.

"Ready!" I say with a grin. "Have you got the key?"

"No," she says. "I thought you had it?"

"But how will we launch the rocket?" I cry out loud, waking myself with a jolt.

It's dark outside and the bedroom's freezing. I check the alarm clock: six a.m. December 29, 2019. Normally, I would grunt, turn over, and go back to sleep for at least another couple of hours. But today I feel wide awake. I shower, get dressed, and put the coffee on. Tomorrow I begin my sessions with Alexia. She explained that her office was closed until January but that she had a treatment room at her house that we could use. It means I have the day to myself and although I have absolutely no idea where I'm going or what I'm planning, I pour coffee in my travel mug, grab my car keys and an old road map off the bookshelf, and leave the house. My trusty old Volvo is parked in the next road. It used to be great when I needed to pick up a piece of furniture from a private sale or drop items off for a customer. These days, I hardly ever use it. I check the tires. They seem fine. I unlock the driver's-side door manually, shoving the key into the rusty lock, and for once, the car fires up on the first attempt. There's half a tank of fuel too. I pull away and head toward Gloucester on the A40.

I'm out on the open road in the quiet of a late December morning, and it feels great, liberating even. I've been putting so much into trying to travel back and save Amy that I've barely stopped to take a breath. This morning, some other part of me has taken over, my internal compass maybe. I left Cheltenham on a whim, but I have a powerful feeling that I am right where I am supposed to be, that everything is unfolding just as it should.

Just after Gloucester, I turn off the A40 and onto the smaller road toward Newent. I wend my way through country lanes and deserted villages, Christmas trees and festive lights illuminating my journey. I'm a bit worried the car might break down, and I don't have a contract with any of the recovery services. At Leominster, I carry on as the pale golden sun appears above the horizon to the right, until I get to a sign for Ludlow. It's like a tuning fork reverberates through me, infusing every cell with energy. This is the way. I turn left at the roundabout and drive till I get to the town. It's still only eight a.m., and it's only just got properly light. Unusually for me at this time of day, I'm so wired I don't need to go on the hunt for coffee, so I decide to explore, to see where my feet take me. I park the car, grab my jacket, and walk up the hill toward the church.

As I approach the center of town, I wonder why I've never come here before. It's beautiful. And when I get to the town square, it reminds me a bit of Stratford and the Seabrook building I saw in my viewing.

I feel a prickling on the back of my neck, a strong sense of being in the right place. At the highest point of the town, I come to a junction and hesitate for a second. My instinct is always to go upward, but my feet turn left and I walk down the hill toward the river. I feel a kind of magnetism drawing me, leading me toward something important.

The road ahead bends to the right. As I round the corner, I see it. Standing before me on the other side of the street is the building I saw in my viewing, illuminated in the afterglow of the camera flash. I know it beyond a shadow of a doubt. It's burned into my memory, and now, the scene before me matches perfectly, with its three peaks, ornate wooden carvings, and overhanging floors.

"Yes!" I murmur triumphantly, not wanting to disturb the peace of the early morning. "Found you!"

The building, as I suspected, is a hotel. There's a blue plaque on the outside wall, and I cross the street to read it. It describes the history of the building, which has stood here since Shakespeare's time. It must have some stories to tell, this place. I feel my excitement growing. Can it tell me about Amy? Did something happen to her here? Or is this linked to the photographer and his girlfriend? I try the entrance, but the door's locked. The hotel doesn't open today till eleven a.m.

I don't get it. The building doesn't have "Seabrook" written anywhere on it . . . so what's the connection?

Farther down the street, and just past the hotel, I spot a narrow lane through a low stone archway. I feel an inexorable pull to enter the cul-de-sac. And there in front of me, like something out of a Jane Austen TV remake, is a sign. Charles Seabrook Antiques.

I've found it.

The shop is beautiful. The paintwork is olive green, and "Charles Seabrook Antiques" is painted in white lettering above the door. Flanking the door are two bay windows with curved glass set into fine wooden frames.

I walk up to the door, shield my face with my hand, and peer inside. To my surprise, I see a face looking back at me. It's an older woman, perhaps in her seventies, wearing a gray tweed dress and a green scarf. She appears momentarily shocked. I smile and try the door. It opens, the bell jangles, and I walk in.

"Good morning," the woman says warmly. "Sorry, I didn't expect any customers yet!"

"Hello," I say. "No problem. It's great you're open so early." I scan the cabinets filled with ancient items of interest, objects people have loved, lost, or thrown away. "Lovely shop."

"Thank you," she says. "We've been here forty years this year." She pauses, proudly. "Can I help? Are you looking for anything in particular?"

"Maybe," I tell her. "I'll just have a browse first, if that's okay?"

"Of course," she replies.

I turn away from her and close my eyes, tuning in to whatever it is that's brought me here this morning. I feel energy ripple up from the floor, and I know in that moment that the camera, *Barry's* camera, is here.

In the back of the shop, I find a cabinet wedged behind a tall wooden palm tree. On the third shelf down, there's an empty plinth, with dust marks around the edge and a dark dust-free space in the middle, about the size of a camera. It was here.

"I collect old cameras," I call to the woman. "I'm particularly interested in Leica models from the '50s and '60s. Do you have any in stock?"

"Funny you should ask," says the woman. "We had an old one here for about fifteen years. It was badly damaged. It sat in that cabinet beside you all that time. We just couldn't sell it."

With my heart in my mouth I ask, "Do you still have it?"

She considers this. "I think it's in the storeroom somewhere, ready to be taken to the next auction. I wouldn't have a chance of finding it now, it's like a war zone back there."

Once more I tune in, and I see it in my mind's eye. I'm not leaving here without it, so it's time to roll the dice. "Actually, I called the other day and spoke to . . . I can't remember the name. Who would it have been?"

The woman scratches her nose. "Um, Diana?"

"Yes. That was it. She said it was in the storeroom, on the top shelf, next to the maps. Would you mind having a look?"

"Oh, of course." The woman disappears through the door behind the till. A minute later she reappears. "Well, you were right. It was exactly where you said, up there with the maps." She turns it over in her hands. "Unfortunately, I was right too. It's badly damaged."

I study the camera. There's no flash, it's lost its strap, and there's a vicious crack across the lens, but it's Barry's camera. I know it.

"It's a Leica IIIf 35mm Rangefinder, a classic," the woman says, shifting into sales mode. "This one has the more popular black casing. It was made around 1955. I could probably confirm the year, using the serial number, if you'd like?"

"Thank you, but there's no need," I say. "I'll take it. How much?"

"One hundred twenty pounds?" suggests the woman.

I pay her. She looks surprised that I don't bother to haggle, but I just want to get out of there as fast as I can. I run all the way back to the car. I feel like my lungs might burst, and my hands shake as I fumble to get the key in the lock. I climb in, shut the door, and lock it.

I take the package out of the bag, then slowly unwrap the paper. The camera lies in my lap, its unseeing lens facing upward. Holding my breath, my shoulders so tense they're up by my ears, I turn it over and undo the little door that hides the film canister.

The compartment is empty.

Despair washes over me, then exasperation. What did I expect? Did I really think the undeveloped film would be inside, that I would just pop to the pharmacy, get it developed, and within hours have the final clue to the mystery?

I bang my hands on the steering wheel. Why is this all so difficult? Every step only brings more questions. I close the film compartment and hold the camera in my hands. It starts to hum quietly, like a bumblebee in a matchbox, reminding me gently that I don't need the film.

Objects don't just launch stories at me out of the blue. I have to treat them with kindness and respect, let them know I *want* to listen. I quiet my mind, open my heart, and invite it to tell me its truth. "What do you want to tell me?" I say aloud. "Why did you bring me here? Show me."

I close my eyes. At first all I see is the dark red inside my eyelids. The red fades to dark gray, and the viewing begins. My mind assembles the scenery, painting details like an artist, stroke by stroke. I'm back at the fairground. This time though, I'm seeing everything from a completely new angle, a new perspective. This time I'm seeing everything as Barry.

Debbie reaches up to kiss my cheek, then sashays across the grass and over to the corner of the Hall of Mirrors. She turns to face me, cocks a hip, tosses her hair, and takes a lick of her ice cream. I lift the camera to my face and start to line up the shot through the viewfinder, positioning Debbie in the center. Just as I'm about to take the photo, the young Joe runs into the far left of the shot, pauses, and looks around desperately. He glances at me briefly, and then I shift the camera to the right to get him out of frame, and press the shutter release button. I focus back on the viewfinder and see that when the younger me entered the frame, Barry moved the camera a couple of millimeters to the right, capturing not only Debbie and the Hall of Mirrors on the left side of the shot, but also a thin slice of the field beyond on the right. And there, off in the distance, is Amy. Her little blue cardigan is flapping behind her, and her right foot is off the ground, midstride. As her hair blows in the summer breeze, I can see that one of her ribbons is missing. She's halfway up the hill, heading for a coppice at the top of the slope. And she's alone.

"Amy!"

My eyes snap open. Tears stream down my face. It's the first time I've seen her since the day she left my side. It's wonderful beyond words, but not being able to reach her rips my heart in two. I try to reassure myself that at least for those few minutes after I lost her, she was still okay. That means *something*. But I didn't expect her to be on her own. I blink at the camera through a haze of tears. "Okay, Amy," I say out loud. "I see it now. I can see you. But what am I supposed to do?"

I'm still half an hour from home when I ring Vinny. It's midday now, but the December sun is respectfully low in the sky. Vinny listens patiently to the whole story and doesn't ask any awkward questions about how an old camera summoned me sixty miles.

"I've gotta be honest," he says after I've finished the story, "it's a massive surprise that she was on her own, Cash."

"I know. I always imagined that she was snatched by a kidnapper or lured away by someone she knew."

"Well, at least you know which way she was headed."

"I do, but it doesn't explain what happened to her, or where she was going," I reply. "She was afraid of the dark. Why would she go into the woods on her own like that?"

"What if she was going to meet someone?" he suggests.

I consider this. "Maybe."

"Joe," says Vinny, carefully. "Did the police . . . did they . . . search properly up there in the woods?"

"They combed the area for three days, had volunteers from the public too. They didn't find anything."

He's silent for a moment. "I dunno, Cash," he says. "Where does this leave us? What next?"

I reach the outskirts of Cheltenham, where all this began.

"I don't know yet, Vinny," I say, feeling calm determination wash over me, "but I'm going to get some help, and I'm going to get back to Amy if it's the last thing I ever do."

As I PULL UP OUTSIDE MY HOUSE, it feels like the camera's agitated, and I can sense the ribbon stirring too. I open the front door and run upstairs to Amy's room.

The jewelry box is just where I left it, of course. But everything else is different. The air feels ionized, fizzing with potential. Soulful, binaural melodies wrap themselves around me, and a golden glow emanates from Amy's jewelry box on the dressing table, as though a miniature sun is about to rise from behind it.

The camera falls silent. I place it on the bed, cross the room, and open the jewelry box.

Amy's ribbon gleams, shot with threads of pure gold. I reach out to pick it up, and as I touch it, I get a tiny shock, like a hit of static electricity. Then I feel the energy flood into me.

I sigh with relief. It's like an ice-cold beer after a day in the desert. With its last dying breath the ribbon guided me to the camera. My viewing allowed me to observe a new angle on a familiar scene, and the power of that process has reenergized the ribbon.

This is it. This is my chance.

I grab my sports bag from the bedroom, shove the ribbon inside, and run downstairs, straight out of the house. I kick a box with my foot as I turn to lock the front door. A small package wrapped in brown paper sits on the ground by the wall. It's from Mark. I tear it open and unwrap a chunky black digital watch. It's old, a Casio G-Shock, military style, like something my Action Man would have worn back in the day. With the watch is a piece of lined paper, ripped from a notebook, and a simple handwritten message:

Joe, give me a call and I'll explain.

—Mark

As I walk toward Leckhampton, I ring Mark. He picks up straight away. "Joe, how are you?"

"I'm okay. I got the watch, thanks."

"Great. I was thinking about how I could help, and I remembered that old thing. I don't wear it anymore. I used to use it on survival weekends. Do you remember I did those?"

"I do." Mark used to disappear into the Welsh mountains to learn survival skills. They must have worked because he always came back.

"It's got all the bells and whistles," he says. "Compass, barometer, heart rate. But the reason I've sent it to you is that the time updates automatically, and it tells you the year too. Just press the button and it'll reset itself to the current time."

I process that for a second. "Will it work in the past?"

"Well, you need to test it obviously."

"Obviously," I say obediently. Mark sees this as a terrifically exciting experiment.

"These watches use satellites, but they also have a back-up mechanism that uses the MSF radio signal from Anthorn to set UK civil time."

There were a few words in that sentence that I didn't quite grasp, but I don't want to open a can of worms. "So you're saying it'll tell me the time no matter how far back I go?"

"No. The MSF signals only started in 1950. But presuming you won't be heading back that far, you should be okay."

"Thanks. It's brilliant, Mark. And the timing is perfect too. I'm on my way to Leckhampton Hill right now for another attempt. I can test it out today."

I fill him in on my trip to Ludlow, finding the camera, and seeing Amy in Barry's photograph.

"You've got the photo of Amy with you?" he asks.

"I don't, but I saw it through the viewfinder of Barry's camera. And when I got home, the ribbon had fired up again. I had this feeling of inevitability, like everything's come together finally, and I have another chance."

Mark's quiet for a moment. "I have a theory," he says, almost to himself. "I think you've just experienced the observer effect . . ."

"How do you mean?"

". . . and then if we lean toward the Copenhagen interpretation of quantum entanglement . . ."

"Mark, I'm not following you." I'm not far from my jump location now, so if Mark can shed any light on this, he needs to do it soon. "Can you explain in English?"

"Sure. Sorry. Quantum entanglement is a physics theory which, loosely speaking, suggests that two separate particles can be linked, or entangled, even if they're very far apart in space and time. Got it?"

"I think so," I say.

"And the observer effect says that just looking at something, witnessing it, can change it in some way. Make sense?"

"Yep." I try to silence the sanctimonious voice in my head that's telling me I should have tried harder at school. I wait, but Mark's quiet. "Mark?"

"Sorry," he says after a beat. "It's just that I'm taking particle physics and applying it to hair ribbons. I'm struggling with my professional credibility and twenty years of dogma here. If you ever tell anyone about this conversation, I'll kill you."

"I won't," I say. "I just want to understand."

"Okay," he says and takes a deep breath. "I'm guessing here, but I think the camera and Amy's hair ribbon are connected. You altered the state of the camera, which in turn altered the state of the ribbon. They're bound to each other somehow, perhaps via Amy and her story. All things are connected at some level . . . Man! You're creating a working model of the theory of everything. I need to get you into a lab."

"It sounds amazing, and I'd love to talk more about it, but I'm nearly at the hill now. I need to go."

"Joe, I just want to say something." Mark's voice is sober. "You sound good, you sound positive, and I'm pleased. But the last time you jumped, you hurt yourself so badly you ended up in the hospital. I'm worried you're going to do the same again. Or worse."

"I'll be fine," I say.

"It's the definition of insanity, you know."

"What is?"

"Doing the same thing but expecting a different result," he says. "We talked about this. We agreed you need to try a double jump."

"But everything's changed, Mark! I can't tell you how . . . ready I feel, how powerful. I'm charged up to full! I've got a good feeling about this."

He sighs. "Just be careful."

"I will, and if I save her, you'll be the first to know."

"If you save her," he says flatly, "you won't need to tell me, because she'll never have gone missing."

"Good point," I say cheerfully.

"Good luck, Joe," Mark says. "You can do this."

I GET TO THE TOP OF THE HILL, near the triangulation point. I pull the ribbon out of my bag and tie it around my wrist, staring over the valley to the distant park where the fair took place. When I land this time, I know where to go. I'm going to try and arrive a little bit earlier, stop Amy from going to the wood, maybe even catch her before she heads off.

I close my eyes and focus on my breathing. Slow and controlled.

The first hint that this isn't right is a feeling of severe turbulence. I'm being tossed around like a plastic bag in a tornado. I feel my hair on end and my stomach in my mouth as I'm spun upside down for a few seconds. Then my body rights itself, and I'm pedaling my legs in midair like a cartoon character hurtling over a cliff. I open one eye, and I'm rushing headlong toward spinning rides and flashing lights in the darkness. I close it again, feel a familiar retching, and clamp my hands over my mouth.

The wind speed drops a little, so I open my eyes and see that it's daytime. I aim myself toward a huge red-and-blue bouncy castle, but then the air's knocked out of my lungs, and I land on the hard, sunbaked earth with a WHUMP. Where the castle was is now an empty patch of ground. Around me are trailers, a crane, and a collection of worn-out caravans. Fast-food packaging, cotton candy sticks, and burst balloons litter the ground.

It takes my poor disorientated brain a moment to work it out, but it appears they're packing up. The fair's over.

"No!" I cry in dismay. Mark's watch confirms it's 1997, but I'm four days too late.

A man in an orange safety vest calls over to me. "Oy!" he shouts. "What's your game, son?"

Before I can answer, brain freeze takes a nip at the back of my head, an icy snake come to paralyze me. I gasp. Safety Vest walks toward me, a confused expression spreading over his face.

Cold fingers grip my skull, and as their crushing weight squeezes the breath from my lungs, the daylight darkens. Safety Vest fades from view as the blue veil of time descends.

I'm catapulted back, flung through time like a rag doll.

When I open my eyes, I'm back on Leckhampton Hill. The whole trip over in just a few exhausting seconds. With a heavy heart, I sit and rest my head in my hands. How could I get it so wrong? I was so certain I would succeed today, felt so sure that the ribbon would connect me back to Amy, with enough time to save her.

A terrible thought crawls up my back and settles at the nape of my neck. What if time is always moving? What if it's always dragging my window of opportunity along with it, and I've missed my chance?

On the way home, I call Mark. He sounds like he might be in a busy restaurant.

"What happened?" he asks.

"I went back as far as I could, but I landed four days *after* Amy went missing. They were packing up the fair."

"I was worried that might happen."

"What are you thinking?" I ask him.

"I'm not sure."

"Tell me anyway."

"Hang on, let me go outside." The line crackles, the sound of cutlery and conversation fades away. "Right, that's better. You remember we talked about time travel working like an elastic band? The farther back you travel, the less time you have there?"

"Yes," I say wearily. "I remember."

"It's possible that the elastic band is always the same length. Imagine it stretched over pegs on a board." I can visualize what he means exactly. He's a natural teacher. "As each day goes by, the elastic band spans the *next* two pegs."

"And so time marches on," I say. "Each day in the present is another day I can't reach in the past. It's too late." My voice catches. I don't think I've ever felt so tired.

Mark clears his throat. "Joe, listen to me. It might not be. I maintain that the best option you have is to break the trip down into two achievable jumps."

"But why would splitting the jump make any difference? I'm still traveling back just as far."

"Dean Karnazes."

"Who?"

"He's a long-distance runner. Amazing man, totally dedicated. He ran nonstop for eighty hours, covered three hundred and fifty miles in one go. He didn't stop to eat or sleep, he just ran until he couldn't run anymore." Mark pauses as a large vehicle passes by. "Now. If you let Karnazes rest in between his runs, allow him to fuel up, give him longer to do it . . . well, you get a very different result. He can run thousands of miles. Same runner. Split the mileage. Different result."

My mind whirs. "I get what you mean," I tell him, "but I just don't know if time travel works like that."

"Neither do I," Mark replies. "All I'm saying is the split jump *might* make a difference. Maybe you won't stretch the elastic band so far. Think about it. First, you jump back to, say, 2005. You know you can do that pretty easily, and you'll have time to regroup when you get there. To follow the running analogy, you refuel, you rehydrate, take a breather. Then, refreshed, you jump again, back to 1997." His voice wavers a little. He sounds cold and I visualize him pacing outside a bar in a ski resort somewhere in Austria. "On the second jump, you'll only be traveling back eight years, perhaps even giving you a bit more time when you get to 1997. You don't need long, just need enough time to save Amy."

"It sounds good in theory, but I'm exhausted after the first jump," I tell him. "There's no way I can jump again. We already tried it when I came to see you."

"The wonderful thing about all of this," says Mark, unperturbed, "is that, in the nicest way, time traveling is all in your head. You're not pushing your body to the limit, you're not using a machine or a magic potion. I don't understand how, but you're doing it through the power of your mind. And the mind has plenty of room for expansion. I'm convinced that you can channel your power and manage a double jump."

I heave a massive sigh. "Thanks, Mark." I hope he's right.

"Have you spoken to the hypnotherapist?"

"Yes. She wants to help. I'm seeing her tomorrow."

"I'm pleased to hear it," he says. "We both know there aren't any guarantees, but it's got to be worth a try."

21

Alexia hands me a coffee. It's an instant, but today is an exceptional day, so I accept it with a smile.

She's wearing a dark-green sweater, turned up jeans, and white trainers. Her hair is pinned up in a ponytail, but strands are trying to escape, falling over her eyes.

I hear snuffling and snorting behind a door.

"Are you okay with dogs?" Alexia asks.

"Friendly ones," I reply.

"He's very protective of me, but he won't hurt you. He's more likely to kiss you to death." She walks to the door and opens it. "Come on then, Jack. Come and meet Joe."

Jack gallops in. He's a lurcher, large, gray, and very hairy with a shiny black button nose and intelligent eyes. He bounds up to me.

"Keep your mouth closed, by the way. Jack kisses like an anteater." He bounces up to my face and licks my cheek.

"Hello, Jack," I say. He lies at my feet and rolls over for a tummy rub.

"You are honored," says Alexia. "He doesn't let just anyone do that, you know."

"How long have you had him?" I ask.

"Two years altogether," she says. "He belonged to my ex, but I got custody when we split up because Will moved to Argentina. It's been just the two of us for six months now. Jack was the best thing to come out of that relationship, weren't you, boy?" She leans down and caresses his ears.

I find myself thinking that whatever was in Argentina must have been pretty spectacular for Will to leave these two behind.

Alexia sits opposite me at the kitchen table with a cup of chamomile tea. "You said you had a new lead?"

"I've found out that Amy left the fair on her own. She was last seen running toward a nearby wood."

"Do you know why?"

"No, it's all guesswork. I think maybe she was meeting someone or running away. Either way, it's given me a new focus. I at least know where she was heading. So if I can travel back far enough—and it's a big *if*—I might be able stop her from running away or find her in the woods and bring her back to safety."

Alexia nods, a serious expression on her face. "And how can I help you?"

"If I travel all the way in one go, I can't stay long enough. And now, I can't even reach the night she went missing. I think I need to try what I'm calling a double jump." I take a sip of coffee to disguise the lump in my throat. "My friend Mark thinks if I split the jump in two, I'll be able to go back to the night I lost her and stay there long enough to save her."

"Have you done a jump like this before?"

"I tried, but I couldn't do it. I didn't have any energy after the first jump, none at all."

Jack walks around the table to Alexia and sits beside her. She strokes his head as he peers up at her adoringly.

I tell Alexia about the ribbon, my unexpected trip to Ludlow, the camera viewing, seeing Amy running alone toward the wood, and how the ribbon seems to have charged up since I brought the camera home.

Alexia's looking at me with a bemused look on her face.

"What?" I say.

"So . . . now you're saying you see things when you touch objects?" she asks.

"Oh . . . sorry, I thought I'd told you that before," I reply sheepishly.

"No." She raises her eyebrows and lets out a little laugh. "I just thought you could time travel." I watch her processing this new information and get a sense of what Vinny and Mark have been through. Disbelief, suspicion, denial, the whirring cogs of reality being disassembled and reconnected. Now it's Alexia's turn.

She blinks, in deep thought, then asks, "So how does it work?"

"Certain objects seem to absorb the past. They want us to find them, want to tell us their stories. When I touch them, I just happen to be able to hear them."

She shrugs. "Well, I suppose if I believe in time travel, that isn't so far-fetched . . ."

We both laugh a little. Jack seems to like that. He wags his tail enthusiastically, tapping a rhythm on the table leg.

"Right," Alexia says. "So what do you think's stopping you from doing one of these double jumps? Why can't you charge back up after you've jumped the first time?"

"I don't know," I tell her. "I suppose it might be a focus thing. The landings are very messy. Last time I tried, I was all over the place, tumbling around like clothes in a dryer. Maybe if I could focus better, and land more accurately, I'd still have some juice left in the tank."

She considers this but then her expression becomes pensive. "Joe, there's something we need to discuss."

"Okay," I say.

"On your travels so far, have you ever changed the past?"

A little reluctantly, I tell her about winning the lottery, making sure I stress my shared win and good intentions for the proceeds.

She appears to have no opinion about my motives. "Therefore, you know it's possible."

I nod.

"So . . . you save Amy, what then?"

"What do you mean?"

She swallows, draws in a breath. When she speaks again her tone is thoughtful, a little sharper. "Right now, although it's unbelievable, incredible . . . this still feels relatively small. It's just me and you. I know we're talking about potentially transforming your life and that of your family, but on a global scale, it's a drop in the ocean. If I help you to hone this skill, and you manage to save Amy, you could continue to improve your ability to time travel, and end up with the power to change anything you like."

"No." I frown. "This is all about Amy."

She nods gently. "You say that now, but if you get that power, who knows what you could do? Where would you stop? You could believe you were doing good, avoiding wars, undoing huge disasters. Wouldn't that be tempting?"

"I wouldn't do that," I tell her. "I know I could just as easily end up making things worse. Honestly, changing anything else . . . it hasn't even crossed my mind. I believe I've been given this gift so I can save my sister. As far as I'm concerned, this starts and stops with Amy." She waits, studying me. "I promise, Alexia. This has only ever been about her. I never wanted to be a time traveler, but now that I have the chance to save her, I want to give it one last shot. I just want to be happy, get Amy back, and give her the life she deserved."

Alexia nods. Jack lays his chin on the table, and they both regard me softly. "Okay," she says. "Let's try."

HER TREATMENT ROOM IS COZY. It's just off the kitchen, with a window looking over the garden. I guess it was once the dining room. The garden is well cared for, with neat flower beds on either side of the lawn, a couple of fruit trees, and a summerhouse in the corner by the fence.

"It faces west," she says. "Lovely spot for a G&T on a summer's evening. Hard to imagine at the moment, isn't it?"

"Yeah, it is." I feel unexpectedly nervous.

There's a large taupe leather chair next to a triangular coffee table with a potted plant and a box of tissues on it. The dark-blue velvet sofa is well used, and the pile on the arms has worn away. Above the sofa is a large whiteboard, plastered in Post-it Notes. The opposite wall is floor-to-ceiling bookshelves packed with serious hardbacks. The text on the spines is mostly too small to make out, but a particularly large red one says *EMDR: Desensitizing Trauma*. Sounds painful.

"Take a seat, Joe." Alexia's smiling at me. "Do you want the chair or the sofa?"

I sit on the sofa, and it's a long way down. I'm not sure I'll be able to get up again without rolling out of it.

"Wow, this is . . . low," I say. "Is it designed to trap patients, make it harder for them to escape when things get hairy?"

Alexia smiles. "Relax! There's nothing to worry about. You weren't this nervous last time, were you?" She takes a seat in the chair, folding one leg under her and stretching the other out, resting her right foot on the floor. She's purposeful, but she moves with grace and balance, like a cat. I like watching her.

"Maybe not," I reply. "But the second time is always harder, don't you think? No one expects you to know what you're doing the first time."

She studies me. I shift in my seat.

"What made you choose hypnotherapy anyway?" I ask, not ready yet to turn the spotlight on myself. Martin told me Alexia had her own reasons for getting into therapy. I'm curious to learn more.

"I actually had hypnotherapy myself," she explains, "to help me through a difficult part of my life. It was so transformative, I decided to train as a hypnotherapist so I could help others in the same way. I grew up in a household that was very focused on money and achievement. I tried my best to fit in, but I learned early on that what gives me a sense of purpose is helping other people."

A shaft of sunlight illuminates Alexia's cheek. Her skin is soft and clear, a strand of hair framing her ear and the small amethyst earring that adorns it. She pulls a notepad and a pen from one of the shelves nearby and pushes her glasses back up to the bridge of her nose.

"Which brings me back to you," she says. "Let's go over what you want to achieve, and see if we can agree on a plan of action. Does that sound good?"

"Great," I say. "Action sounds great."

"Okay, let me see if I've understood so far. You've tried a double jump before?"

"From Mark's house, yes. I managed to do the first jump okay, and

I really tried to focus and prepare myself for another jump, but it was impossible."

"You mean it *felt* impossible?" Alexia suggests.

"I suppose so, yes."

"But you're open to the fact it might *be* possible?"

"It's got to be," I say. "It has to be. It's the only way for me to get back to Amy."

"Okay," she says. "Let's take a step back. When you decide to travel to a certain date and time, how do you make it happen?"

I think about the first few times, how random and frightening they were. I guess I am getting better. "First, I get hold of an object that links back to that time," I say. "So for Amy, it's her ribbon, which I found at the fairground the night she went missing. Another time, I traveled back to 2005 using some horse-racing tickets from a trip my dad and I went on."

"All right. What next?"

"I make sure I'm somewhere safe. I need to travel from a spot that's the same in the past as it is now, so I don't hurt myself when I land." My nerves twang painfully as I recall the barbed wire fence.

Alexia scribbles as I talk.

"Then, I set my intention, and I focus. Through the object, I connect to where I want to go, and I do the breathing exercises you taught me. Sooner or later I feel myself fall back through time, and I land in the past."

"What are the landings like? Does it make any difference how far back you've traveled?"

I think back to my last jump, to 1997. "It seems like the farther back I go, the rougher the landing."

"What causes the turbulence, do you think?" she asks.

"I don't know." I smooth the hair at the nape of my neck. "I've been assuming it's because I'm trying to jump so far in one go. But it could be the fact that I'm so tense. Every time I go back, I relive the panic of losing Amy, the terror, the guilt . . . I was in charge of her that night, and I let her go." I swallow and glance at the box of tissues. I don't want to cry.

Alexia makes a few more notes, then gazes out the window. After a few seconds, she turns back to me. "I have a theory. And a plan." She leans forward and puts her hands on her knees. "I'm thinking that maybe all your challenges are fundamentally the same. You need to learn how to be more present . . . more *mindful*, if you like that term."

I don't. *Mindfulness* is a word bandied about by hippies and tree huggers as an answer to everything. Apart from the fact that one idea can't be the answer to everything, I have no idea what *mindfulness* even means.

"More present?" I ask. I hope I sound more positive than I feel.

"It's just a hunch," she says. "Go with me on this."

"Okay, I'll try."

She smiles patiently. "When people learn to be more present, they live in *the now*. They worry less about the past and the future, and they focus more on what's happening in the moment, on what's happening right now. Does that make sense?"

"Yes," I say cautiously.

"Good. So I'm thinking about that double jump you tried. Am I right in thinking that the first jump was okay? You weren't worried about it?"

"Yeah, I guess so."

"I'm wondering whether that's because you were jumping from your true present. With me so far?"

I am, but I wonder what she's driving at. "Yes."

"So let's say you do your first jump back to 2005. If I can teach you how to connect more to the present, you may be able to feel as though 2005 is your new *now*, rather than the past. And that might help you recharge for a second jump back to Amy."

She looks excited.

"I don't know," I say. "It's a nice idea, but I feel like I've already been doing a load of focusy breathing stuff."

"Maybe not the *right* focusy breathing stuff ," she says, a smirk hovering. "And it might help with your landings. Maybe all those negative emotions are causing the turbulence, and if you could master your thoughts, you could master your landings too."

I don't know what to think. It all sounds pretty tenuous, but I don't have any better ideas. In my mind's eye, I consult with my friends. Mark tells me to test it. Vinny tells me to go for it and to bring some snacks for the journey.

"All right," I say. "Let's give it a try. How quickly can you teach me?"

"The better question is, how quickly can you learn?" she says and winks. "I usually work with people on this kind of stuff in twelve sessions over three months." My face must give away the surging panic, because she adds quickly, "But I know you'll want to go faster than that."

"We *have* to go faster," I say. "Every day that goes by takes me farther from Amy. Even if we can work out this double jump, there's no guarantee I'll get back to the night of the fair. And even if I do, we don't know how long I'll have."

"We have to be realistic," Alexia insists. "People don't acquire new skills like this overnight. It takes time to build new ways of thinking. And a lot of the magic happens in the time *between* sessions, as people assimilate what we've covered and apply it in their lives."

"Okay, but we already agreed that you're not treating me as a therapist. I just need this one skill, and I needed it yesterday. Can't we do some intensive sessions?"

Alexia peruses her shelves of books, no doubt seeking advice from the gurus whose work lies within. "I've never used it, but a little while back I studied a kind of accelerated approach to treatment," she muses. "I don't know if it'll work for us, but some people have had astounding results with it, sometimes in just a few hours."

"I like the sound of that," I say firmly. "Can we try it?"

"I know you're under pressure, but we need to go at a pace that works for me too," she says. "I'll do a session with you every day, as long as you promise to practice at home. We'll start tomorrow, do it for ten days, then see where we've got to." She shoves her pen behind her ear and puts down her pad. "Does that sound all right?"

"That sounds amazing." Honestly, ten days still feels like an eternity, but it's a lot better than three months. "Alexia, are you sure you can spare me all this time?"

"I told you I wanted to help, and I'm not due back at work until the second week of January."

"Well, I'm going to pay you."

"There's no need."

"I am though. But is there any chance we could do two sessions a day?"

Alexia opens her mouth to speak, but then clearly changes her mind. She offers me a wry smile. "Sure. A crash course in therapy, coming right up."

OVER THE NEXT FEW DAYS, I feel as though I'm on a kind of retreat. I keep Mark and Vinny updated via text, and they send back messages of support, but other than that, I see and speak to no one except Alexia. I don't want to be distracted.

I give up coffee. An addiction to caffeine is not helpful when you're trying to meditate. Alexia gives me some supplements to help with the withdrawal symptoms. They work brilliantly.

Every morning I arrive at Alexia's at eleven a.m. We make tea, I spend a few minutes fussing over Jack, then we move into the treatment room for another session. During morning sessions, Alexia teaches me new techniques and practices. In the afternoons, we workshop. I give her feedback, and she helps me to hone my skills. For the first couple of days, I go home for a bite to eat between sessions, but on the third day, she invites me to stay for lunch, and we share a pot of soup. We take Jack for a walk afterward and I'm surprised when Alexia wishes me a Happy New Year. I'd completely lost track of the date. I wish her the same, but we don't discuss it again, perhaps because we both know there is only one way this year is going be a happy one.

I'm putting all my faith in this process, but fear often snaps at my heels, telling me I'm running out of time. At first, I fight with it, ordering it away so I can concentrate on meditating. Then Alexia explains that engaging with fear is what gives it its power. I try and ignore it, intensifying my focus on the present. The better I get at filling myself with *nowness*, the more everything else falls away. Fear, doubt, and guilt all fade, giving way to peace and clarity. At first, these moments are fleeting, but as I practice, there are longer periods of time when I feel truly at peace.

I wonder why I didn't get help years ago.

On January 2, I knock on Alexia's door at 10:55 a.m. She opens it and beams a welcoming smile. Her hair's in a braid today, and she's wearing a pale-pink sweater and black dungarees. I don't know if she wears makeup or not, but if she does, it's that clever stuff that makes her face radiate natural beauty. There's a moment when I think we're about to hug, but then we don't. We're just friends working on a project together. It's probably just that lifeboat mentality thing I've read about, where people get really close to others that they're flung into intense situations with.

"How did you sleep?" Alexia asks, standing back to let me in. Jack noses at my hand, and I ruffle his ears.

"I slept like a log," I say, and it's true for a change. "How are you?"

"Fine," she says. "Come on through. I've made peppermint tea. And I've got a new technique for us to try this morning. Something that'll help with your landings, hopefully."

We go into the kitchen, and Alexia pours me a mug of tea.

"I want to try a pattern reset with you," she says. "You're going to practice control, so you can stay calm and focused during your landings. I think it might help with the turbulence. And it makes sense to me that if your first landing is less traumatic, you might have a bit more in the tank for the second jump too."

"Sounds good," I say, taking a sip of tea. I've got a plan to steer the conversation. "Alexia, you know this is really working for me. I feel like I've had quite a few breakthroughs already."

"That's great to hear," she says.

"Because you're brilliant at this," I say earnestly.

"You think?"

"I know you are."

"Well, thank you," she says. "I absolutely love it. In fact, I want to write a book about my approach and some of my case studies. I've made a start. I have a ton of notes, but I haven't got very far."

"I'd buy it!"

She smiles. "Thanks. I think my parents might buy one too, so that would make two copies sold."

"They must be very proud of you."

Her apparent happiness fades. "I have two brothers. One's a doctor and one's a vet," she says. "I'm the disappointing one, I'm afraid."

"No way," I say, gazing at the warm, talented, passionate woman sitting opposite me. "I doubt that very much."

She blushes, stands up, and takes our empty cups across to the sink.

"Alexia," I say, deciding I just need to go for it, "I'm ready."

"For what?" she asks.

"To try the double jump."

"Wow, Joe," she says. She's silent for a good ten seconds. "Look, you *have* made great progress, and that's brilliant, but there's still a lot we haven't covered."

"Part of me could spend the rest of my life in therapy with you," I tell her. "The past few days have been amazing. Our sessions, the meditation, walking Jack, the soup lunches, our chats—all of it. Here, it would be easy to forget all my problems. But time's running out. I've been patient, I've worked really hard, and when I woke up this morning, I felt like something inside me had really shifted. I feel totally different, like a new man!"

"I can't tell you how happy I am to hear you sounding so positive," she says cautiously. "But are you sure? We agreed we'd do this for at least ten days. It's worth taking the time to let everything embed. There's almost certainly more that needs to come out too. These things take time."

I won't give up. "We agreed to ten days because we didn't know how long it would take. I feel full of energy and peace. And I can feel the ribbon calling me too. It's time to go!"

Alexia leans back in her chair. She undoes her braid, runs her fingers through her hair to loosen it, then puts it back in a ponytail.

"Okay. It's your choice. You're in complete control, and I do understand. But I promised to help you. So if you're determined to go now, then I'm coming with you."

"With me? What do you mean?"

"I want to time travel with you."

"No, Alexia. It's too dangerous."

"I want to." Steely determination flashes in her eyes.

"But you said you'd never travel again."

"Well, I've changed my mind. That was before I . . . got involved."

I have to admit, it's seriously tempting.

"If I come with you," she presses on, "I can help keep you focused. It'll be just like we've been practicing."

"I'm not sure . . ." I say, weakening.

"I want to help you get Amy back, Joe," she says finally. "But I'll worry about you if you go on your own. Let me come with you."

I relent. "Okay. But on one condition: You only come for the first leg of the journey. You can help me set up for the second jump, but I'm going back to the fair on my own."

"Agreed." She smiles warmly and gives Jack a hug. "When do we go?"

"Tomorrow." I realize that I feel nothing but excitement. Alexia's become more than my therapist, she's become my friend, my ally, and with her by my side, I'm not afraid of anything.

22

Friday, January 3, 2020

It's eight a.m., and Alexia and I are standing on top of Leckhampton Hill. We've left Jack with Alexia's neighbors for the day. The winter sky is dark and ominous, a storm's brewing, and it's bitterly cold.

"Why are we traveling from up here again?" asks Alexia, shivering. "Why can't we travel from the field where the fair was? We'd land nearer to where you're trying to get to, wouldn't we?" She pulls her collar tighter around her neck. "And it'd be less windy."

"I've traveled from here before," I tell her, "and I know it's safe. Nothing up here was that different in 2005, so I know we'll land on solid ground." I've got the Gold Cup tickets with me again today. They're my focus object for the first leg of the trip. Amy's ribbon is in a matchbox in my pocket, ready for later.

"Once we're safely in 2005, we can move down the hill and get a bit closer to the fairground," I say. "But it needs to be a place that works for both of us. I'll need to jump back to 1997 from there, and you'll need to bounce back home from there too."

"Okay," says Alexia. "You're in control. I trust you."

"Close your eyes," I advise her. "It's easier that way." I reach out my hand and she takes it, her skin soft and surprisingly warm. I hold the Gold Cup tickets in my other hand, and I feel the pull of time. I visualize the shape of 2005 and how it's going to feel to land there. I have a powerful sense that Alexia is meant to be here, she's supposed to do this with me, and then I feel the present slipping away like an avalanche.

For what seems like a few seconds, there's nothing. I'm floating in a void. Then I become aware of solid ground under my feet, and on the cool breeze I hear distant voices and traffic sounds.

I open my eyes. It takes a second or two to adjust to the darkness. I was expecting daylight, but it's night, probably early evening judging by all the activity down in the town.

Alexia lets go of my hand. "Wow!" she gasps. "This is so weird!"

"It is, isn't it," I agree. "I'm not sure I'll ever quite get used to it."

"And we're definitely in 2005?" she asks me.

I press the reset button on Mark's Casio watch. It takes a few seconds to update, then displays the date: March 18, 2005.

I show Alexia. She gazes out over Cheltenham.

"Somewhere down there a nineteen-year-old me is pulling pints for race-goers in the Old Restoration," she says. "You're down there too somewhere."

We stand together for a while, looking over the town, a twinkling mass of white and golden lights.

"Where's the fairground?" she asks.

"Over there," I tell her, pointing to a dark patch among all the lights. "That's where it happened. Let's get a bit closer. We need to get to the next jump point."

I lead the way down the hill along the narrow footpath. We use the flashlights on our phones to see. A few minutes later, I find the gate I'm looking for. I hold it open for Alexia, and we walk to the middle of the open field.

"This is the spot," I say.

"How do you feel?"

I take the opportunity to check in with myself. "You know what? I feel good. Calm and positive. Thanks to you."

"You're a good man, Joe," she says. "Fighting for your sister like this. She'll never know what you went through to get her back, but I will."

"It's what you do when you love someone," I say.

She faces me. We look directly into each other's eyes.

"Ready?" she asks.

She talks me through the presence meditation, the one I've been practicing. It's designed to help me reset, to think of this moment wholly as *now*.

"I want you to listen to my voice now, and just my voice," Alexia says. "Can you do that?"

"Yes." I could listen to her forever.

I close my eyes. As she talks, I set my intention, imagining that every cell is grounded. I repeat each line inside my head as she says it, like a silent mantra.

"This moment is all there is."

This moment is all there is.

"Every moment is now."

Every moment is now.

"This moment is my new present."

This moment is my new present.

"This moment is now."

This moment is now.

Just like we practiced, I envisage strong green roots growing from the soles of my feet, down into the earth, down, down, down to the center of the planet, wrapping themselves around its core.

"I am here now."

I think about the years that have passed since I lost Amy, all of the pain of that loss compressed into one single moment. Time is relative. Now is absolute; the only time we can ever truly be.

I become aware of Alexia's voice again, growing more distant now.

"You're calm and safe, Joe," she says.

I'm calm and safe.

"You're going to find Amy and save her."

I'm going to put this right.

A tingling sensation moves through my body. Yes! It's happening . . . My eyes flicker open in surprise.

Alexia smiles at me. She isn't afraid, so neither am I.

"This moment is all there is."

I close my eyes again. I feel amazing, waves of energy coursing through me. I could travel back a hundred years.

This moment is now.

Gravity shifts around me, like a wave lifting me off my feet. It's a calm transition, refined and graceful.

And then, nothing.

When I open my eyes, the field is gone.

It's pitch black. I'm standing, but I see no ground, no horizon, no defining edges. Just lightless, endless space. Holding a hand out in front of me, I realize the only light comes from within me. My skin is silvery, translucent.

What is this place? Where am I?

When am I?

"Alexia?" My voice is flat. There's no atmosphere to carry it.

No answer.

There's a flutter of movement to my right, weak and pale in the darkness. It makes me jump. More now, streaking multicolored explosions skitter around me. Gradually they take shape, colors sharpen into defined surroundings, seven huge canvases spinning silently around me. They move so fast it's hard to make out specific detail, but I focus on one and move my head with it, and then flick it back around like a ballet dancer. It's nauseating, but I work out that it's a window onto the fairground. It evolves further, and I realize it's the day they packed everything up.

In another window I see an empty field, a bright blue sky. Before the fair arrived? Afterward?

I'm in the eye of a storm. An unimaginable power has created this gallery of animated scenes, windows alive with pictures of the past. Each is recognizable. I take a step closer, and the scenes begin to crackle and hum with static, drawing me toward them.

I could run, jump, and land in any one of these snapshots and find myself days from Amy and my goal. A swirling ball of panic forms in my gut. How do I do this? My chest tightens, and as my breath gets shallower and my throat constricts, the canvases whizz faster and faster around me until all I can see is a continuous blur of color, imprisoning me.

"This moment is all there is."

Alexia's voice finds me again, quiet and calm amid the maelstrom. "You're calm and safe."

I focus, breathing slowly, with purpose.

"You're going to find Amy and save her."

Little by little, the windows lose speed, until they are slow enough that I can see each one clearly as they revolve around me. I am in control now.

Out of the seven, one draws my attention. As it moves past, I see the fairground, the lights, the Ferris wheel lit up and brilliant in the twilight.

Then it hits me. I'm like the center spindle of a record player, the world is a vinyl record, and time is the song etched into its surface.

A song plays in my mind, clear and loud. "Tomorrow Never Knows" pours from my subconscious and fills me with confidence, its drumbeat and vocals timeless. The Beatles have been the soundtrack to my life. Why would that change now? I need courage, determination, and a good old dose of British rock.

John Lennon tells me to turn off my mind, relax, and float downstream. To lay down all thoughts, surrender to the void. He asks me if I see the meaning of within and insists that love is all . . . that love is everyone.

I'm listening, John. I'm with you, mate.

The fairground window passes in front of me a few more times, and I learn the rhythm, feel its pace. I count down, bobbing my head with each revolution. Three, two, one. Without hesitation I leap. It's like leaving a swing, high on the arc. For one perfect second I'm motionless, but then gravity beckons me and I begin to descend, not rapidly though—this is a gliding down, like the tone arm on my record deck. I am the needle at the end of that arm, and all I have to do is land right in the gap between the songs. The slower I drop, the smoother the listen, the neater the entry.

It's perfect.

Slowly, I sink down, static drawing me toward the rotating ground. My body tingles with nervous excitement. My feet finally touch the ground, and I feel the undulating rotation of Earth itself, grounding me.

I land gracefully in the field near the fairground. There are people nearby, but it seems they can't see me, at least not yet. I'm still catching up with time.

Houston, the needle has landed.

The warmth of summer floods over me. The smell of grass, the feel of it. I made it. I'm here! I take in the familiar surroundings. I remember this night, walking here as a fourteen-year-old boy, with Amy. She was so excited. The horizon is the burning red glow of a setting sun. Above me, the dark blue of early evening. The fairground lights flicker to life, and the crowd roars its appreciation. Not far from here, Amy and I have just arrived.

PART 6

"PINKIE SWEAR?"

March 1997

Like any younger sibling, Amy hated the fact she had to go to bed earlier. She would hear me come upstairs and call out to me, want to chat, ask to me to read her stories, anything to squeeze a bit more out of the day. On one particular occasion, I found her sitting on the edge of her bed, clearly afraid.

"What's up, Pip-squeak?" I asked, leaning around her door. "Can't sleep?"

She shook her head.

"What's going on?"

"Nothing," she replied with a sniff.

I walked in and stood by her bed. "Come on, you can tell me."

Eventually, in a quiet, trembling voice she said, "I'm scared the Hairy Toe Man is going to get me."

To this day, I'm not sure how I kept a straight face. I clenched my jaw and in a serious voice asked, "Who is the Hairy Toe Man?"

She sniffed again, wiping her sleeve across her nose. "He isn't very nice, his toes are hairy."

"Yeah, I guessed that much."

"He lives down there," she said, pointing under her bed, "but he only comes out when I'm asleep."

I had a good rummage around. "There's no one there, Amy."

"He is there . . . but you can't see him."

"Why not?"

"Because you're a grown-up," she said flatly.

This time I did laugh. I was thirteen.

She swallowed and let out a little sob. Clearly, I wasn't helping. I asked her to move up a bit and sat on the edge of her bed. Amy looked genuinely scared. "Who put this idea in your head?" I asked her.

"A girl at school," she said. "Emily Jenkins."

I nodded. "Well, I don't think Emily Jenkins knows what she's talking about. Did she even tell you what he wants?"

She screwed up her face. "What he wants?"

"Yes, everyone wants something."

"I don't know," she shrugged, "but he's horrible."

I considered my next move. Complete denial rarely worked with Amy. "I think, considering that he's very small, he's probably way more scared of you than you are of him."

"How small is he?"

I stretched my thumb and forefinger. "About four inches tall."

She blinked, wiping her cheeks. "Why would he be scared of me?"

"Because some people can be really nasty sometimes. For example, I know they pick on him just because he's got hairy toes, but he can't help it!"

She shook her head. "No."

I was making this up on the fly, but Amy didn't seem as worried anymore. "And you know, he just wants to look after his wife," I explained.

"The Hairy Toe Man has a wife?"

"Oh yes. They are actually called Mr. and Mrs. Belly Button. They have seven children." Amy giggled at this, the best sound in the world. "They call their children little jelly tots. They love them very much, even though they've all got hairy toes as well."

Amy pulled her duvet up around her neck and yawned. "Tell me more about them."

"Well, like you, they get cold, so they collect fluff from around the house."

"What do they do with it?"

"They . . . make it into a blanket."

She stared at me. "Can we leave some fluff out for them tonight?"

"Sure," I told her, "hang on." I found an empty matchbox, and much to Amy's fascination and mock disgust, I picked fluff from my belly button and between my toes and placed it inside the matchbox. "Hopefully they'll find it, and in the morning it'll be gone."

Amy smiled. She seemed quite happy with this explanation. I'm aware that when Dad said I could teach Amy stuff, this probably isn't what he had in mind. And replacing one bogeyman story with another is not exactly the recommended approach. But storytelling was part of our thing. Living in the real world was nowhere near as much fun.

She peered up at me, eyes glowing in the reflection of her plug-in nightlight. "And you're sure he isn't going to hurt me?"

"Positive."

"How do you know?"

"Just trust me, okay?"

Amy frowned. "Pinkie swear?"

This was serious. A ritual based on trust, a lever we only pulled occasionally. I considered my response carefully. On this occasion, Amy's question had been specific. Could I promise that the Hairy Toe Man wouldn't hurt her? Yes. I was good with that. I held up my little finger, she linked hers through it. "Pinkie swear," I said. "Now, go to sleep."

23

None of the people around me seem to notice my arrival. Perhaps we only see what we can comprehend. Either way, I'm here and no one is screaming, a positive result. I remain still for a few seconds, breathing and soaking in 1997.

I remind myself that although I'm close to Amy, I'm still nowhere near saving her. As if to remind me, the chill of brain freeze nibbles at the nape of my neck. I'm getting better at estimating this. I reckon I have thirty minutes, tops. I need to make every minute count.

As I run toward the entrance to the fairground, the dark outline of the Ferris wheel bursts to life, multicolored lights travel its spokes in a pulsing, hypnotic rhythm. People cheer. A shudder of familiarity runs over my entire body. It's one thing to remember a place in time, but it's completely different to relive it, especially as an adult. I pass under a sign that reads Welcome to King's Funfair! It's lit by a string of light bulbs and shaped like a giant horseshoe.

I've viewed this many times, of course, but now I'm here, I can't seem get my bearings, in place or time. I just want to scream Amy's name, grab her, and run, but that could cause a scene—which in turn could change things. I don't want to create new problems if I can help it. Plus, this may be my only chance. I need to be smart, keep things simple. I'm going to head to the rifle range, try to talk to Amy after she wanders off, and perhaps distract her long enough so she doesn't go to the wood in the first place. All I have to do is break the sequence.

A song I recognize plays in the distance, KWS's "Please Don't Go," an earworm of a tune. I scan the fairground and head in the direction of the rifle range. A girl walks past me. I recognize her from school. I almost say hi. She glowers at me and then sneers. "What are you looking at?" she asks. It's a fair question. I'm about to apologize when brain freeze nips at the base of my neck again, causing me to let out a stifled groan. The girl looks even more worried now.

"Can I help you?" a deep voice from behind me asks.

Turning, I discover the voice belongs to a heavyset middle-aged man with *Security* embroidered on his shirt in gold lettering. His dark hair is sharp, cut into a flattop. His blue eyes pierce me.

"Er, no, I'm good," I say. "Thanks though."

He studies me with growing suspicion. I don't blame him. The girl is waiting to see what happens.

"I'm watching you," he says, holding my gaze. Then he heads off toward a group of kids who are way too young to be smoking, shouting and pointing.

It's a relief, but I'm burning minutes here. I need to get to the rifle range!

Icicles form in my skull as I work my way through the crowd, hoping I'm heading in the right direction. The lights and sounds make me feel queasy with anticipation and worry. I have seen this fair in my viewings many times, but nothing could have prepared me for actually being here. The weirdness, the shock of familiarity; the depth of my past seen through adult eyes. Unlike my viewings, I can interact now, and everywhere I look I see *new* memories. Kids wearing crazy clothes, which appear retro to me. Music that belongs on a classic radio station plays, fresh and new. And there's something else different too. Everyone has their heads *up*, either looking at each other, or where they're going. They seem . . . present.

No mobile phones.

Despite all the pressure I'm under, I laugh. I can't help it. I remember liking 1997 immensely. I was fourteen, and the future was all there for the taking. My smile fades as I realize that this very night was the last time I felt that way. I assure myself that if I change this night, if I save Amy, then it might change other things for the better too.

Save Amy, and I change it all.

I push through the crowd. Everyone is a potential suspect. Someone here knows what happened to Amy.

In the distance I see the carousel, golden horses spinning. As a fourteen-year-old I staggered toward it, panicking and shouting after Amy went missing. I'm close. At last, I see the rifle range. It's smaller than I remember, but enticing, with large gifts for those with an eagle eye. And just when I think I cannot stand the suspense any longer, I see Amy.

Everything becomes still. Sound drifts away. My sister. Not in a dream or a viewing, but alive and beautiful. Seven years old. Innocent and smiling. I see myself too, fourteen years old, unaware of the horror that is about to unfold. The Artful Dodger running the stall leans down and whispers in Amy's ear. Amy giggles, charming him, telling him her brother is a good shot. He laughs as a crowd gathers around him. I inch forward, closing the gap between the past and a potential new present with each step.

"Roll up, roll up, ladies and gentlemen!" the Dodger cries. "The world-famous Burning Joseph Bridges is about to take the stand."

My brain freeze reminds me that time is the one truly calling the shots. I grit my teeth against the pain that rips from the base of my spine over my skull. This is the worst it's been, but I'm damned if it's taking me yet. I watch the young version of me step up and take the gun. I follow his gaze to Sian Burrows, flanked by her two cronies. Once a vision of beauty and utter perfection to me, Sian now looks impossibly young, hidden behind a veil of youth and heavily applied makeup, yet I can see who she will become. She smiles and winks at young Joe, then Mark's future wife turns in my direction and fixes her gaze on me. I look away. When I glance back, she is still looking at me, tapping her friend's arm, and pointing in my direction.

Someone taps me on my shoulder. The security guard is back. "What are you doing now?" he asks, following my line of sight. "Are you here on your own?"

"What? Er, yes. Why?" My attention darts between him and Amy. I hear the first metallic *ding* of a target being hit and the rippling cheer of the gathered crowd. "Listen, this isn't what you think, I'm not here to cause any trouble." I stop talking then, because I see pure determination in his eyes. He is not going to buy any story I might tell him. He's probably a father too, suspicious of blokes who hang out at fairgrounds watching children.

"I'm going to need to ask you to leave," he says, pale lips tightening.

Another shot rings out. I see my younger self celebrating. Amy backs away slowly. She looks around nervously and then appears to commit to leaving. She's going right now, fleeing the rifle range, heading out to the woods alone. If I don't act now, I'm going to miss her. I came too far to let this guy stand in my way. I turn back to him. "I'm really sorry about this," I say, "but I have no choice." He looks confused. My hand curls tightly into a ball, and I punch him as hard as I can on the nose. He falls to the ground, clutching his face.

There are numerous gasps around me. Someone calls out angrily, "What did you do that for?" A man holding his daughter's hand scowls and heads in my direction. He is now blocking my path, and I realize that I've attracted a lot of unwanted attention. Not my plan at all. Against every internal alarm in my body, I run away, heading in the opposite direction to the wood.

My legs howl their disapproval, my barbed wire injuries not yet fully healed. I dart left and run straight into the middle of a potential pileup. Electrified bumper cars, with long poles attached to a crackling metal ceiling, whir and spin violently around me, headlights flashing, around an oval thirty feet in diameter. I time my movements, lunging and jumping between the cars. I almost make it across, but at the last second, a car veers toward me, catching my shin and sending me spinning. I pirouette and fall flat on my backside. I stare up at the drivers, a woman and a young girl.

"Are you all right?" the woman asks nervously. She places a hand protectively around the girl. "Yes, I'm sorry." I crawl away on my hands and knees to the rubberized edge of the track. The bumper cars ride is a wooden construction, raised about three feet from the ground and surrounded by fencing. When I'm sure no one is watching, I climb up and over the fence, crunching down into stinging nettles nearly as tall as I am. The prickling sensation is instant, but adrenaline is a wonderful thing, and the feeling wears off quickly. I crash through them, reach a nearby tree, and wait, panting like a wounded animal. In the distance I hear shouting mixed with the screams of nearby teens being flung around by powerful machinery. I'm praying I haven't been followed. Every second feels like an ax above my head.

Cutting back around the edge of the bumper cars, I lean out from behind the safety of a boxlike outbuilding—the pay desk, I realize—and see the rotating horses of the carousel in the distance. I run across the main drag of the fair and cut behind another ride, some horrible pirate ship noisily churning the stomachs of its victims, managing to stay out of sight. Between two stalls I peer out to get my bearings. I'm near the rifle range again. The Artful Dodger talks to a concerned group of people, who begin searching the area. They might be looking for me, but more likely they're searching for Amy, on the request of my fourteen-year-old self. Carefully, I work my way along the amusements until I reach the last, a tame children's ride. It offers little cover.

But there, in the distance, I see the wood. And with a colossal surge of relief, I see Amy, running like a ghost in the darkness. I follow her into the night.

Everything is falling into place.

A brilliant flash lights the field, as Barry takes the photograph of Debbie, which means that fourteen-year-old me is running to the carousel. But I am here now, and Amy is close.

My eyes adjust to the moonlight, and I make out Amy among a dark line of trees. I run toward them, calling her name, but she doesn't stop. I close the distance and shout louder this time. She turns, and her features, initially masked in shadow, resolve into those of my long-lost sister. She is glowing with life and vitality, but her eyes are wide and filled with fear.

She peers into the wood, and then back at me. "Who are you?"

"A friend of your brother," I say, forcing myself to appear calm. "He's down there looking for you. He wants you to come back to the fair. Will you do that?"

In the half-light of the moon, she studies me. "I don't know you, and my daddy says I shouldn't talk to strangers." Amy takes another step back. She glances over her shoulder toward the wood, and when she looks back at me, her eyes are narrowed. "You said you were a friend of my brother," she says, her voice calculating. "What's his name?"

"His name is Joe," I reply, "and Amy, he really wants you to come home."

Amy's fearful, suspicious gaze remains fixed on me. I draw in a breath and ask her the question that has haunted me for all these years. "Amy, can you tell me where you're going? Are you meeting someone here?"

She chews the side of her mouth nervously, pulling at her dress with its pattern of white birds swooping and gliding. I want to lift her up in my arms, to hold her and never let go. She looks at me, puzzled. "Why are you crying?" she asks with a tenderness that sets a fresh tear coursing down my right cheek. I wipe it away.

"I didn't realize I was," I answer instinctively. Brain freeze takes another bite, making me wince.

"Does your head hurt?" she asks anxiously.

"Yes," I say, trying to avoid scaring her, "but it's not too bad." Amy's innocent expression, her obvious empathy gives me hope. "Whatever it is you're running away from, maybe I can help?"

She replies in a cold tone way beyond her years. "You wouldn't understand."

"Try me," I say quietly, transported back to the many times, late at night, when I would read to her, reassure her, build her trust. "Amy, just tell me what's going on. Why did you run away?"

I'm convinced she's about to share her secret, but then she stares back down at the ground, nibbling her bottom lip. "I can't," she says, her voice catching. "I can't tell you, and you can't make me."

"I'm not going to make you," I assure her. My mind races to compute what her words might mean. "No one is going to make you." The distant music is broken by a clear and angry shout, a man's voice calling Amy's name. I glance back toward the fair and see a group of people gathering at its edge, black shapes cut against colored lights. A triangular beam of flashlight scans the field like a lighthouse, followed by another, and then more shouts. When I turn back to Amy, she is running again.

"Amy, no!" I burst into a run after her.

The wood is darkness itself. Amy slips from view, and I am consumed by the terrible notion that I came this far only to lose her again. I reach the tree line and enter the wood. The trees are old, their thick trunks packed tightly together. I push between them, calling her name continuously, the pitch of my voice escalating as panic sets in. I glimpse her briefly, a flash of her dress like a sheet in the wind, but then she's gone again. Behind me, close now, I hear the concerned shouts of the people who followed us. They sound like the howls and barks of wolves closing in.

"Amy!" I cry, my voice breaking.

I stumble and fall flat on my face, cold wet earth plugging my nostrils. I snort it away, rubbing my face, and pause just long enough to see a strip of blue cloth hanging from a twisted branch. Again I call out, but my mouth is so dry that nothing comes, just a croak, accompanied by the bitter tang of fear. Stumbling hopelessly, I crash through undergrowth and spill out into a clearing. It is lit from above by sharp moonlight. My impending return jump renders the scene a cool blue.

No! Not yet. Please . . .

Amy stands in the center of the clearing, her back to me. Warm flashlight cuts through the trees behind us, passes over her, and then flicks back suddenly, illuminating her fully. She turns, eyes wide.

"I've found her!" a man's voice shrieks, then others join him, distant but closing.

I'm out of time and options. I can't leave her here when I still don't know what will happen to her. My decision is made. I'm going to drag Amy with me and travel home. I run and launch myself at her. My fingers brush her arm and then gain purchase around her wrist. She cries out. "It's okay," I whisper to her.

We are falling as we travel.

The shock is instant.

Vicious.

All consuming.

We are plunged into dark, freezing water. I can't think. I scream, but all that comes is a garbled drone. Amy slips away. I kick and thrash until my arm catches something. I blink, trying to focus in the murky water. It's Amy! She's drifting away, thrashing and clawing at the water, as though surrounded by some invisible foe. I swim as hard as I can but fail to close the gap between us. The pain in my chest is agony, my lungs burning. I recall a trick my dad taught me: exhale a short blast of air to trick your lungs into believing they are operating normally. It works, just enough to give me a chance. I turn and kick with everything I have, reaching for Amy. Our fingers meet, and she wraps her hands around my right forearm, her nails digging into me. I pull and kick hard toward the surface, but we don't move. I try again, but a fierce current is dragging us down. Amy's grip loosens. No . . . No! A brilliant flash of lightning illuminates us, and in that dreadful moment, I see Amy's eyes stretched wide in utter panic, her mouth open to the water in a terrifying scream. Silvery bubbles dance up and over me. Her last, precious breath.

Her hand slips from mine. The edges of my sanity fray like rope. No oxygen. Nothing left. Lungs on fire. Another bolt of lightning cracks the world in two, and my body's natural instincts take over. I rise up, heart pounding. When I finally break the surface, I gasp, sucking in the sweet air.

But Amy is still down there.

Thunder rips the sky, the sound deafening. I draw a breath and dive, searching the terrible, all-consuming darkness. Despair weighs me down, but I rise to the surface, breathe, and dive again. Eventually, exhausted, all I can do is tread water. It laps against my face as I cough and gag.

This is a lake, I realize as I finally catch my breath. To my right a large storm drain, open like the mouth of a whale. It empties into the lake, creating complex undercurrents. I dragged Amy here—wherever here is— and I killed her.

Killed my own sister.

Gradually, I stop treading. The water no longer feels cold. It fills my mouth, and I allow myself to sink into the willing embrace of the lake.

Death will release me from my pain.

Alexia's voice stops me. *What if she isn't dead? What if she's on the bank, calling out your name?*

Rain pummels the surface of the lake. It's deafening. If Amy were calling, I would never hear her. I kick again and break the surface, ejecting gritty water, and it takes every ounce of my remaining strength to swim to the shore. I drag myself slowly from the water and collapse, panting and crying, the rain pelting me. Lightning tears at the sky like swords in battle.

"Amy!" I cry. No reply. I cough, heave, and then puke.

I haul myself up and take in my surroundings. Around the edge of the lake is a path. This is still Cox's Meadow, the site of the fair, but it's completely flooded. I press the reset button on the watch Mark gave me. It takes a few seconds, finds its signal, and reads July 20, 2007.

Why didn't I return to 2005?

A brilliant blue fork of lightning splits the sky. Brain freeze descends in a sudden rush. The whole world turns cyan, and I realize I'm about to travel again.

In a heartbeat, I am transported.

Daylight. Warmth. Silence. Safety.

But I am alone.

An early morning sun breaks through a layer of mist that hovers over the now dry and empty meadow. I'm soaking wet, disoriented, and nauseous. I drop to my knees as an intense feeling of déjà vu consumes me. Has this all happened before? Is this the way it *always* happens? Am I responsible for Amy's death? I peer down at my right arm, Amy's nail marks still fresh and raw. She was petrified, as I dragged her through time and drowned her.

Tears come, and I let them.

When they finally stop, I walk the path that winds its way to the exit of Cox's Meadow. With each step, my mind gradually coheres. I pass the storm drain, *the mouth of the whale*. At the exit is a yellow sign that reads Danger: Flood Storage Area. Water Levels Can Rise Rapidly.

Yes, they can.

I call Alexia.

"Joe?" Her voice is quick and nervous.

I almost cry again, just hearing her worry, feeling her care. "Yes, it's me."

"Did you do it?" she asks.

My mouth opens and five things try to come out all at once. I try again. "I lost her," I murmur, the words tightening my chest.

"Where are you?" Alexia asks.

I tell her, and twenty minutes later she picks me up. She doesn't ask any questions, just offers me a kind smile.

"Come on," she says. "Let's get you home."

Her Toyota Prius is immaculately clean. I apologize for getting the seat wet. She tells me it doesn't matter and turns the heaters to full blast. I sink back and keep quiet, glad to feel some warmth returning to my body.

When we get back to my place, Alexia says, "I'll make us some tea. See you in the kitchen when you're ready. Take your time."

I take a long hot shower, trying not to think. It isn't hard. I feel numb. I put on fresh clean clothes and join Alexia in the kitchen. She tells me again not to rush, so I sip my tea, watching through the window as clouds scud across the sky, marking the passage of time. Everything feels different. Everything feels the same.

Eventually, I begin to talk.

"Oh, Joe," Alexia says when I've finished relating the story. "I'm so sorry. But you couldn't have known. It isn't your fault."

I stare at her. "What if all I did was change the way she died?"

Alexia fixes me with a determined gaze. "Listen to me now. This won't get you anywhere. We need to think it through, figure out what happened, and make a new plan."

A new plan.

I frown. "We traveled to July 20, 2007. I dragged her back to the night of that awful storm. Cheltenham flooded. Do you remember? Were you living here then?"

"I was," she says. "I remember it well. Worst storm in a hundred years, they said."

I sigh. "It took two jumps to reach her, so I guess it makes sense that it would take two to get back." Guilt and confusion hit me again. "Was it something I did?"

Alexia places her hand over the scratches on my forearm. "You can't blame yourself, Joe. We could never have planned for this." I meet her eyes, which are fired up, confident. "Now we know what might happen, we can avoid it next time. Right?"

"Next time," I say, voice flat. I stare at the table.

After a few minutes of silence, Alexia asks, "Did she tell you why she ran away?"

I rub the back of my neck. "No, although she did seem scared, like there was something she wanted to tell me, but didn't feel she could."

Alexia nods thoughtfully. "And what about the suspect, did you see him?"

I blink a few times, considering the question, but I draw a blank. "I'm sorry, what?"

"The suspect," she repeats. "Did you find out who he was? Manage to stop him?"

Frowning deeply now, I say, "I'm really sorry, but I have no idea what you're talking about."

She looks at me, as confused as I am. Then she pulls an assortment of newspaper clippings from the tattered old wallet I've held onto all these years. She spreads them over the kitchen table and taps one of the articles. My heart skips a beat. It features the photograph Barry took of Amy, familiar but slightly different. I scan the articles, and most of them are like this, familiar, but laced with new information.

I shake my head in disbelief. "If you've ever wondered if my actions in the past affect the present, you can stop wondering now."

"So you saw him?" Alexia asks.

I stare at the photo. Amy runs toward the woods, chased by a man. "Alexia, I *am* him."

24

The midmorning sun has burned away the clouds. Alexia fans the contents of the folder across the table. There are so many more clippings than I remember. Most of them are from local rags, but three or four are from national newspapers. The majority show the photo of Debbie, but it's been zoomed in. Only Debbie's right ear and some of her hair is visible now, and the new focus of the image is Amy, running toward the wood. The picture is the same as I saw in my viewing, but with one crucial difference. There's a man running after her.

It's blurry and indistinct, but there's no doubt. It's me.

I pick up the paper nearest me.

MYSTERY MAN INVOLVED
IN GIRL'S DISAPPEARANCE

Police are searching for a seven-year-old girl whom they suspect was abducted from King's Funfair on Thursday night. Amy Bridgeman was last seen running toward the copse at the top of Merlow Hill. A man was seen running after her, captured in this photo taken by a local photographer. Anyone with any information as to his identity is asked to contact Cheltenham Police at the number below.

"Oh god, Alexia, what have I done?" I fold my arms tightly across my chest, to hold the panic in.

"What do you mean?"

"Before I went back to 1997, this photo showed Amy running toward the wood. Now it shows me too. I've never seen this before."

"That can't be right," Alexia says, looking at the clipping more closely. "It's always been like this."

I shake my head. "It only had Amy in it before. But now I'm in it. I'm in all of them!" I pick up another and study it closely. "If I didn't know this was me, I'd be obsessed with finding out who this guy was."

"You have been!" Alexia says. "It's all you've talked about since you decided to travel back to the fair. You thought that if you could uncover his identity, you'd find Amy."

I sit back in disbelief. "There's something else," I say. "This photo of Amy running up the hill wasn't part of the original investigation. It never turned up. It was never in any of the papers. It was only in my head."

"Seriously?" says Alexia, incredulous. "But it's been the focus of the investigation for the last twenty years. Whenever there's an article about Amy, that's the picture they use."

"I'm sure it is," I say grimly.

"So how did *you* know about it?" she asks.

"I got a viewing from Barry's camera, the guy who took the photo. I went to Ludlow to pick it up."

"To pick what up?"

"The camera! I found it in an antiques shop. It triggered a viewing, during which I saw photo. It's how I knew Amy had gone up to the wood. Remember?"

Alexia looks at me askance.

"It's in my study. I'll get it." I go to my study and open the bottom drawer of the filing cabinet. It's empty. I walk back to the kitchen. "It's not there."

"I've never heard you talk about the camera before, or—Hounslow?"

"Ludlow," I say, my voice distant, my mind piecing together a new set of rules. "So you don't remember me telling you about the camera?"

She shakes her head.

"Okay," I say, thinking through the timeline. "What did I say I was going to do when I got back to 1997?"

"You said you were going to find the man in these pictures and stop him before he gets to Amy."

I've changed the past significantly, and Alexia remembers things differently from me. And that's when the penny fully drops. Only I remember a world without this photo of Amy, without "the suspect." When I had that feeling of déjà vu, was I sensing the ripples of time flowing through me, while the universe reconfigured itself as a result of my actions?

"Alexia, do you remember the week we spent training together at your house?"

"Of course," she says.

"And did you travel back with me to 2005?"

"I did," she says. "We traveled from Leckhampton Hill. And then I helped you focus, and you jumped back to '97 on your own."

"Same for me," I say. "That's a relief. But I suppose there still might be other things we remember differently. I guess we might never discover all of them."

"Well, you've solved part of the mystery at least. So you need to try again." Alexia's voice is firm, her eyes bright with confidence. "We know more now. We can send you back prepared."

I lean back and stare at the ceiling. In my mind's eye, I see Amy's terrified face, her expression a harrowing mixture of desperation and disbelief, her mouth stretched open in a silent scream, her hands clawing at the water in panicked frenzy as the current drags her away.

"I don't know if I can go back again," I say.

"But Joe—"

"You don't know what it was like," I say, the words tumbling out. "I can't stand the thought of watching her die again. I can't bear the thought that by trying to save her, I become the cause of her death." I stare at nothing, my thoughts everywhere. "But if I don't go back again, I'll have to live the rest of my life knowing that I killed her."

Alexia hands me a tissue, and it's only then I realize I'm crying. It's a shock because I rarely cry. I bottle things up, like my dad did. Maybe I drove myself insane, and I'm only just realizing.

"Joe, it was an accident," Alexia says softly. "You were doing your best."

My throat tightens. "But what if it was always me who killed her, and I just can't remember because I've reset my memories by traveling back again? What if I'm destined to murder my own sister, again and again?" I lean my face into my hands and sob.

Alexia places her hand on my back. "If there's one thing I'm sure of, Joe," she says, "it's that you had nothing to do with Amy's disappearance. You were fourteen years old. You loved her. You made one mistake, lost your concentration for a split second. It's a tragedy, but these things happen sometimes. You need to try and forgive yourself."

I wipe away my tears.

"And I'm sorry your trip back was so traumatic," she adds. "It sounds horrendous. But listen to me. We've come this far, and you nearly saved her. And everything that happened can be *undone*." She says the last word with such commitment that it sends a ripple of goose bumps over me. She leans in. "And there's a positive angle to this, you know."

"What's that?" I ask, failing to see one.

"It's absolute proof—if you needed it—that when you change things, you alter the outcome of everything." She takes my hand and gives it a firm squeeze. "You're a time traveler, Joe, and you've been given this opportunity for a reason. I know it."

I let this sink in. I had faith the first time, but that was before I let Amy drown, before I messed it all up and delivered my sister up to a potentially worse fate.

"Let it all go," Alexia says kindly. "Don't forget, it's fear that will hold you back, and it's testing you now."

I relax my shoulders and exhale. "Okay. Let's give it another go. Will you help me again?"

"I'll help you," she says, "but not now. You're exhausted, and you need to regroup. Rest today, recharge your batteries, and we can try again tomorrow."

I swear, Alexia does something to me, gives me a confidence I can't remember ever feeling. She gives me faith, makes me feel like I'm part of a greater story than myself and my little life.

"Okay," I say. "And Alexia? Thank you."

25

I sleep badly. In my dreams I awake in my bedroom to see Amy standing there, dripping black water onto the carpet, waggling her finger at me. "No, Joe," she mouths, rivulets of lake water coursing down her ghostly face, her eyes glassy, her hair floating bizarrely as though in deep water. "You're not doing this right. Do it again."

The next morning I wake up exhausted but determined. I meet Alexia at our jumping point on Leckhampton Hill at eight a.m. It's a chilly morning, but there's no wind. The earth seems to be holding its breath in anticipation. Alexia reassures me and we discuss phase one of our plan, the jump to 2005. When she asks if I'm ready, I offer her my hand. Her skin is warm and soft. She smiles, and it fills me with much-needed confidence.

So much of this is guesswork. If we are holding hands, will it work the same? Will she always come with me?

We arrive calmly in the early evening of March 18, 2005. As we make our way down to the jump field, Alexia's hand is still in mine. I wonder if she feels the same as I do. That if we let go, we might lose each other.

I'm more nervous than last time, and I need to break the silence. "I used to walk here a lot when I was younger," I say. "It's such a great view of the whole of Cheltenham."

"It's beautiful, isn't it," she agrees, gazing out over the valley.

I turn to her. "It is." I want to tell Alexia that she's beautiful too, but

I bottle it. "Thank you for helping me. No matter what happens, I'm so glad you're here."

"Joe," she says, "I know we don't have long, but I want to tell you something."

"Okay," I say, my nerves immediately on standby.

"I accused you of emotionally blackmailing me into helping you."

"Yes," I say. "I still feel embarrassed about that."

"You mustn't. When you showed me that picture of Amy, I wasn't ready to see it, but it was brave, actually, showing your vulnerability like that. Once I talked to Martin, I was able to step back and see the bigger picture. Whatever happened to your sister, it was wrong, and it tore your family to pieces. Good people helped me when my life fell apart too, and now . . . maybe, just maybe, if I can be part of saving Amy, then the universe will balance out somehow."

She holds my gaze for a second longer than I expect.

She swallows, looks down, then back up at me, her eyes glistening in the moonlight. I could get lost in those wise, slate-gray eyes and not mind one bit.

"And I've seen how you fight for your family," she continues, "the way you'd do anything for them, it's inspiring. And I care about you . . . That's why I said that I couldn't treat you as a therapist anymore."

Her expression suggests she's done a very bad job of something extremely simple. My heart is banging in my chest. A few minutes ago, it was racing from fear, but now I think it might be jumping for joy.

Alexia waits.

I am terrified of talking about how I feel. I haven't really had any practice, not since I lost Amy and my world fell to pieces. But now I know how dangerous the past is, and I might not make it back this time. I have to try and tell her the truth.

"Alexia, do you think that somewhere, in a parallel universe maybe, you and I might have got together?"

"Why not this one?" She's so close to me, and the air's so still, that I can smell her perfume and see the long lashes at the outer edges of her eyelids. The corner of her mouth dimples as she smiles.

"Because in a parallel universe, I might be a better version of me, more sorted . . . In this one, I feel broken."

"Oh, Joe," she says, shaking her head, "we're all broken in our own way." She takes my other hand. "Have you heard that Leonard Cohen song? 'There is a crack in everything, that's how the light gets in'? I feel lucky to have met you."

I clear my throat. "Do you think, when I get back, we could maybe . . . maybe . . . ?"

Very slowly, she leans in and kisses my cheek. I feel the reassuring warmth of her lips against my skin, the soft smell of her hair. She holds the kiss for a few seconds then pulls back. "That was for luck," she says.

"Thank you," I manage, hoping the darkness might hide my shock. "I'm going to need it."

Something shifts in my chest, I actually feel it move, and I sense myself opening up, to Alexia and to possibility.

I cup her face in my hands and kiss her on the mouth. There's no awkward buildup this time, no snappy one-liners or artless gestures. Our kiss deepens, and it feels like coming home. My fears melt away. I move my arm around her back, holding her close, and finally allow myself to imagine us together, how it might be.

When we pull away, Alexia shakes her head. "You're a hard man to read, Joe. I wasn't sure how you felt. But I needed to know. Before I let you go again."

She looks worried.

"Is everything okay?" I ask her.

"It's perfect," she says. "But, Joe, I've been thinking. I really want to go with you this time, back to the fair. Your last trip really took it out of you. I know you can do it, I know you'll be okay, but if I could come along and help you too . . ."

I can hear the worry in her voice, and it touches me. "No," I say, stroking her cheek. "I appreciate you caring so much, but it's too dangerous. We talked about this. The best way you can help is by getting me focused so I can travel back to the fairground safely."

"Okay, if you're sure," she says reluctantly.

I breathe a quiet sigh of relief. There's no way I would take her with me, but the fact that she would even consider it makes me glow inside.

"Right," I say, sounding a lot more confident than I feel. "This is the part where you refocus me and tell me I need to concentrate."

"It is," she agrees, "but first I want to lend you something." She lifts a silver pendant up and over her head. It glints in her hands. "This is my Saint Christopher," she says. "My granny gave him to me when I was little. He's kept me safe ever since." She places the necklace over my head. "I want you to have him for your trip. He's the patron saint of travelers. Just promise me you'll bring him back?"

I seal my promise with a kiss.

We make our way to the center of the field and turn to face the lights of Cheltenham, which radiate from the darkness in the valley below. I reach into my pocket and find the remnants of the matchbox. Amy's ribbon is still there. Alexia ties it around my wrist and fastens it with a double bow. "You're all set," she says.

I close my eyes and see Amy's pale, terrified face floating before me, her silent scream wrenching my soul, as lightning tears the sky to pieces.

The ribbon's energy fades. My breathing quickens, but the harder I try to hold on to it, the more I feel the ribbon shutting down, drifting away from me like Amy's lifeless body. Panic flares in my gut, and I stumble.

"Alexia?"

"I'm right beside you," she says. Her voice is warm and reassuring. "You've carried this your whole life, losing Amy. You and your family have suffered so much. But you've paid the price, Joe. It's time to let it go now."

"I'm afraid," I say.

"I know," she says soothingly, "but you're also brave and honest and kind. I know you'll do everything in your power to save her. You can't do any more than that." Her voice helps me remember the imaginary roots growing from my feet, connecting me to the center of the earth, and my heart rate begins to slow. "Whatever you do, it will be enough," she says. "And when you get back this time, Amy and I will be waiting."

As Alexia speaks, I feel it again. That gentle but insistent tug, the anticipation of coming back to a new life. *Hope.* Only now do I realize it's been absent for most of my life.

Energy rolls up from the ground in waves. Soon, I'll be traveling back in time again. I wonder what gives me this ability, whether some benevolent being is looking down, or whether it's all just a trick of the mind. But as the earth dissolves beneath me, and I feel myself traveling back to Amy for what I hope is the last time, I guess I don't need to understand.

I just need to trust.

26

The mass of the familiar world drops away, and I am delivered into the dark void. As before, the only light here emanates from me, my skin glowing faintly like silver beneath pale moonlight.

This time, though, there is nothing around me, just an endless ink-black sky.

Where are the windows?

With trepidation I move, walking on a sea of nothing. Each silent step brings fresh despair. There is nowhere to go, nothing for me here. I cry out, my voice lacking any resonance in this dead place. What if I am stuck? What if I am between worlds or somehow outside of time? What if there is no way out? I peer into the blackness for any sign of the fairground. Did I really believe that I could just keep returning to the past and tweaking it to suit myself? Fear tightens my throat and chest.

Holding Alexia's pendant, I close my eyes. I can rewrite this. Just one more jump.

When I open my eyes, I see a flicker of movement. The ghost of a window spins around me, as though caught in a powerful tornado. I think my mind is playing tricks on me but then I see it again, a glimmer of color, like oil on a wet road, barely visible against the void. Silently, it moves. I'm terrified that if I take my eyes away from it for a second, it will disappear for good. I follow its arc, its rhythm. Gradually it sharpens, this single window until—in a euphoric burst of clarity—the carousel, fairground lights, and a candy-pink sunset resolve. This time, only one window. All the others have gone, drifted away. This will be my last chance.

With each rotation the window increases in size. It flickers past me, big as a house now, the sound bleeding through, the screams of children, machinery, music rising and falling with each rotation. It continues to increase in speed. The last time I traveled, I felt like a needle, easing down and connecting with vinyl. It was controlled, calm, like a bird landing on a serene lake. This time will be different, more dangerous. The wind of time howls in my ears as I nod along with the rhythm of the window, counting down just as Amy and I used to when we were kids.

Ready or not, here I come.

I break into a run, the lights of the fairground strobing against the void. I launch myself, close my eyes, and pray for either a smooth landing or a quick death.

I get neither.

I'm slammed into reality as though hit from behind by a wall of air. The world turns over itself as I cartwheel into the past. My momentum drags me along the ground, my fingers clawing at the dry soil. Finally, I slide to a stop in a cloud of summer dust. I'm in the field next to the fair in 1997. It was a terrible landing, but I made it.

The void is behind me, the past is now.

I pick myself up and reset my focus, adjusting quickly. I have a plan, and if I'm going save Amy this time, it needs to work.

I run in the direction of the shooting range. The dark outline of the Ferris wheel bursts into life. KWS sings "Please Don't Go."

As I run, I consider the fact there are now three versions of me here. My fourteen-year-old self at the rifle range, the version of me who came back and failed, and yours truly. I replay the events of the night in my head as I move toward the carousel. There, I see the previous, time-traveling version of myself being questioned by the security guard.

"I'm watching you," he said. And now I'm watching him. I get the usual sense of repulsion when I see myself. I decide to refer to him as Other Joe, for the sake of my sanity. Other Joe backs away from the security guard and works his way through the crowd, toward the rifle range. Running behind the stalls, I follow him, carefully timing my interception.

"Joe," I shout as he passes me.

He turns and jumps at least a foot backward. "Jesus!" he cries, face contorted in shock. "What the hell are you doing here?"

I beckon him into the shadows.

He glances nervously in the direction of Amy.

"We need to talk," I tell him.

Reluctantly, he joins me. He seems to go through the same set of emotions as I do. Confusion, revulsion, fascination. We face each other, seeing ourselves anew in this grotesque Hall of Mirrors.

"What the hell is going on?" he asks.

I talk quickly. "What you're about to do doesn't work, you don't save her."

"What do you mean?" He glares at me as though I am the enemy. "What happens?"

"It doesn't matter," I assure him, banishing visions of Amy in the icy water. "You just need to do exactly as I say and everything will be all right."

Other Joe takes a step forward. "Tell me what happens. Who takes her?"

I almost tell him that *he's* the one who takes Amy, but I think better of it. "We don't have time for this," I say sharply. "Listen carefully."

I explain my plan. With Other Joe briefed—if a little reluctantly—I position myself at the side of a food stand, with a clear line of sight to the rifle range, the bumper cars, and the wood. From here, I observe Other Joe watching my fourteen-year-old self and Amy at the rifle range. The world feels claustrophobic, dangerously close to madness.

On cue, the security guard questions Other Joe. Brain freeze announces my fifteen-minute warning as the first *ding* of a target being struck rings out. The small crowd cheers. As instructed, Other Joe clenches his fist and swings a good hard punch, knocking the poor security guard to the floor. So far, so similar. Other Joe runs, but he doesn't head for the bumper cars, like I had. Instead, he creates a fantastic, very odd diversion. He whoops and shouts, taunting the man on the floor. He points at the gathered crowd and shouts something I can't hear, then runs deeper into the funfair. Some people converse and then follow him, shouting angrily.

Silently, I congratulate us. If you want a job done properly, ask yourself to do it.

My plan is that Other Joe's diversion will buy me some time alone with Amy. I have considered running directly to the rifle range and negotiating with her there, but I'm worried that might cause more problems. A man hassling a young girl is just too risky. Instead, my plan is to cut her off before she enters the wood and persuade her to return to the fairground. If it works, it should stop this eternal loop for good.

I reach the edge of the fair and slip into the dark embrace of the field. Running toward the wood, I am all but invisible. That's when I hear the third and final shot ring out. When I look back, the fair is a bright jewel in the darkness. Although I have put some distance between me and the stalls, I see Amy drifting away from the rifle range, leaving my younger, distracted self. She breaks into a run, heading in my direction. Brain freeze ripples over my skull. I estimate I have ten minutes or so, easily enough time to do this right. The field is suddenly illuminated by the distant flash of a camera. Amy is captured, bright and crisp, her shadow stretched long over the field.

The infamous photograph.

This time though, I am far enough away to be out of shot, and Other Joe is on the other side of the fairground. Yet again, I have altered the outcome of the photo, which should now be back to how it was originally with Debbie posing and Amy alone in the background, destined to be lost in time again.

The flash steals some of my night vision. Multiple echoes of Amy dance across my vision. I blink them away, desperately searching for the real thing.

And then, out of the shadows, she appears.

This time there is no search party. It's just me and Amy. She stops when she sees me, covers her mouth, and looks terrified.

"Amy," I say, holding out my hands. I'm mindful to speak softly, desperately trying not to scare her. "It's okay, it's all right." I need to gain her trust.

"Who are you?" she asks, glancing beyond me, toward the wood.

"A friend," I tell her. "Your brother, Joe, sent me. He's down there now, looking for you. He sent me to ask you to come back to the fair."

Amy studies me, just as she did before, with nervous curiosity. "My daddy says I mustn't talk to strangers."

"And he's right," I agree softly, crouching down to meet her gaze. "But I'm not a stranger, I'm a good friend of Joe's. Why don't you come back with me now, we'll find your brother and—"

"I can't." Amy sniffs away tears.

"Why?" I ask. "Has someone scared you? Did someone ask you to come here?" I'm guessing now, clutching at one of a thousand straws that have grown in my brain over the years. "Please, just come back to the fair."

"I've seen you before," she murmurs. "In the other place." The life in her eyes dims, and when she speaks again, her voice is disconnected, resigned. "Anyway, it doesn't matter," she says. "I'm going soon."

Time seems to stop.

Her skin shimmers, and in an almighty rush of understanding, it all makes sense.

Amy is a time traveler, like me.

27

Amy turns and runs.

"Amy!" I shout. "Wait! I know why you're running away. You find yourself in strange places with no idea how you got there!"

Amy stops. She turns, her eyes searching mine. "How do you know that?"

"Because it happens to me too," I say, walking slowly toward her, desperately searching for words that might make sense to a frightened seven-year-old. "And it's scary, isn't it?"

She nods mutely, looking like she might cry.

I continue toward her, very slowly. "Tell me what happens to you."

Her words come quickly. "I can't help it, it just happens. I feel dizzy, then I stop being here, and I'm somewhere else." She frowns. "It's the same place, but it's different."

I do my best to hide my emotions as the elusive puzzle finally reveals itself. "What do you see?"

"I see Mummy sometimes. She's got gray hair. I don't see Daddy though," she says, staring at the ground.

Her words send an icy chill through me. I process what she's saying, what this means, and realize I was wrong when I thought the puzzle was complete. Amy said she recognized me. She's seen me before, and Mum too—but not Dad. Fresh understanding crashes over me. Amy's time traveling in only part of the story. She travels, but she isn't like me. Amy travels *forward*, into the future. All this time, I've been blaming myself for dragging her into the lake, but I don't think that's what happened at all. When I held her, she dragged *me* into the future, and that means . . .

My whole body shudders.

Finally, I understand.

This *isn't* my fault, but Amy remains in grave danger. She's going to travel into the lake again, any minute now. If I'm going to save her, I need to act quickly. "Amy, do you want to know something really cool?" I ask, trying to stay calm, knowing that if I get this wrong, I'll lose her again.

"What?" She frowns.

"I can come with you if you like."

"Really?"

"Yes," I say with a smile. "I know where you're going next, and I can come too. All we need to do is hold hands."

"You know where I'm going?"

"Yes, and I want to come, so I can make sure you're safe." I hold out my hand. "Trust me, it will be okay."

Her bottom lip trembles. "How do you know?"

"I just do." I kneel beside her and hold out my hand, little finger outstretched. "Pinkie swear."

The suspicion drops from her face, and she locks her little finger around mine. "Who are you?" she asks again.

"Someone who loves you very much," I reply. I don't want to scare her, but I need to make sure that when we hit water, I can hold her tightly enough. I place my hands loosely around her wrists, ready to grip when we travel. "You know when you jump into a pool on a warm day, and the water is so cold it takes your breath away?"

"Yes," she says nervously.

"Well, this is going to be a bit like that, but don't be scared, okay? I'm right here with you."

Amy frowns. "So we're going swimming?"

"Yes." I swallow. "Do you know when you're about to leave? Can you tell me when, exactly?"

She nods and begins to count down. "Ten, nine, eight . . ."

No more planning. No more time to worry or wonder or panic. The lake is waiting. But this time, Amy is going to live. I hold her wrists tightly in both hands. When she reaches three, I tell her, "Take a big deep breath now, and hold it, okay?"

She does. Her cheeks bulge; her eyes are wide.

And bang on cue, we travel.

Knowing that we're about to land in pitch-black, freezing water doesn't make it any less of a shock. We arrive, submerged. The icy water crushes my lungs like a vice, but this time, I maintain a firm grip on Amy and feel her hands squeezing mine.

A flash of lightning illuminates the surface of the lake. Momentarily, I see Amy, her wild hair snaking outward from her head. She's holding her breath and looking directly at me. There is a focused determination in her eyes. Like me, she's kicking against the current, which feels like giant hands tugging us down. It's no use, we're going to lose if we carry on like this.

Against my instincts, I swim with the flow rather than against it. Amy tries to pull away, but I draw her close and continue, swimming with the current but edging slightly toward the shore with each stroke. We begin to rise. Amy thrashes and slips free of my weakened grip. I watch as she shoots upward, legs kicking wildly.

I follow, breaking the surface as another huge crack of lightning flashes overhead, followed by an angry roll of deep thunder. The raindrops pound the lake like ball bearings. Amy is near, coughing and spluttering. She cries out, and I call back, telling her not to fight. When I reach her, I tell her to lie on her back so I can pull her to safety. She wraps her hands around my neck, and my legs go to work. The safety of the shore is only twenty feet away but it feels like a mile. I look back and see the storm drain, the vortex of deadly water that dragged Amy to her death. Not tonight. My lungs are on fire, my head thumping as fast as my heart, but I don't stop until we reach the water's edge. We crawl together through thick, cloying mud before collapsing onto the bank, exhausted.

I hold Amy close. I never want to let go of her again. She's coughing and crying, but she's alive, and as the lightning and thunder continue their angry exchange, I laugh. Amy looks up at me, scared and confused. Lightning strikes again, and to me it is fireworks, multicolored bursts of joy, the night itself celebrating. The air crackles, and Amy joins me, initially smiling, then giggling. We lie side by side on our backs and laugh like a pair of demented hyenas.

Thunder shakes the ground, and Amy pulls herself against me, still giggling a little.

I've tempted fate enough for one day. In the distance, at the edge of the flooded meadow, I spot a small building. I lift Amy to her feet. "Come on," I say. "Follow me."

Amy blinks up at me. "Where are we going?"

"Somewhere safe."

We run, feet splashing in the mud, toward the building. Amy whoops, shaking her fist at the sky as though she knows she cheated death tonight. We reach the building, but it's been boarded up for years. In the future, it will be a café. For now, its roofline offers some shelter and, more importantly, a safe departure point for us both.

Our elation subsides a little as the adrenaline wears off and the chill sets into our bones. Amy's jaw chatters. "I'm cold," she says. Her lips are dark.

I begin running in place, like a crazed hamster on a wheel. "Do this," I say. She does, and within a minute or so, we're laughing again. When we get our breath back, I say, "I'm sorry that was so scary."

"It's okay." She shrugs. "You saved me."

I turn away. Tears come, and I let them. For once, they're tears of joy.

Amy peers out over the lake. "Where are we?"

"This is the same place as the fair," I reply, wiping my eyes. "But it's a different day."

As I stare out over the worst flood in Cheltenham's history, new understanding rolls in like thunder. Before I intervened, Amy must have drowned here, dying in the depths of the flooded meadow. I will never know for sure, but I suspect she was pinned by the storm drain's powerful current. Logic dictates that if her body then traveled back to 1997, she would have been buried twenty feet deep. Back then, this area hadn't been excavated and turned into a flood defense area. No wonder we never found any trace of her. No one would ever have thought of digging that deep. I grimace at the thought and banish it by taking a good, long look at my sister. Amy stares back at me, pale and cold, but alive.

Lightning flickers in the distance, followed by a low rumble. The rain thickens to a heavy downpour.

"So what day is this?" Amy asks.

"Amy, do you understand that you travel into the future?"

She nods.

"This is 2007."

She looks around and then up at me. "Is this where you're from?"

"No," I say. "I've come from 2020."

"Wow," she says. "That's a long way."

"Yes, it is." I keep my tone light, but my thoughts are racing ahead. "How many times have you traveled like this?"

Amy thinks. "Lots of times."

"And what have you seen?"

"I go to the big house sometimes," she says. "I see the old man, and we play in the garden. I see the lady too."

"Your mummy?"

She shakes her head. "No. She's nice though, they all are. Everything's different there, but it's okay, because I always come back."

This prompts me to consider my next challenge, because she isn't home yet. I've saved her, but for how long? I need to think fast.

"Amy," I say, trying to disguise the urgency I feel, "I need to tell you some things that are very important, okay?" She gazes up, wide-eyed and innocent. I wish I could hug her, reassure her, as her brother would. "Where we're standing now is right by the entrance to the fairground, the place with the hanging colored lights . . . you said it was like a rainbow, remember?"

She bobs her head.

"When you get back, people will be looking for you," I say. "I want you to go straight to the stall with the fluffy bear and the guns, and I want you to wait there. Joe will come and find you. And Amy, you mustn't tell your brother anything about this, about what happened tonight."

"Why not?"

"Because it might change things," I say softly. "This is our secret. Just for you and me. Okay?"

She considers this for a moment, and then looks up at me, her expression serious. "Don't worry, I won't tell him. I'm good at secrets."

"I know you are," I say.

She stares down at her muddy hands, nibbling her bottom lip. "My dress is all dirty," she says. "Mummy's going to be really cross with me."

I sigh, shaking my head. "Don't worry about that. Everyone's just going to be so happy that you're safe."

"But what will I say?"

"Just tell them you got lost and you fell in some mud. They won't care, I promise. You won't be in trouble."

Her concern seems to melt away, and her eyes glaze over. "It's all gone blue," she says in a monotone voice. "I'm going back soon." She attempts a smile, but her teeth are clenched.

No time left. Amy gazes out over the flooded meadow, and then back at me. "Will I see you again?"

"Yes, I think you will."

And then, she travels.

Her departure is instant. All that remains of her is an outline, momentarily shrouded by rain that hasn't yet realized it has nothing to cling to. A hollow, glass-like sculpture of Amy lit by distant lightning. Then, the water falls away, and she is truly gone.

For a few seconds I just stare, praying that what I just told her was true, that I will see her again. The minutes pass, the wind dies down, and the sharp pain of my own brain freeze arrives. The world takes on a familiar blue sheen. I look at the sky and step into the rain.

28

My watch is gone. It probably fell off in the lake. I don't need it to know that I'm home though, because the boarded-up building is a café again, and the sign in the window advertises a music quiz for next weekend. Thankfully, no one seems to have noticed my arrival. I cover my face against the bright morning sun and peer out over the excavated meadow. I have traveled years into the past, but in real time, it's just over an hour since I set off from Leckhampton Hill with Alexia.

What now?

For the first time in weeks, I don't know what to do next. I don't have a plan for after the plan. The familiar sense of déjà vu ripples through me, rolling and building to disconcertingly powerful waves as the universe reconfigures itself. I lean against the side of the building and wait, hunched over, blood pulsing in my vision, my ears ringing.

Slowly, the waves subside, and the ground is still again.

My body feels like it's made of metal, cooling and setting hard. I drag myself toward the road. All my adrenaline is gone. I have nothing left.

A woman in a brown jacket and dark-blue jeans approaches. I look up and shield my eyes from the sun, but it makes me feel light-headed and I begin to sway. I think I'm going to pass out.

The woman breaks into run and calls out. "Joe!"

My heart races at the sound of my name. "Alexia?" I call back, but my voice is weak.

As I lose my balance, the woman takes hold of my arms to steady me. "It's all right," she says in an unfamiliar voice. "I've got you."

I shield my eyes again to get a better look at her features.

"Hello, Joe," she says softly. "It's good to see you. After all this time."

She smiles. Her loose, golden-brown hair falls around her face in soft waves. Her skin is pale, with faint lines around her mouth, but her cheeks are pink from the chill of the morning air. Her face has lengthened, and the line of her jaw reminds me of Mum's, but those green eyes, sparkling with life and curiosity, are the same as they were just a few minutes ago, in seven-year-old Amy's face.

"Amy? . . . Amy!"

I fling my arms around her, as intense relief sears through me. I want to sing with the stars, shout from the rooftops, dance like a madman, and curl up in a ball and weep, all at the same time.

"Is it really you?" I reach out and gently touch her cheek. Her skin is soft and warm. "Please tell me I'm not dreaming, that this isn't some kind of cruel trick?"

"It's really me," she says.

"Oh my god, I did it. I did it! I saved you. You're really here. You're all right."

"Yes, I'm all right," she assures me.

I think my heart might burst. I jump up, pulling her with me, take her in my arms, and spin us both around and around, till we're both laughing and dizzy like children again.

I hold her tight, like I'll never let her go. The tears come freely now, spilling down my face in a release from the pain of all those years without her.

"Don't ever leave me again," I say, voice cracking. I remember when Mum and Dad brought her home from the hospital, knowing from that moment I would do anything to protect her. I messed that up, but now I have a second chance. "Promise me. Say it."

"I won't leave you again," she says, and then with a kind smile, adds, "pinkie swear."

Amy helps me back to her car, which is parked nearby. I'm close to useless, but she came prepared, brought me a towel.

"Here you go. Dry yourself off with that," she says. "I'll drive us back to mine and you can get cleaned up. It's only a few minutes away." She turns on the engine and puts the heater on full blast. "You'll be frozen. I know I was only little, but I remember."

As I dry my hair, I watch the streets whiz past. "God, Amy. I just left you in the rain, and now I'm here . . . and you're here. I don't know how to process this."

She offers an understanding smile. "I know. It'll take time. There's no rush."

We stop at a crossing to let a young couple with a stroller cross the road.

"Amy, are Mum and Dad all right?"

"Yes, they're fine. They're on holiday at the moment, actually."

"So Dad's still . . ."

"Dad's fine. They're both absolutely fine."

It's too much. I break down in tears again. I'm going to be a mess for a while. I have a lot of crying to catch up on. My family were ghosts that haunted me, but now they're real again. It all makes sense. The pain and suffering that tore through my family never happened. Amy never went missing. Dad never killed himself. Mum didn't become depressed, and perhaps the onset of dementia hasn't hit yet, if it will at all. My parents are okay.

Amy reaches for my hand. "It was different for you, wasn't it?"

"Yes, very."

"I saw them a few times," she says, "when I was younger, when I traveled. What happened?"

"It doesn't matter now," I say, squeezing her hand. "None of it matters now."

Amy pulls in and parks the car.

"Here we are," she says. We're on a wide street, flanked by trees and tall grandiose buildings. It reminds me of the building Alexia's office is in. My heart swells with excitement and pride as I imagine her reaction when she hears that we did it. I decide to call her as soon as I've cleaned up a bit.

I follow Amy into the foyer of the nearest building and up the stairs to the second floor. "This is home," she says as she unlocks the door and pushes it open. "Go on in." I walk through a hallway and into the main living area. Its high ceilings and big windows look out over a park. The room is full of color, the shelves crammed with interesting things, a bit untidy, but it smells of incense, and I like it. It's exactly the kind of place I imagined Amy might live.

"Bathroom's just through there on the left," she says. "And there are some clean clothes in the spare room next to that. Help yourself. I'll get the kettle on."

"Thanks, that's kind," I say.

She smiles. "I've been preparing for this for a long time."

After a long hot shower, I go to the spare room and get dressed in the clothes Amy's left out for me. On the walls are photos of Amy with her friends, and some family shots too. There's a big one of just the two of us. Amy looks about eighteen, and I'm in my twenties, goofing around. We're doing leapfrogs in a white photography studio. I don't remember it of course, but I'm going to have to get used to not knowing.

One step at a time, Joe.

I join Amy in the kitchen, an untidy but cheerful mixture of styles. Original oil paintings adorn the walls, and piles of recipe books line a floating shelf above the worktop.

"How do you like your tea?" she asks, a spoonful of sugar hovering over the mug she's holding.

"I'm more of a coffee man, to be honest," I say.

She hesitates for a split second. "Of course. Instant okay?" she says, recovering her composure.

"Fine, thanks," I say. "White, please. Oh, and maybe one sugar." I think I need it.

Amy makes the drink and hands me the cup. "How are you feeling now?" she asks.

"Better," I say, taking a sip of the hot sweet liquid. "Thank you for the coffee. And the clothes."

Amy smiles, sunlight dappled across her face. "Do you want to sit down?"

"Actually, do you mind if I make a quick call first?"

"Of course," she says. "If you don't mind me asking, who do you want to speak to?"

"I don't mind," I say. "I want to call Alexia."

"You said her name when you first saw me this morning," Amy says. "Who is she?"

How do I answer that? I decide to keep it simple. "She's a friend. She helped me figure out how to save you."

Amy's eyes widen. "God, Joe, of course, you must call her, let her know everything's okay. At some point I'd love to meet her," she adds enthusiastically. "For now, if you don't think it's too weird, please just thank her for me."

"Sure," I say. "I don't have my phone with me though." I make it sound like I left it at home or in the car. The truth is, I think I left my phone in my old life.

Amy unlocks hers and hands it to me. "Give me a shout when you're done. I'll be in my room."

"Thanks, Amy." I watch her go, knowing I will never take her life for granted. It's going to be strange, because Amy isn't back from the dead for anyone except me. No one here is going to feel what I feel, understand the chasm she now fills. For them, the void was never there.

I find Alexia's website. When I go to the "About Me" page and see her face smiling back, my heart leaps. If anyone understands what I've been through, it's Alexia. Bursting with excitement, I key her number into the phone.

She picks up almost immediately.

"Alexia Finch," she says, her voice cheery and professional, stirring up butterflies in my stomach.

"Alexia," I say excitedly. "It's me!"

"Sorry, who is this?" she says.

"It's Joe!" I cry.

"Joe! Sorry, I didn't recognize the number."

"Of course. I'm calling from Amy's phone! Alexia, we did it! We saved her!"

There's a pause. I'm expecting her to whoop with joy, to congratulate me, to break down in tears of relief. What I'm not expecting is silence.

I reach for the St. Christopher. In all the turbulence and the elation of the last few hours, I forgot all about it. I feel a flash of panic. It's not there. Like my watch, it probably got torn off in the lake. My subconscious has another idea though. *Perhaps she never gave it to you.*

"Alexia?" I say, hoping that perhaps we've been disconnected. "Are you there?"

"I'm sorry, Joe, but I have absolutely no idea what you're talking about."

My mouth dries up. She doesn't remember.

"I . . . just wanted you to know that she's okay, we're both okay," I murmur.

"Who's okay?" she asks. "You sound a bit . . . Look, do you want me to call someone for you?"

My mind struggles to grasp this new reality. Amy didn't go missing, so my life didn't fall apart. Martin didn't send me for hypnotherapy, so I didn't meet Alexia, and we didn't fall in love. The earth feels like it's shifting beneath me again.

"Joe?"

There are a thousand things I want to say. *I need you to remember us, to be the version I was falling in love with. You were feeling the same, I think. You said when I came back, you'd be waiting. But you were wrong.*

"Are you still there?" she asks, a little impatiently.

"Sorry," I say. "I'm fine. I had one too many whiskeys, and I had a bad dream about my sister. That's all."

"Okay," she says, clearly unconvinced.

But . . . wait, hang on, she knew my name. "Alexia, we do know each other then?"

"What? You know we do."

"Right," I say, brain scrambled.

"Joseph, if you're not feeling well, maybe you should call an ambulance," she says. "You're actually scaring me now."

"I'm sorry," I tell her, and I am. Devastated, actually. "I didn't mean to bother you. I'll be fine."

I disconnect the call and gaze longingly at her face on the screen. This time, she is a stranger. Without Alexia none of this would have happened, and I've lost her. I can't share the joy of our success with her.

But how can I complain? I have my family back. Amy is safe and well and all grown up; we have a lifetime of memories to catch up on. I made my choice, and I accepted that changing time comes with inherent risk, unexpected potential changes like this. It's clearer to me now than ever: Time travel gives with one hand and takes with the other. The best things in life may be free, but there is always a cost.

Amy walks back into the kitchen. "So how did it go?" she asks considerately, clearly reading my expression. I glance up at her, unsure what to say, how to approach this. I don't want Amy to feel guilty for anything, for her to think I'm pining for my old life already. She deserves better than that, but my heart feels like a can that's just been crushed flat. I can't hide it.

Amy's expression mirrors mine. Pain. Loss. She sits opposite me, takes me hand, and asks, "Are you all right?"

My chest tightens. My eyes burn. "She doesn't remember me," I say, the words making it real. "Doesn't remember what we had, anyway."

"Oh, Joe, I'm so sorry."

"It's okay," I tell her, doing my best to sound like I mean it. "We hadn't known each other that long and I knew some things might change. I just hoped this wouldn't be one of them."

Amy studies me for a second. "You were close," she says, her voice tender. "Maybe you could get to know her again?"

"Yes, I hope so."

Amy makes me a fresh cup of coffee. I thank her, and she regards me with real empathy. Although the pain of losing Alexia is raw, I dig deep and focus on my family, the things that matter the most. "Tell me about Mum and Dad," I say, taking a sip of coffee. "Do they still live in the same house we grew up in? Leckhampton Road?"

"Yes," Amy says, "they are still there." I smile. The ghost of my past self no longer haunts that place. It's good to know my parents still own the house, that its walls hold some happiness now. "They have a place in Cornwall too, that they visit a few times a year. They're there at the moment. It's good timing, means you can adjust for a while."

"Wow," I murmur, mind reassembling this new reality at speed. My parents both alive and doing well by the sound of it. I'm not surprised they still live in Cheltenham. They both loved the place. It makes me think of Vinny.

I wince a little, "I'm sorry to hit you with more questions but—"

"It's fine," Amy says, smiling and leaning back in her chair. "We are going to be doing this for weeks. I'm prepared."

I laugh but it fades. I'm nervous, almost afraid to ask. "I had a friend called Vinny."

"The record shop guy," Amy says, looking pleased.

"Yes!"

"Oh, you're still friends with him," she says. "You buy all your vinyl there."

My shoulders drop. "That's really good news."

It feels like the first stitch in my efforts to sow these two worlds together. I plan to call Vinny later, maybe pop in and see him. Although we know each other, I'm aware that he might not have any memories of helping me. It stands to reason, doesn't it? If Amy never went missing, Vinny and I will probably have no time-traveling connection at all. Erase and rewind. I glance back at Amy. "What about . . . Mark D'Stellar?" I ask.

She considers this. "I remember you being friends with a guy called Mark at university. He was in your band, wasn't he?"

"Yeah, that's him," I say. "Is he all right, do you know?"

"Well . . . like most older brothers, you didn't exactly tell me everything that went on." She smirks, pursing her lips in thought, and then says, a little reluctantly, "I don't think you really stayed in touch. Was he a good friend?"

"He was, but to be honest, it sounds like things are pretty similar in this timeline. We reconnected recently; we can do it again."

I can't deny feeling a little robbed of recent progress. Mark and I mended some bridges, Vinny and I went through some bonding experiences too. But I learned from the process and it's always easier to do it again, second time around. It's the wonderful benefit of hindsight. It seems my questions are like a boomerang; they circle, return to me, and then I throw them again at a slightly different angle. If my parents still live in the family home, the place I lived until this morning, then—

"Amy, where do I live now?" I ask.

She grins playfully, just like she used to when she had a plan. "Why don't we go and take a look?"

29

It's a beautiful winter's morning, cold and fresh; glimmers of sunlight break through gray clouds. Amy drives us through Cheltenham, a town that feels friendlier now. We don't talk much and after all the recent revelations, the silence is surprisingly golden. Amy is giving me some space, I suspect, some time to acclimatize to this new reality. I try not to stare at her, but it's difficult.

I am struggling to reconcile the woman next to me and the seven-year-old girl I saved this morning. We have so much to catch up on, and there's so much about her I don't know. It's the first time I think about how the previous me had all those years with her. Years I can never have.

Eventually, we pull up on Montpellier Road, an impressive row of beautiful houses and smart-looking shops. We get out of the car and walk. If I live here, I'm doing pretty well. Amy pauses in front of one of the shops. The majority of its frontage comprises of two huge windows, through which I can see a multitude of delights.

I read the shop's sign, gold letters on a dark-gray background: Bridgeman Antiques and Curiosities.

My heart pounds in my chest.

"This is yours, Joe," Amy says.

My gaze settles on the entrance: a wooden door, painted royal blue, with a brass handle. The sign reads Closed—Please Come Back Later. I try to speak but words don't come. In my previous life, I neglected my modest antiques business, another casualty of losing Amy. I often wondered if I could have made a go of it. Those dreams always felt like they belonged to a different man. It seems they did, and now they're real.

"I can't believe it," I say, mumbling. "I'm finding it pretty hard to comprehend what I'm looking at. Amy, this can't be mine."

"It is yours," she says, "and you love it here. You often joke about your morning commute." She points to the first floor. "You live up there, above the shop." She pulls a set of keys from her handbag. "Now, come on, let's go inside and have a look around, shall we?"

My legs carry me inside. As we enter, a tiny bell rings above the door. I like the shop immediately. It has a reassuring smell, old furniture laced with history, a hint of brass and polish with the subtle undertones of damp and aging dust that perhaps only an antiques lover can appreciate.

Slowly, I soak in the contents of the shop, feasting on every little detail. It's an eclectic mix of ornate furniture, oddities, rarities, and antiques from all walks of life and corners of the world.

"This is *real*, Joe," she says, as though reading my mind.

"I know, but it's almost too good to be true," I reply, still working my gaze over the shop. "I don't feel like I deserve this. I haven't worked for it," I tell her honestly.

She takes my hand, her expression serious. "I need you to listen to me, Joseph Bridgeman, and you listen *good*." She takes my other hand, keeping her attention on me. "You worked hard for this. You kept on believing and you never gave up, even when it seemed impossible."

I look back at her, unsure who she's talking about, me or him, or maybe both of us.

"There's no one on earth who deserves this more than you. You never stopped."

"No." I agree with her on that. I didn't.

"I've been preparing for this day for such a long time," she says. "It's so lovely to finally be able to show you this. Let me tell you a bit about the place."

She walks ahead, past a cabinet of shiny colored glassware, toward a desk in the center of the shop. It's big and covered in paperwork, and a captain's chair has been pushed underneath. "You'll find your own way of running things of course, but just so you know, this is how it's done at the moment. You normally open around ten a.m. and close at five p.m., or a bit later when you feel like it," she says. I regard the desk and then look back around the shop. It's a fantastic place, and in another world, I can imagine I'd really enjoy hanging out here, but it's all too much. I feel the weight of my new reality on my shoulders, and for a moment wonder how I'm ever going to step into another man's shoes, even if they are, technically, mine.

"And like I said, your house is upstairs," Amy continues. "It's pretty amazing. You have your own terrace and . . . well, you'll see for yourself, but I think you're going to like it."

"Amy?" I murmur.

She walks ahead, pointing at things like an air hostess. "You don't open on Sundays unless you get one of your feelings, in which case sometimes you open up and wait to see who walks through the door—"

"Amy," I say again, louder this time. "We need to take things a little slower."

She looks worried and walks back toward me. "Sorry, Joe," she says, shaking her head. "I'm such an idiot, I was determined to get this right and I'm just bombarding you." She shrugs and finds a smile. "I've been thinking about this since I was seven, knowing this will happen, that it *has* to happen. I so badly want it all to go well."

There's a hint of sadness in her voice. My recent conversation with Alexia gives me a sense of what Amy might be going through. With Alexia, I'm mourning the loss of something that grew over just a few short weeks, but Amy lost decades of shared memories when I replaced her brother.

"You're doing great," I tell her. "You're coping with this amazingly well. It must be hard for you too."

She squeezes my hand. "We're in this together. The main thing is, we take it one day at a time, and we keep talking."

I feel a lump in my throat. It's going to take me a long time to get used to the fact that I have my sister back. I spent so many years wondering what she might be like, wishing I could talk to her. Now, here she is, standing right in front of me, and although I'm a bit out of practice, I know she's right. We do need to talk.

"Amy, I'm worried. I don't know anything about my life here. We're going to have to say I've got amnesia or something, aren't we?"

She nods. "Yes, exactly," she says. "I've been thinking the same. To be honest, it's the only way."

"So how do we do that?" I'm overwhelmed by the prospect of spending the next few months lying to everyone, in order to cover up something that's impossible to explain. "What shall we tell people?"

"Look, it's the weekend. Keep the shop closed, don't answer your phone, and don't answer the door. Come over to mine tomorrow, and we'll plan it all out. I think you'll find that once we start telling people, it'll get easier." She offers me a tentative smile. "We can do this, Joe."

She's so confident that even though I know it's going to be hard, I believe her.

"Okay," I say.

"Great," she says. "For now, I think you should have some time to yourself, and get familiar with Casa Bridgeman." I know some time alone to settle in is a good idea, but I'm worried that when Amy leaves, my subconscious will go to town, persuading me that I imagined the whole thing. I don't want to be a burden on her, though, so I dig deep and manage a smile. She hands me a set of keys. "I labeled these for you. The alarm is pretty straightforward and the code is my birthday. That was your idea, not mine. Now, all you need to do is . . ." She pauses, searching for the word.

"Decompress," I finish for her.

"Exactly." Amy gives me a hug. "Give me a call if you need anything. My number's on speed dial, just press one. Oh, and I checked, there's plenty of food in the freezer."

"Thanks, Amy. I'll be all right," I tell her. "Can I call you later though?"

"Of course," she says, "that would be nice."

She can see I'm struggling. "Joe, just remember: you deserve this. Okay?"

I tell her I'll remember. She leaves the shop, the one with my name above the door and half my life under its belt, and I'm alone again, except

I'm not. I've got my family back. It's probably a good thing my parents are away, though. Although my head is quickly assimilating this new reality, it's going to take my heart a while to catch up.

Over the next hour or so, I continue to explore the shop and then venture upstairs into Other Joe's flat. Every angle is an assault on my senses. It feels as though I've sneaked into someone else's home.

My bedroom is huge. Modern and a bit clinical for my taste, if I'm honest. I browse my wardrobe and chest of drawers. I own some good clothes, much better than the ones I left in my old life. Amy's influence maybe. Either way, I find myself thinking again that once I have adjusted, life might be good here.

Of course, I can't shake the feeling that any minute now the previous version of me is going to burst through the door and demand his life back. Mirrors kind of freak me out a bit now too. Once you've seen yourself, I mean in the flesh like I have, you kind of expect the man opposite you to shout *Boo!* I know it isn't going to happen, but it still feels weird to be here, home but not yet . . . home.

When I walk into the study, I finally feel a sense of connection. There is a beaten-up leather chair with the studs missing in places, so similar to mine it makes me grin. He has a decent vinyl collection too. I wonder if the albums are the same. I browse through them and am relieved to find a pretty good Beatles collection, along with a few rarities I never owned. He also has many of my favorite classics and of course, some new ones to try.

I decide that's enough for one day, that I need to compartmentalize, to ease myself in, one floor at a time. The terrace sounds amazing, but it can wait. I have the rest of my life to get used to this.

As my first day in this new world draws to a close, my thoughts return to Alexia.

I wonder how we know each other here, in this version of the present. It really does seem that certain things echo through time. My life here feels like a jigsaw puzzle, the same shapes but a different scene. All I can do is hope that Alexia and I might be able to start again. Imagining her makes me feel safe, more complete. That feeling is laced with sadness of course. She taught me so much in such a small amount of time. She taught me the importance of living in *the now*, not worrying about the past or the future.

In this moment I realize that I spent all my time and energy utterly focused on saving Amy. Never once did I stop to think about what might happen if I succeeded. It means that I must live in *the now* and cope with whatever life throws at me here.

I will manage, somehow.

EPILOGUE

My decompression continues slowly. On Sunday morning I pluck up the courage to venture downstairs. It's early. I wanted to come down here and spend some time in my shop, while it's quiet. It's a chance to familiarize myself. Apparently, I have a shop manager called Molly. Amy assured me that Molly takes care of almost all the technical aspects of running the place. She has been given the weekend off, meaning the shop has remained closed. I know that tomorrow morning I'm going to have to open the doors, act like the owner, but I'm not ready for that yet. I still feel like an impostor, a clone who has inherited a life from some poor bloke who was *me* not so long ago. It's just plain weird. As I browse his place of business, trying to imagine it as my own, I think of all the years he has spent here, in this shop and in this life. I feel a strange mix of envy and guilt. I'm envious because he got to watch Amy grow up, lived with my family, created memories I can only imagine. I missed all of that. But I also feel guilty, because I robbed him of his life, the one he'd built here, and I've taken over. I try to remind myself that I didn't *murder* him. It wasn't deliberate. It helps to think that together, we saved our sister, that we've shared this life to a certain degree. Either way, it's me here now, picking up the baton, and all I can do is run what remains of the race the best I can.

For an hour or so, I explore the shop, familiarizing myself with the various antiques and collectibles. It's much bigger than the one I rented many years ago, and the stock is more varied. In the numerous glass cabinets, the previous version of me has amassed an impressive collection of desirable pieces. It's all organized by period or a specific collector's specialty: jewelry, silverware, rare and collectible coins, as well as some interesting Second World War memorabilia. There is also some rather nice art deco and art nouveau furniture, all fascinating in their own right, each item waiting for someone to come along and claim them.

I'm not surprised that some of the objects in here are whispering to me already. I resist the urge to tune into them. I don't want to connect and certainly don't plan to trigger any viewings. I'm going to take a break from that for a while. It makes me wonder if the previous version of me had any psychometric abilities. Mine only began after Amy went missing. I've always presumed they were triggered by that. I guess I will never know. I suppose it doesn't matter. Now, I could do with familiarizing myself with some paperwork, the general running of the place. As I head toward my desk, I catch my reflection in a large gilt-framed mirror. I imagine the previous version of me here. I hope this shop is where our souls can meet, converge maybe.

The bell above the front door rings, making me jump. I must have left the door unlocked. What kind of shop owner am I?

A tall man, dressed smartly in a striped shirt, light-gray trousers, and matching waistcoat, enters the shop. He approaches my desk. I would guess he's in his midsixties. His salt-and-pepper hair is neatly styled and swept back. He has the look of man who pines for a bygone era. I'm about to explain that I'm not open today, but he beats me to it. "Good morning," he says, pushing a gold pocket watch into his waistcoat. "You have a beautiful shop here." His voice is precise and clipped. He offers me a warm smile.

"Thank you," I say, mind racing.

His blue eyes sparkle. "An item in your window caught my fancy. May I show you?"

"Of course," I say, feeling like I've arrived halfway through a play and don't have a clue about the plot or who the characters are. I follow the man to the window, picking up the faint odor of sweet tobacco. It reminds me of lazy Sundays with my grandfather.

The man points out the item in question, a Victorian zoetrope. This one is taller than the others I've bought and sold over the years. It looks a bit like a table lamp. "I've always liked these," I tell him, glancing at the label beside it. "This is a lovely piece, in excellent condition considering it was made in 1889."

"Indeed," he says, and then politely asks, "May I take a closer look?"

"Yes, of course." I lift the zoetrope from the display and place it on a nearby table. Its base is metal, with a polished mahogany cylinder, slits cut vertically into the sides. It's lined with a decorative card, featuring twelve hand-drawn illustrations. Unexpectedly, I find myself enjoying the thrill of a possible sale, the storytelling that accompanies the process. It's been a while. I've missed it.

The man admires it. "Would you mind if I gave it a spin?"

"Be my guest," I tell him.

He pushes the outer edge of the zoetrope. It flickers into life, spinning silently. Inside, a man in a bowler hat chases the devil. It offers a surprisingly good representation of motion.

A cog of familiarity clicks inside me. Flickering motion. My final couple of jumps. The dark place with spinning doorways. Since getting back, it's been playing on my mind. I knew it reminded me of something.

"This is a beautiful piece, Joseph," he says, "but it's not quite what I'm after."

I stare at him, unsure what to say. This could be my first encounter with someone from Other Joe's life and the first test of my "amnesia protocol."

After a brief smile, his expression becomes inquisitive. "You didn't think you were the only one, did you?"

I place my hand against the zoetrope, stopping it dead. "Who are you?" I ask him, my nerves beginning to sing.

He straightens his back, draws in a breath, and says, "Please forgive me, Mr. Bridgeman, where are my manners? My name is William P. Brown, but my friends call me Bill. I am very pleased to make your acquaintance."

He doesn't hold out his hand. I'm relieved because touch has taken on a whole new meaning to me over the last few weeks. He waits patiently for me to speak.

"What do you want, Mr. Brown?" I ask warily.

His eyes remain fixed on me. "I represent a small but organized group of time travelers, and I am here to make you an offer."

"What kind of offer?" I ask, questions building. An organized group? Do they know about Amy? About what I've done? Panic bubbles up from deep within my gut.

"I am here to offer you my mentorship." He says this with such sincere and intense conviction, I almost laugh. Wistfully he adds, "A double jump in order to reach her. Ingenious . . . extremely creative."

"How on earth do you know so much about me?" I ask.

"I am drawn to people . . . people like *you*." He smiles kindly and it feels genuine. My initial concern shifts more toward worry, about how I'm going to let him down gently.

"I'm sorry if you've come a long way to tell me this," I tell him, "but I have literally just got back. The last thing I want to do is time travel. To be honest, ever again."

He grins confidently as though we are in total agreement, like he genuinely thinks I'm going to jump at the chance to risk my life all over again.

"You don't believe me?" I ask, folding my arms.

"I understand you feel this way *now*," he replies. "And it's your choice of course, but you have opened Pandora's box, Joseph. You will miss the winds of time in your hair, the thrill of the chase. I've seen this before, many times. You will come around."

"Mr. Brown," I say, adopting a more empathetic tone, "I belong *here*, in the present. I am totally done with time traveling."

"That's as may be, Joseph," he says, "but time traveling is not done with you." He fixes me with his wild blue eyes, and when he speaks again his voice is deep, confident, and laced with excitement. "The Magical Mystery Tour starts here. You are a time traveler, my boy,"—he pauses just long enough to flash me a mischievous grin—"and saving Amy was just the beginning."

ACKNOWLEDGMENTS

Writing this book was an amazing, transformative experience for me. I wondered what it would it be like for an average Joe to discover he could time travel. I wanted to really go there, explore, and share his story as he struggled against the odds to save his sister. It was fun, and the process assured me that I wanted to become a full-time author. It was no longer a choice. I wrote like the wind, released the story in episodes—before my fear could ask what on earth I was thinking—and crossed my fingers. Then, something amazing happened. People read it, they seemed to like it, and Blackstone Publishing got in touch. It's how this book got into your hands.

For me, the process of writing a novel is a heady mix of creativity, periods of doubt, flashes of self-belief and inspiration, plus a healthy dose of collaboration. It might start with me, but the end result is a team effort. And that means I have plenty of people to thank.

Thanks to Josh and Rick at Blackstone for seeing the potential in Joseph Bridgeman. Thank you to my agent, David Fugate, for his advice, wisdom, and patience, and for believing in me as an author. Getting to this stage in my career would have been impossible without him. Many thanks to my editor, Jason Kirk, for understanding my vision and helping me to realize it. I couldn't be more proud of the result. Thanks to the team at Blackstone who have helped make my books look and sound so awesome. Thanks also to the following who all played their part in my journey: Ian Hughes, the Beatles, Toby Hyde, Simon Wallis, 200 Degrees Coffee, Louise and Andy, Murray Bruton, Steve Parolini, Isle of Harris Gin, my mum for being proud of me, and you, the reader—double-love if you've been with me from the start. And finally, thank you to Kay, my partner in life and collaborator in fiction. It's pretty simple: without you, none of this would have happened.

Thanks for reading my book. I love to keep in touch with my readers, so if you're interested, please sign up for my mailing list:
http://NickJonesAuthor.com/SignUp
Subscribers receive regular emails about my writing life, and I like to share stuff that I find inspiring.

You can also follow me in the usual places:
Website: http://NickJonesAuthor.com/
Facebook: https://www.Facebook.com/AuthorNickJones/
Twitter: https://Twitter.com/AuthorNickJones
Goodreads: https://Goodreads.com/AuthorNickJones
BookBub: https://BookBub.com/Authors/Nick-Jones

If you like, you can email me at Nick@NickJonesAuthor.com. I read everything I get.